100 Erotic Quickies

The Train

Frustrated, I took my seat, an hour delay, I was not impressed but there was no one around to vent too so I sucked it up. At least the train was almost empty so I'd snagged a table, spreading my bags beside me to deter company.

Twisting open a bottle of wine, I propped up a book and poured myself a glass, in two hours I would finally be home, or at the station at least.

The carriage doors opened and my eyes glanced up, walking towards me my ex, the arsehole who had dumped me the year before unceremoniously for some slapper at his office.

As If this day wasn't bad enough, do not see me my mind emitted, walk on by. But, of course he did, greeting me with a smile as if a long-lost friend, half-drunk as usual.

"Is anyone sitting here" he asked, what does it look like? I wanted to answer, but instead, "No; have a seat." Shot out of me friendlily. I cursed myself, rolling my eyes as he jammed his bags overhead, this day could not get worse.

Bla Bla Bla, Bla Bla Bla, I nodded along to his incessant crap, did he expect me to agree that his girlfriend was a boring nag trying to control him or point out that he was a complete dick and she deserved a medal for putting up with him for as long as she had.

As he droned on I noticed the man across the aisle looking on amused, he had seen me frowning and seemed to read my thoughts as he smiled sympathetically.

Our eyes met and he winked, I looked away, well this was

awkward. I continued to listen to the ex, drone on and poured myself another wine, I glanced across and noted he was still staring, so quickly looked away, no chance to check him out.

I couldn't put up with this conversation for another hour, so seizing a gap in his whining, I excused myself, waving to an imaginary friend and advising I would be back shortly.

I stepped out of the carriage and stood in the vestibule. Behind me the man coughed, I hadn't heard him approach and there he was behind me. He didn't speak just stared suggestively.

"Yes" I asked, wondering what he wanted.

"I thought you were hinting for me to follow" he answered. I laughed, seriously how far was this man up his own arse?

On the other hand, I could do with the distraction, he opened the door to the loo and gestured for me to follow. I stepped in pulling it closed behind me. Crammed into the loo I had second thoughts, but before I had chance to bolt, he leaned in and kissed me, his hands circling around my waist and I kissed him back, eagerly, he was hot and he knew it.

He sat on the closed toilet seat and unbuttoned my top pulling me close, distracted by his kisses on my breasts I hardly noticed his hand creeping up my skirt and before I knew it he was inside me, rubbing my clit with the palms of his hands as he probed his fingers around.

The train rocked and I shuddered, his mouth enclosed my nipple as he bit gently and as I moaned he looked up at me, a smug smile on his handsome face. I pulled his face towards me and kissed him to avoid his stare.
As he continued to probe into me with his fingers I pulled him

to his feet and unfastened his belt, releasing his penis, already throbbing, I wanted to suck it but there was no room to bend so I settled for groping it with my hands pulling the skin back to the shaft and jerking forward.

As he began to groan I smiled back at him, equally smug.

A knock on the door froze us temporarily and from outside we heard my ex asking if there was anyone inside, we ignored him and I began to move my hands over him again, cupping his balls in my hand and squeezing gently. He began to moan and I held my hand over his mouth stifling the sounds.

He wrenched my skirt up over my hips and pulled my knickers aside, rubbing my wetness across my clit and pushing his groin towards me.

I pushed him down to sit again on the toilet and sat astride him, slotting my vagina onto his penis and forcing myself down on to it, before standing slightly and rising again to the tip, teasing his hardness against me.

His tongue lapped my nipples and he bit playfully, grabbing hold of my hips and pulling me down to him, grinding my body in circles onto his dick. The train ground on its vibration adding to our pleasure.

My lips parted and my moans escaped it, unable to contain myself, no matter whether he was outside or not, the man planted his lips on mine to quieten me, I thrust my tongue into his mouth, grasping at his body as I turned onto the road to the climax, no avoiding it.
His mouth pulled away from me and his head pushed back as he angled his groin to push further into me, "Oh God" he uttered as his pleasure matched mine, we were thrusting

together intent to rush into it, his eyes opened and he rubbed his mouth across my breasts.

His hands gripped around my ass and he lifted me up and away from him, before slamming me down again, jerking erratically against me, then letting out a strangled scream he released himself into me, holding me firmly.

I had held off for this moment and now I orgasmed my mouth pressed against him to drown out the inevitable screaming. We rocked our bodies together as we reveled in the moment our breaths short and as the intensity settled we kissed, finally our bodies relaxing.

I was a sweaty mess as I dismounted as gracefully as I could muster, straightening my skirt I stood and attempted to use the tiny sink to wash my hands. Behind me he stood and fastened himself up, before letting himself out of the loo without uttering a word.

I cursed myself in the mirror for acting like such a slut, what the hell had come over me. I tidied myself up as best I could and set off back to my seat.

I sat back down, avoiding eye contact with the men across and before me, taking a sip of wine.

"Were you in the toilet" he asked, I looked up but didn't offer an answer.

"I walked down the train and couldn't see you."

"I was in the loo" I answered shrugging my shoulders.

He leaned in towards me "you stink of sex, were you in the toilet with him?" he asked angrily.

I looked up at him and then across at the man who smiled in amusement.

"Yes" I answered, "Best sex I've had in years," he scowled, stood, collected his baggage and shuffled away in disgust. In peace at last I finished my wine and took my book out.

The Lifeguard

I watched her from the shore, laughing and joking with her friends commanding their attention as the alpha female. Yesterday she had checked me out, but she was a tease, when I had tried to get her attention in the sea she had swam off rejoining her friends.

I watched as she peeled off her clothes leaving them on the bench, her tanned body glistening with oil under the tiny red bikini.

She glanced at me, aware I was watching still from my lifeguard station, my colleagues nudging my shoulder as she undressed, yes, she was something, but too aware of it, full of herself. I flirted instead with the friend, also hot but not in the same league.

The inflatable ball the friends were kicking around ended up beside the station more than could be coincidental, but it was the same with all the girls, a new group each week fantasizing over the lifeguards, bouncing around them, all giggly, encouraging each other.

This time the friend retrieved the ball and I jumped down from the chair, break time, I made contact, offer of a drink, of course agreement, I was hot too after all.

We headed up to the beach bar and I grabbed us a couple of cokes, small talk followed, would she like me to take her for a drink later, of course she would. Date set, back to work.
The hot one now flirted more openly, I ignored her, she ran across to retrieve another stray ball, I looked away. The friends headed in the hot one remained, glancing across to make sure I noticed she grabbed a surf board and headed off

into the sea.

Of course, I followed, hard to resist the body, I wanted it and I was not scared to ask. She swam around the rocks heading to the shallow water of the coves and floated there, laid on the board, arms and calves hanging over, I swam near, she knew I was there but gave me no acknowledgement.

I stood beside her, the water chest high and grabbed the bottom of the board, pulling it closer to me. She raised her head and glanced at me, a hint of a smile and lay back again, I pulled the board around so that I faced out to sea, my actions hidden from the shore by my body and walked with it further out.

My hands ran up her legs to her thighs and she continued to ignore me, I pushed the briefs aside and rubbed my thumbs across her clit, a sigh, an involuntary response.

I pulled her body to the edge, walked deeper and thrust my tongue into her, the salt water lapping around us as I expertly licked her clit, pushing my fingers, her arse rose from the board as she pushed towards me, sighs, moans as she flicked her head to both sides in surprise, making sure we were alone.

Her hands gripped the edge of the board as her breath quickened, I had her now but I withdrew. She hovered towards me, enticing me to return.

I reached into the water and placed my hand on my penis, good and ready I wasn't surprised, she lay exposed on the board, her body shimmering. I moved to the side, spinning the board around and pushed the bikini aside taking her nipples in turn into my mouth until they pierced upwards, ignoring her mouth I pulled her down from the board and held my arms around her, pushing her and the board further out to sea.

As we pushed out my penis pushed against her and she pressed towards it, my hands reached around and I massaged her breasts roughly then lowered my hands and entered her, driving my fingers into her vagina as my palms massaged her clit, her head leaned back on my shoulders as she writhed.

Her hands reached round and she took my penis softly massaging its tip. I spun her around, hoisted her legs around my hips and shoved into her, voices could be heard from the shallow waters, coming nearer, we had to be quick.

She clung to my shoulders, her mouth clasped to my neck, she bobbed up and down as the tide helped me, lifting her with me, her hips ground round, her voice in my ear, yess, yesss, too right I thought, gripping her firmly and feeling her throb around me as she came, her eyes squeezed closed, her brow tight in concentration.

I let myself go, the orgasm shuddering through me as my arse clenched and I drove into her squeezing her tightly against me. Clinging together we kissed deeply, our bodies relaxing as the high passed.

I unwrapped her legs from around me and lowered her to the floor, she spun and swam to the board retrieving it as it bobbled away from us.

A frown settled on her face as she looked beyond me towards the shore, a voice now near shouted her name accusingly, her friend, guess our date was off. I turned and swam off into the water, I'd leave them to it.

In the Woods

We had settled on a campsite at last and I dragged the rucksack from my back gratefully, settling myself onto a rock and taking a well-earned drink. The sun beamed down, bursting through the gaps in the trees around us.

Several tents were dotted around the clearing, there occupants unseen, probably hiking in the hills around us. Dan had unpacked the tent and we built it quickly, now experts after almost two weeks of rambling.

Our task completed we unpacked and settled in for the evening grabbing a beer. Eventually our neighbors returned to their tents, offered friendly greetings and for the most part ignored us getting on with their trips.

Our nearest neighbors a couple our age asked us to join them, their set -up superior to ours, fire already in place, we agreed and filled each other in on our adventures. We were all students, travelling for the summer around Lake Tahoe.

As the night grew darker the campsite emptied, the four of us continued to chat quietly, wine and beer had lightened the mood and I was beginning to feel quite light headed.

The couple were quite touchy feely and I looked away embarrassed as they kissed openly, their hands lingering across each other's bodies, I looked at Dan and indicated that it was our cue to leave but he lingered there and watched intently. I smiled, the perv, he was getting off on it and he pulled me closer sitting me on his lap.

As they pulled apart they looked over and saw us watching, eating us alive with their eyes, I cringed, had this been their plan, get us drunk and attack our bodies. I was paranoid, my parents had panicked when we'd told them our plans, warning us of any possible danger of being taken advantage of, robbed or murdered in the vast woods.

We had laughed, we could take care of ourselves. I pushed my fears aside, they were our age, drunk and horny, nothing more.

Below me I could feel Dan harden, the couple continued to embrace, I scanned my eyes around the campsite we were alone, Dan's mouth lowered to my neck and he kissed me, his hands holding me tightly to him.

As always butterflies flickered across my stomach, I couldn't resist him, his touch drove me crazy, I pulled his chin up and his mouth to mine, kissing him deeply. The sounds of the couple's kisses joined those of the forest, blending with the sounds of distant animals and the wind.

I flinched involuntarily as I felt Dan's hands push into my trousers, panicked I looked across at the couple and saw that they were ignorant to what we were up to, their own hands actions invisible within each other's clothing but clearly busy as their faces flushed and their kisses grew more passionate.

I continued to stare at them, facing forwards away from Dan as he brushed around making his way into my underwear, I groaned as he found my clit rubbing his fingertips against it, I reached round and returned the favor, releasing his now bulging penis and rubbing It gently, safely hidden behind my back.

The couple looked towards us as our breaths grew louder, and he pulled her onto his lap as their positions mirrored ours, her face flush as his hands drew across her breasts, releasing them over her vest as he twisted his nipples between his fingers. Dan watching her from behind me hardened still as his hand rose to copy, clutching at my breasts.

The woman dropped to the floor in front of her partner and she took his penis into her mouth, her head bobbing up and down as she sucked him, his face lit up, the fire flashing before him between us highlighting his pleasure.

Dan dragged his hands down my hips pushing down my trousers and threw them aside, I quickly checked my top hung down enough to cover me as he lifted me up, seating me closer to him, his penis angled to push inside me as I was forced back downwards.

The man stared from across the fire his moans now coming in short blasts as he held his partners head encouraging her deeper and deeper onto him.

My body rocked as Dan bulged against me his hands held me close pinning me to him, his hands spread across the front of my vagina heightening my feelings. The man squeezed his eyes closed, obviously about to come and my movements quickened, his pleasure contagious.

Dan's hand closed around my mouth, trying to stifle my moans as I neared orgasm, I bit his fingers to stop myself screaming, as I heard him groaning and felt his penis throb as he shot into me.
Across from us the man's shoulders relaxed as he also came, she withdrew from him, licking to the tip of his penis. I came with a shudder, squeezing onto him, taking his hand from across my mouth and letting him squeeze me close as we softened together our bodies trembling.

In the Office

I waited patiently, my guest would arrive shortly, a hooker. I had no shame, my time was precious, the pressure in my head mounted I needed release.

She arrived, my assistant announced her, dressed in a suit she could be anyone. She stood opposite me, I didn't want a chat her instructions had been made clear.

She undid the jacket, tossing it aside and stepped out of the skirt. Her body glistened, taut and tanned, black leather and lace, her nipples and crotch naked, straps around them, suspenders, fish net stretched across her long legs her thighs solid, heels lengthened her body, her hair pulled tight back from her face. Perfect I thought, let's begin.

I pushed back from the desk, naked lower half revealed, my shirt and tie remained. I held a hand on my penis already warmed up, I watched as she sauntered around the room, bending from the hip as she took cuffs and a whip from her bag.

She crossed towards me taking my hands and cuffed them behind me. She snapped my head back and shoved a nipple into my mouth ordering me to suck it, she replaced it with a finger and I tasted her on it, she had followed my instructions.

She walked to my front and leaned my seat backwards, sitting astride me, she rubbed herself against my leg and kissed me deeply, as I moaned she brought the whip down, sharp against my thighs.

My dick lengthened inching towards it, she teased her vagina over it, close enough to enter but not quite, she pulled away and dropped to her knees. Her mouth closed around my balls, the skin taut as she nipped her teeth around it dragging it roughly.

Her fingers nipped at her breasts, her nipples hard. Her tongue began to rise the shaft of the penis, her hands holding it stiffly in place, I watched greedily yearning for her to enclose it inside her, damn the script I'd prepared I wanted her to suck me. I instructed her so, her response rocked me, the whip cracking down across my balls.

She stood and strode around me, picking up a gag and securing it around my mouth, the ball fixed in me stifling my voice.

She undid the cuffs, dragging me to my feet before securing me once more on the leg of the table, she kicked my legs apart and shoved me forwards, a swift whip across my arse encouraging me to bend further, my arse sticking into the air.

I gasped in anticipation, she had withdrawn again, I knew what was coming.

My arse cheeks were pulled aside a plug entered, pushing through the tip of my anus and rubbing there before advancing further.

My legs almost buckled, I pressed towards the plug as it pushed further settling an inch in, thick and rough against me, she secured it there and reached between my legs to my balls wrapping leather around it and squeezing it tightly.

The pain shot through me my pleasure peaked, groans escaped through the ball of my gag and she stiffened, forcing her shoulder back to gain force in the whip as she flung it against my arse, the skin prickled, a deep red line formed as the blood rushed to the skin.

She stopped listening to my breathing, her hand reached around and she took my throbbing penis into my hand slashing the skin back as she pushed to the shaft, before driving her hand forwards, twisting it at the edge as she tossed her wrist quickly.

Again, to the shaft, my back lengthened, clenching the butt plug against me. I counted the seconds, holding my breath until again she tossed, I began to pump my body with her hand I was going to come, shoot across the desk, but maddeningly she slowed, I groaned my displeasure and felt the thrash of the whip once more against me.

I groaned again loving the pain and stretching into it another strike, followed by another, which whipped the edged of my balls, the pain ripped through me, I tried to cry out but the gag wouldn't allow it, instead my hands thrashed around in panic.

Her tongue ran over the contact points, my arse throbbed, she dropped to her knees beneath me and took the shaft of my penis into her mouth, gagging as she held me deep inside and rubbing her tongue across the tip as she withdrew it.

Further and further she pushed, distant phones rang as the office work continued around us, my staff scurrying around getting on with their work.

The pain eased, the pleasure grew, my hips gyrated, her hands held my arse close, the butt plug pushing inwards, I trembled. Standing she slipped around me, releasing the cuffs and shoving me into the chair once more.

The butt plug strained deeper as it pushed against the chair, as she secured my arms behind me I wriggled loving the pressure in my arse as I vibrated against it. She faced the desk and stood before it, lowering her chest to drape across it.

Her legs lifted and she pulled the chair towards her, slotting her legs between my arms and waist, her heels scratching against me, she pushed her hand down and pulled my dick forwards, angling it towards her, then pressed her hands against the desk as she pushed me into her, dragging the chair on the wheels forwards and back as she circled against me.

I looked down at her bare arse pushing against me and struggling with the cuffs around my waist, I wanted to grab it and hold her closer, the pressure of her around me teased too softly I wanted to rip into her and grind her against me.

The circles continued my dick maddeningly teased against it still the pleasure rose, I yearned for her to quicken, desperate for the finale.

Her body position adjusted and at last she squeezed onto me, pushing me into the chair and the plug deeper inside me, I began to gasp, her resolve fell and her control weakened, her back arched, she reached up and released her hair letting it fall and onto my face.

Suddenly the script seemed to dawn on her and she rose, leaving my penis throbbing beneath her, she ripped the gag from me and released my cuffs.

I rose towering over her and pushed her flat against the desk, her cheeks glowed her lips spread as she struggled to catch her breath, she had gotten carried away, so close to coming, satisfied she hadn't I let her breath settle, running my hands across her breasts and then felt it quicken again as I lowered my knees and rammed myself into her.

Pulling her hips forward to hold her stiff against me, just in time she began to orgasm, her face pressed tightly against the desk, her arms flailing above her.

I slowed drawing out the moment, feeling her wetness flushed around me, my dick squeezed within her, holding it in place. My knees began to tremble, my body shivering I couldn't hold any longer, my pace quickened once more pumping in and out of her, her wetness squelching around me, mine joined it as I burst inside her. Driving my arse forward and jerking desperately.

Satisfied I had had my monies worth I pulled away withdrawing and discarding the plug unceremoniously. She dressed, securing her hair back in place, and sipping water as her breathing returned to normal.

She took a seat opposite me and smile. The intercom clicked on and my assistant knocked to enter, checking all was back in order I ushered her in.

"Sorry Mr. Harding I didn't know you had company," she apologized as she stepped forward.

Her head glanced towards my guest, who smiled and nodded back.
"Mrs. Harding, how are you."

My wife smiled, looking over at me.

"Just leaving" she laughed, the spell broken, she stood and planting a kiss on my lips, left taking her bag of tricks along with her.

The Window Cleaner

I woke, my eyes remained closed as I tried desperately to recall the dreams that lingered, they had left me moist and frustrated, there was no rush to get up I had nowhere to get too.

Outside, I heard the scraping of ladders against the house, my eyes flickered open and I looked to the window, it had been hot during the night and the window was open along with the blinds.

I smiled, it would be a while before he got to the window, leisurely I put my hands between my legs under the covers and began to massage myself gently. The sheet pulled down, my breasts exposed I rubbed my nipples.

I pressed my knees together squeezing my hand tighter and rocked there, the ladders remained where they were I was safe for a while.

I leaned over and grabbed my vibrator glancing at the window to check it was clear, it was, I turned the vibrator on and pushed it inside me, the vibrations made my pulse quicken and I steered it deep inside me before withdrawing and rubbing it against my clitoris rolling around under its pressure.

I climbed the ladder and pushed the window inwards so that I could position the ladder more centrally over it, about to head down.

I noticed her, seemingly asleep on the bed her body writhing around the pleasure on her face obvious. I hovered there unable to pull away as the sheet pulled downwards exposing her pert breasts, her hands reached up and she rubbed them seductively. I looked around, I was at the back of the house, no one could see me.

Her body rocked, I could trace the outline of her hand under the sheets rubbing herself against it. Her eyes flickered open and she looked at the window, she must have seen me, but she didn't react, reaching around and grabbing a vibrator from a drawer, she pulled the sheets away from her, her knees bending as she pushed it inside herself, I gasped feeling the pressure in my jeans growing, I pushed against the side of the ladder, rubbing against it.

I listened for ladders, heard nothing, maybe he had been leaving, I thought of him, we had flirted for weeks, his muscles flexed as he washed the windows bare chested late into the summer, when a shirt would surely have been necessary, who would complain, we'd chatted about him, the neighbors and I, joked about dragging him into our houses and seducing him.

The vibrator lingered over my clit and I pulled it up to my breasts, feeling it tingle against my nipples, I threw my head back and bent my knees, turning the vibrator back to my clit before plunging it deep inside me, grinding my hips against it.

The vibrator in place I rolled over onto my stomach and slipped to the edge of the bed, I grabbed a pillow, planting it on the corner and pushed my arms against the bed grinding my clit against it as the vibrator continued to pulsate inside me.

My body throbbed I yearned to come but I wanted to draw

out the moment, my pace slowed wide circular motions my clit pushing against the pillow every few seconds, my fingers clenched around the sheets, my teeth clenched.

She took the vibrator from herself and pulled it towards her chest, its tip glistened with her wetness. My penis stirred in my jeans and I lowered my zip to release it, taking it in my hands and jacking it swiftly, she was putting on a show.

Her body lifted and she again glanced at me, grabbing a pillow she shoved the vibrator deep, impaling it in her as she rammed the pillow against it and ground against them both.

She was facing me, a few feet away her hips ground so slowly, her face shone, her head tossing side to side I imagined standing before her shoving my dick into her mouth, her tongue licking its tip before pulling it deep inside her. My penis throbbed I held it there, waiting for her.

I heard a sound outside, my eyes half opened and I glanced, through the glare from the window I notice a shadow, then a face hovering there.

I squeezed my eyes closed ignoring it, I considered running but the pleasure in me deepened as it dawned on me that he had been watching me, I wondered if he was touching himself, hoped that he was and imagined him with me, writhing beneath me his biceps flexing as he held me against me.

I returned to the bed, improving his view. I lay before him, my legs spread wide I teased the vibrator over my nipples then against my clit, spreading myself and rising my hips against it, my fingers pushed inside me I couldn't hold much longer, desperate to come I shoved the vibrator back inside me lifting my body with my elbows pushed against the bed to watch myself.

Bravely I opened my eyes, the sun had passed, his face clear now, his eyes watched my groin hungrily his body leaning in and out, his jaw clenched, his eyes drew up and met mine.

She lay back on the bed, legs spread wide, her fingers pushed in and out, the vibrator pressed over her body and returning to her clit, her legs held tense, her body tossed side to side, moans escaping her mouth as it lay open, I squeezed my hand around myself, gripping the ladder tightly with the other, my mind wandered I was standing before her.

Her vibrator returned to her vagina and in my mind, I was it, entering her, her hands grabbing around my hips as she pulled me closer.

My hips pumped forward, I stared watching it pushed in and out, her moans deepened I looked up to her face, her eyes met mine, she was watching me.

Her eyes were begging for it, I increased my pace and fell in against the ladder as I came, groans escaped my lips as I tensed my jaw, to shut myself up I pulled down and squeezed my balls enjoying the moment.

She was starting to come before me her body rocking, she rolled into it, withdrawing the vibrator and pressing against her clit as she rubbed against it, her body softened, the vibrator clicked off and she froze there, head laid back.

I studied his face, the eyes narrowed, the jaw clenched, as my pleasure rose his body fell in against the ladder, he was coming it was obvious and I couldn't help but join him. My body exploded I needed the pressure against my clit so withdrew the vibrator and held it against me, on it went until finally the pleasure waned and I collapsed against the bed, my body shivering.

Moments passed I daren't open my eyes, finally I heard the ladder being pulled against the wall. I pulled the sheets back over myself, pledging to go back to sleep and imagine I had been dreaming.

In the Van

She walked past us 20 times a day, strutting her stuff, we wolf whistled of course, they expect it, would be offended if we didn't, the older ones struggled to hide their glee as we include them.

She must live nearby, we had never spoken but we had glared and the job would be finished in a few days so it was high time I made a move, the end of the day neared, the site emptied as I packed everything away, I was in no rush, I knew her last passing for the day was near.

And here she came, I intentionally blocked her path with a wheelbarrow as she neared, she could have gone around if she really wanted to avoid me, instead she lingered as I had known she would do and we chatted flirting openly.

I told her I would be leaving the area shortly and asked her out, she said she couldn't she had a boyfriend. I smiled as if that was relevant, I was hardly looking for a relationship.

I offered a quick coffee, she agreed and as I pulled into the drive through she laughed. I drove back around to the site, pulling around the corner against the trees, she rose her eyebrows as she noted the privacy, but didn't object.

We sipped our coffee and made small talk, she was 27, had had a boyfriend for the past couple of years on and off, both had cheated. I was single, travelled around the county for work had casual relationships, nothing serious.

Coffees finished I leaned in towards her, pretty confidant she wouldn't reject me, we kissed, my hands travelled towards her lap but she stopped me holding it there.

Her attraction was obvious, her kisses passionate, I wanted her but she was making it clear, I had no chance.

Months passed and I returned, I wasn't used to rejection, the number of women I'd had in my van totted up weekly. There she was hot as ever, dressed to impress despite the time of day, I lowered my window shouting her over, fancy a coffee later I asked raising my eye-brows, she leaned in towards me planting a kiss.

I'm working she said as she pulled away – unless you want to pay the going rate. I stared back, she was a prostitute I had had no idea.

My workmates were none the wiser and not seeing a problem, I invited her to hop in, not bothering with the coffee I pulled further up in against the trees and asked her to follow me round to the back of the van.

Scrapping the foreplay, charged by the hour I asked her to strip her own clothes off, and pulled off mine, pulling her down on to the mattress beside me.

Her body was as I expected curves in all the right places, I ran my hands over her, my dick stiffening. She leaned forward and took me in her hands massaging me gently, I lay back on the mattress and she sat astride me kissing first my mouth before settling on my neck and biting my ears roughly.

I would let her do the work seen as I was paying for it, she travelled down to my dick, placing her hands expertly around it before plunging me into her mouth, as she sucked I put my hands on her head guiding the pace.

I pulled her away just in time, so close to coming, my dick

throbbing, I wanted to feel her inside me. She scraped her body up pushing against me, and as it pushed inside her the pleasure rose to bursting once more.

She leaned forward kissing me passionately before shoving her breasts into my mouth and juggled them against me. I clung to her lips dragging her towards me as I came, thundering into her.

With a satisfied smile, I lay back on the mattress, she dressed hurriedly and put her hand out for payment, I reached into my pocket handing the notes over, you paid for an hour and lasted….8 minutes she said, lifting her wrist and glancing at her watch, well done she said sarcastically, stepping out of the van and slapping the door behind her.

The Babysitter

The wife tottered around the bar, drunk as a skunk as usual, no matter, I'd peel her from the taxi and tuck her safely in bed. I checked the time, last orders at last.

The babysitter had arrived dressed for summer, floaty white summer dress, legs bare, she'd been on my mind all night and I couldn't wait to walk her home, our chats on the route through the paths at the edges of the woods had become increasingly flirty, tonight I'd decided would be the night I made a move.

We had had her for years, through the end of school, soon she would leave for college, she had been the star of more of my fantasises than she could ever dream of, I needed a memory for real.

Home, the wife staggered up to bed, time to go. I passed her a jacket it was starting to get chilly, held it open for her, brushing my hands across her bare shoulders as I helped her into it, she turned, smiled, my penis already twitching.

Off the main street we walked single file, her butt tight, skirt flitting over her mid thighs, my thoughts raced ahead of me, in my mind she was already laid in the grass, my hands pushing up her skirt.

She paused, there was a bridge here, over the stream, she leant against its bannister, a signal, she wanted me.

I stood behind her and moved her hair to the side, leaning slowly I began to kiss the back of her neck, she felt like silk, darkness all around us the stream reflecting the light of the moon, she turned to face me and put her arms up around my neck, kissing my lips slowly and deeply.

The path split in two, the first leading across the bridge to her estate, the second deeper into the woods, as we kissed I steered her, feet inching slowly towards the woods, just around the corner a bench awaited us.

As we kissed I pushed the jacket from her, freeing her shoulders her body glistened her long hair soft and tangled in a mass of curls. I pulled her close to me, tracing the curve of her back with my hands as I held her close, she tasted sweet, innocent and yielding.

I sat on the bench and pulled her down beside me, hands continuing to search he body, her breasts softy and high bounced freely beneath the cotton, her nipples stood on end piercing though, I pushed the thin straps of her dress aside, down her arms and slowly peeled the dress down.

I sighed as the breasts were freed, taking them in my hands in turn and squeezing them slowly, the nipples commanded the attention of my lips, I bit them gently swishing my tongue across them and watching them raise higher still.

Her head lay back, a soft smile on her lips, eyes closed. My hand lowered to her lap and I inched up her skirt, her underwear white, I traced the outline of it with my hands, skipping over them and rubbing the tops of her thighs.

She purred like a cat upon me, I smiled and her eyes met mine, so desperate, we kissed again I placed her hand on my crotch and she ran her fingers across the outline of my penis, her face questioning, desperate to be freed of my trousers.

I undid the belt, ripping open the button and zip and placed her hand inside, it lingered there, deliberately teasing, laughter in her eyes as she sensed my desperation.

My thumb pressed against her clitoris as I teased her in return and she groaned, I rubbed across it above the nickers and watched her mouth open softly low moans escaping, her eyes opened and she stared at me shyly, embarrassed at the sounds she couldn't contain.

I pulled her knickers to the side slowly inserting a finger into her, her back straightened and her arms held me closer as she tried to hide her face. I pulled her back, I wanted to watch her, her beautiful face creased as her pleasure increased, with each rub of her clitoris her brows raised her face tensing.

She put her hand on mine to slow me but I continued, my finger dipping in and out of her, I was mesmerised by her face

I wanted to watch her orgasm, my penis stirred, her light touch continued but as her pleasure increased she wrapped her fingers around me and held me more firmly against them, her hand began to rise and fall I stiffened, fighting the desire to lift her onto my dick and push myself into her.

I leaned in and began to kiss her neck passionately so close to her mouth I felt the heat of her breath against me, her head leaned back on the bench, my head lowered to her breasts as I sucked them once more, now more urgently my pressure rising as her head began to flail side to side.

I removed her hand from me, it was becoming too much, leaning her back against me I reached both hands around her, both now passed under her knickers as I paid full attention to her clit, she inhaled sharply as my fingers flicked against it.

Her hips beginning to circle slowly, I smiled I had hit her

sweet spot, her arms flailed as she tried to take me in her hands. I held her firmly against me, my penis pushing into the small of her back, even its pressure was hard to contain as she writhed against me.

My lips ran across her shoulders, her head fell against mine I turned her to face me, her eyes opened, she was so close. I held my breath, calming myself.

I lingered my fingertips over her my pace controlled, she pushed her hand over mine, desperate for me to return, I obliged, at the same time I pushed two fingers into her, surprised at the wetness as I felt her muscles squeezing around them.

She tried but failed to refrain herself, her groans escalating, I stared into her eyes as she came, her jaw clenched with concentration as she lost herself momentarily.

Once it was over I released my hands and held her close, her heartbeat settled, she remained there transfixed. Her nipples softened, I kissed her shoulders as I brought my hands to them, taking my time, I played around, finding the actions that best stiffened them.

I had dreamed of these breasts for so long, seen them behind all manner of material and fantasised of seeing them naked, now I was holding them, kissing them it was blowing my mind.

My hand traced across her stomach, firm and flat and down to her hips, I pushed them across her pubis and watched as she shifted if forward, she told me it tickled but I could tell that she was still turned on.

I lowered her head to the bench and slipped away from her, I wouldn't have her for much longer, I wanted to taste every inch of her, I pulled her legs up and across the bench and kneeled before her.

I took off her shoes, kissing her toes then rubbing my hands across her ankles and following with my lips. I raised to her knees then planting kisses all the way up her thighs, I spread her legs apart and licked across her clit, her back arched and I smiled.

I passed to her stomach kissing it gently my fingers ran across her clitoris and settled on her vagina, quickly teasing in and out of it. My hands rose and gave her breasts more attention, the nipples brought stiff once more.

As my tongue licked across her up and down her heartbeat began to increase once more. Her hand reached between my legs as my slow kisses increased in hardness, she held herself firmly around me rubbing me up and down gently.

My intensity rose and I grabbed her nipples with my teeth, closing them gently as she moaned beneath me.

I removed my trousers completely and stepped over the bench with one leg, she lay flat upon it now, pulling my penis towards her face.

As she held it with her hands she licked up the sides of it before taking it in her mouth and dragging deeply, I felt dizzy my legs almost collapsed as she rode me deeper, twisting herself round it as she rocked it against her cheek.

Her eyes held mine, no longer shyly she was an expert at this I had never been sucked so hard. Her hands held my arse firmly as she pulled me in place. At the last second, I withdrew, ripping myself away from her, my dick throbbed as I hovered over her.

I leaned in and kissed her mouth, she took my tongue and maneuverer her lips around it as she had with my dick. My hands lifted her legs up and my fingers tested her, dipping into her vagina and rubbing across her clit, yes, the power she had over me with her blow job had turned her on.

Her hips rose to my hand as I shoved into her, her eyes hungry. She pulled her hands over my back and pulled me into her, wrapping her legs tightly around me a she gyrated.

I tried to breath slowly and distract myself to last forever but it was no use, her vagina throbbed tightly against me, her breasts bouncing with her thrusts, nipples erect.

Her lips sucked at my neck and ears, her eyes watching me hungrily, her head threw back and she began to shout at me, her voice piercing through the stillness of the night. "yesssss" she screamed, driving me crazy as she began to orgasm.

Her voice pushed me past the brink and realising there was no return I surrender, no longer concerned with quieting her my voice joined hers as our moans rose together.

My pleasure escalated beyond anything I had ever known, her nails dug into me as she squeezed me closer and finally I burst into her, jabbing her fiercely as we came, our lips silencing each other as realisation set in and it dawned on us where we were.

We calmed and I pulled away from her, redressing as she rearranged herself and replaced her shoes. I held her hand as I pulled her from the bench and we continued to walk in silence.

We reached the end of the path, her house across the street, I leaned over and kissed her gently on the lips and watched her go, skipping gently across the street, as she reached her door, she turned and waved as she always did, this time blowing me a kiss.

The Taxi

I picked them up from the club, one man, two women, drunk, but not to sickness I knew to avoid those. They squeezed together into the back of the cab, a woman either side of him, the man draped his arms around their shoulders, he was in for a good night,

I set off, a long fare glancing back to them in the mirror, I adjusted it angling it down. His head lay back, his face glowing, hands pressed against him shifting forwards and back. He turned to his right, kissing the woman beside him, his hands massaging her breasts over her dress.

The second woman leaned over to him and began to undo his jeans, she glanced to them in satisfaction as she released his penis and leant in towards her, her head bobbing up and down as she sucked him deeply.

Moans escaped his lip and the woman he was kissing stared at him in surprise, she looked down and realised why he was moaning, her friends head rubbing against him, she laughed and pulled her friend up, scolding her with a pointed finger and a faked frown.

The man kissed them one against the other, pushing both their hands towards his penis as he pushed both their legs open and shoved there skirts up, rubbing his fingers against their clits.

Three heads lay back absorbing the pleasure as we travelled along leisurely, I was in no rush this was quite a show.

One of the women's eyes met mine as I glanced towards her,

she knew I was watching, I quickly glanced away, had I blown it. Minutes later I looked back she continued to stare at me, seemingly no problem with it, she pulled her top down releasing her breasts and rubbing them roughly with her hands, she smiled.

The man leaned in over her lap, I coudn't see what he was doing but her face lit up, her eyes closed, the woman leaned in to quiet her, snogging her mouth and rubbing her hands across her breasts.

I turned the corner onto the main road, as we turned they fell against each other. The woman on the receiving end of his mouth began to groan loudly, her face thrashing side to side, the others laughed piling on the pressure.

Suddenly she screamed out in pleasure I glanced to the mirror her friend had her hand over her mouth trying to shut her up, her eyes wide she acknowledged her and calmed herself, pulling him up and away from her, wiping his mouth with her hands.

We pushed further into the estate not far now, I chuckled to myself, this was one to tell the wife. The satisfied woman now lolled against the window her eyes closed.

The man pushed his hand against her, checking to see if she was awake, she gave no response. He looked to her friend and they began to kiss passionately, engrossed in each other. He pulled her onto his lap and she sat astride him, her hips gyrating.

Her face lowered to his neck as she kissed him leaving his face revealed, he concentrated intently his eyes squeezed closed.

She continued to push against him, alternating between bouncing around and pushing forward and back.

Our destination neared and I considered taking a detour, but not wanting to be accused of overcharging I figured I better not and pulled into the street, stopping at the kerbside.

I lingered there for a few seconds before the woman shouted from the back, "Could you go around the block please mate" her voice breathless. I looked in the mirror and the man smiled back at me, his face in agreement I smiled and obliged.

I took a turn away and as I did, the woman began to bob more violently and shout out, I raised my eye brows, mildly amused, she thrashed her head dramatically, encouraging him to join her.

He shut her up with his mouth pulling her to him as he held his arms around her, his face anguished. Suddenly he came, earlier embarrassed by her screams his now rose above hers as enjoyed the moment, pumping into her erratically.

Now finished he lifted her unceremoniously and plopped her on the seat beside him. She adjusted her closing and instructed me to continue.

We pulled up and I switched on the overhead light, the sleeping woman now stirred and her friend hopped out of the taxi running around to her side to retrieve her, the man paid and with a wink, joined them outside and led them arms around his shoulders into the flat.

The Gardener

I lusted after him, there was no denying it, I watched as he pushed the mower across the grass his muscles bulging beneath his shirt. I sat in the conservatory, draped across the lounger as I watched him, the grass was short enough my sister had assured me, was she blind this man was a god.

He was young enough to be my son, I brushed the thoughts away I wasn't going to pounce on him, watching was enough.

It had been so long since I'd had the pleasure of a man, I'd shut myself away since my husband had died, no one could match him or even come close. I was consent with my books, the gardener a welcome distraction.

He finished the task, shutting the mower away and stepped in to me, should he start the tree now, yes, I agreed offering him a drink first, he accepted, I poured him some juice from the jug and he chugged it down his Adams apple bobbling in his thick chest.

I sighed, ah to kiss that neck and feel the hands around me. He thanked me and stepped out. The sun beamed down, a line of moisture appeared on his back as he stretched up and began trimming the branches, take it off, I willed silently.

The clippings fell to the floor as he worked, his arms reaching high up the branches, my husband had planted the tree when the children were small, now it stood tall, its branches reaching into the neighbours' gardens much to their annoyance, hence its requirements for the gardener's attention, I required the gardener's attention I thought a smile teasing my lips as the thought occurred.

He took a moment, at last releasing his chest from his shirt, his body glistened his chest bulging, he was tensing it purposely, I could tell, who was he trying to impress, he turned and saw me staring, I blushed.

He returned to the tree, I should pull my eyes away, I had been watching him for months but hadn't realised he knew it, I didn't want him running for the hills. As he headed towards the house I grabbed a book, a distraction, he would see I was not watching him.

He entered and asked for another drink, I told him to help himself, he sat on the edge of the chair as he drank and then he asked me if there was anything else he could do, he was finished.

My answer should have been that no I would see him next week, but I paused, unintentionally I glanced down at his body, feeling foolish and attempting to disguise my mistake my eyes returned to his and I babbled that yes that was it, the garden was finished. He stared back at me, my lust, obvious reflected in his eyes.

He reached out and held my hand, I trembled, he lifted my hand to his lips kissed it softly, his eyes fixed on mine. I hesitated so unsure of myself, panic threatened but he pulled me to him, his strong arms wrapped around me as he held my lips to his and he kissed me soft and long.

My body stirred, old feelings rushed to mind of love and passion, how I missed him. I had shut myself away, turned off my emotions and kept people at harms length afraid to be hurt, but in the process turning away friendships and new possibilities.

It had been too long, the gates crashed down as I began to return his kisses, falling into him, his hands held against the small of my back, firm and strong, rubbing it gently. He paused and led me, quickly by the hand to the stairs and without question I followed him to the bedroom.

He stood me at the foot of the bed and peeled away my shirt, I tried not to glance at myself in the mirror, to catch a glimpse of the woman past her prime against his god like image in the mirror, I scorned myself for being pathetic, I was not so bad, swimming kept me in shape and I was not yet 50, I pushed my self-pity aside.

He lowered his lips across my neck, lowering himself to my breasts as he released my bra clip and took my nipples into his mouth, I sighed as the pleasure pushed through me.

He stood away from me and removed the rest of his clothes, his penis stood impressively, he lowered me to the bed and his kisses continued, so softly brushing against me, lowering to my stomach as he removed my skirt. Then his lips rose to mine and he entered me.

Our eyes locked he ground his hips against mine, his hands holding me firmly, our mouths pressed hungrily towards each other and as I kissed his neck I heard moans escape him and they filled me with joy, to know that he wanted this, that he wanted me, because oh how I wanted him.

My body relaxed, growing with confidence, my legs rose and I wrapped them around him squeezing him tight, he smiled feeling the shift in me his butt forcing forward harder.

I loved sex, I always had done and I realised how much I had missed it, this feeling of abandon where nothing matters, the closeness everything open, eyes windows to the feelings deep within.

His face pressed to my neck and he sucked passionately, his grip tightening. His moans grew louder, his hands running through my hair and holding my face near. I wanted to see him, to stare into his eyes.

I pushed him away from me and he froze, panicked, concerned he had hurt me, as he relaxed I pushed him round to his back, no longer concerned with my appearance I sat astride him, pushing my hands against his chest as I rubbed myself over him, before pushing him into me.

Tears rose to my eyes as my ecstasy increased, he lay below me, pushing his pelvis forward to increase the pressure within me as his eyes lit up.

He rubbed my breasts with his hands as he held himself firm below me, his nose crinkled and he puffed through the pleasure, it was clear he was holding off for me for as long as he could but couldn't wait much longer.

I yelled out as it hit, like an onslaught missing for so long, my whole body shuddered and I pushed myself back, my arms flung above my head as my rhythm slowed and I pinned myself to him, immediately he joined me as jabbed at me violently, pumping himself up and into him as he came murmuring softly.

We twisted together as we rose and fell and my body dropped to his as the pleasure passed and we clung together, him softly running his hands across my back.

We lay there for a while, everything had changed, there was so much time left I couldn't keep hidden away. I stepped away from him and wrapped myself in a gown, I sat on the edge of the bed and dropped a kiss on his lips, silently thanking him, before leaving him to alone to dress.

The Mistress

I strolled around the shops, passing time, the hotel had a wealth of them, the room tab would be settled, one of the benefits of having a rich older lover.

The disadvantage, no say, our meet time had been delayed three times now and I'd been hanging around for two days, he didn't like me to have had a drink when he met me, so I'd remained almost sober, throwing time away.

I returned to my suite, time to prepare now, soon he would arrive and the time would fly and then he would leave me again, hanging around. I lounged in the bath, soaking my skin, but not for too long, he wouldn't like my skin to be dimpled.

My hair shimmered, styled to perfection to look bedraggled and fresh. My lips red, otherwise make up thick but looking barely there, everything as he wanted, nothing to my taste but all I really wanted was him.

I dressed, satin underwear at the skin, long gown above, I dressed to go out but doubted we would, we rarely did, he wanted to spend every moment making love to me, we barely spoke in fact.

I imagined us laughing in a restaurant, him hanging on my every word, but that was not my job, I wondered if it was his wife's, but if that was the case why the need for me. He loved her that was clear and she was beautiful, I'd spotted them splashed across the pages of the magazine and they were snapped staring lovingly at one another.

I'd screwed the pages up when I had seen them, before

rushing out and buying another copy. It now rested on the coffee table, I wanted to check his reaction when he saw that I had seen it wondering whether he would offer an explanation.

At last I heard the card in the door and he entered, he headed straight to me, lifting me up and throwing me straight on the bed, briefly annoyed his kisses soon settled me and I returned them passionately.

He laid on the bed and pushed my head downwards, he loved me to suck him, said I was an expert. I pulled his trousers off, he didn't bother with underwear and took him into my mouth, sucking to its core and releasing before driving down again, his penis stood to attention, proud and erect.

I took it by the base and pulled it back, holding it firmly whilst I licked it roughly with my tongue, taking care not to miss an inch of it.

He lay silently on the bed his eyes closed, I wanted to sit upon and feel him inside me, hold him close while he fucked me but that was not my option, if he wanted it he would tell me.

I continued to lick and kiss, rubbing my hands across his balls as I again took him deeply, squeezing into him with my hands as my mouth held him tight.

Without warning, he ejaculated into me, shooting himself down my throat, I pulled away to disguise my gags, discretely wiped my mouth and pulled up, laid beside him. His eyes closed, a smile on his face, I laid my head on his shoulder, I had missed him.

He smiled at me, ruffling my hair with his hands before pulling away. He stood and waltzed in to the bathroom closing the door behind him. I grabbed a gum from the dresser and flopped annoyed on the bed.

Impatient for my own release I tapped the sheets with my fingers as I awaited his return, I wouldn't complain, that was a wife's job, over the months I had perfected the ability to hold my tongue, never complain, determined to become a perfect mistress, convinced he would one day ditch the wife, but the dream appeared to be distancing itself I was a prostitute, serving his every whim without complaint. And if I was a prostitute I needed a pay rise, I realised. So, two choices get something out of it or call it a day.

He returned and I propped myself onto my elbows, he had showered, his body shimmered, god he was so hot, he made me squirm, I told him so and he joined me on the bed, pulling my dress of roughly as his eyes ravished my body, touch yourself, he commanded.

I paused, this was a new one, intrigued I ran my hands over the satin, he stepped from the bed and sat beside it, his legs spread as his penis rested between them, as I released a nipple from the top of the satin rubbing it gently it throbbed gently, stiffening.

I pulled my nipples to my mouth, teasing them gently with my tongue as my hand dropped, I pushed it down under my knickers as my hand, hidden rubbed around my clitoris, tweaking it gently.

He gulped as he watched. I sat and pulled down my knickers, tossing them from my ankle, I spread my legs before him, slowly pushing a finger inside me and holding my thighs apart.

As his dick hardened I moaned imagining it inside me as my

pace quickened, the finger rubbing harder against my clit before driving inside me, quickly pushing me close, before withdrawing again.

His hand dropped to his penis and he began to flick his hand over it, his pace quickening as he watched, I signalled him to join me, my eyes begging to be fucked. He smiled and refused, continuing to rub his hands against himself.

Annoyed I spun away from him, rising to my knees as my arse faced him, I reached through and pushed my fingers into myself, my groin pressed towards the hand as I rubbed against it, fuck him, I could do this myself, I tried to block his groans from my mind as I absorbed myself in my movements, I didn't want to tease, I needed to come. I would not let him see my face, I knew he loved too but this time, no chance.

As I groaned in pleasure I felt him behind me, he ripped my hands away, replacing them with his dick, solid hard inside me, his body leaned over me as he grabbed my breasts, gripping him to me, I felt his lips on my back biting at my flesh as he tore into me.

My anger dissipated as we rocked, he was huge I felt him so deep inside me, his hand against my clit I rubbed desperately onto him. Suddenly I was coming, screaming out as he fucked me, pushing into him as he drove deeper, finally crushing me as he came, we shuddered together, locked in time as the waves passed.

He dismounted and we lay together, finally intimate. I was a fool I knew it, for this moment it was worth it. For now, this would do, it would have too.

The Windows

Dark set in and we watched, my partner and I, in eager anticipation. For the past few nights we had been given quite a show, in the opposite block, recent occupants either didn't know or didn't care that we could see them, having sex openly in the window.

We had pulled the sofa around especially, our light remained dimmed, they couldn't see us, or at least we hoped not as we sat eating pizza and drinking wine. There light flicked on and we laughed and gripped each other's arms excitedly, yes, we were sad, but it was free porn, who would look away.

A knock at our door, our friends had arrived, yes, we had invited them to watch with us, sad we knew but it was too funny. We sat together awaiting the start of the show.

In walked the woman and we cheered, dressed in underwear and heels we debated whether she was a prostitute, we couldn't see their faces clearly so didn't know if the man had been the same, three nights in a row we had watched them fuck. A man joined her and we cheered again, raising our glasses as we laughed.

He stood behind her his hands circling her waist before rubbing across her breast, releasing them from the lacy bra, her legs spread as he reached down, rubbing her. We realised they were not alone, another man stepped into view, he walked before her and kneeled licking between her thighs. Jesus my friend exclaimed why are we not filming this, we shushed him as we continued to watch.

The woman bent forward pulling the man up to her and they embraced, kissing passionately, her hands were on them both, their bodies rocking against her as she worked her hands up and down over their penises.

She dropped to her knees, her back to us taking them in turn into her mouth, they held their hands on her head as each of them coaxed her back to them, taking turns, she shrugged each of them away, her head bobbing rhythmically as she sucked.

They must know they are on show, they are stood right in front of the window my friend observed astonished. As she did the woman stood and seemed to look straight at us, a smile on her face, we shrunk back in to the sofa maybe she could see us, I think she is looking above us someone observed, I bet they are at it as well, putting on a show for each other, made sense, we agreed.

She stood and lowered one man to the floor, he lay apparently on the window sill, his dick stood firm, she lowered herself on to him writhing her body against him, as she did the man shoved himself back in her mouth and she continued to suck him greedily.

His face flushed his pleasure clear. He stopped her, holding himself to delay himself and pulled her to her feet away from the man laid there, he stood looking pissed off, before grabbing a chair and seating himself before her.

She leaned over in front of the window, her face almost pressed against the glass and the second man entered her, hands held around her hips as he pushed into her, her face stiff she pushed against him, her breasts bouncing up and down as her body was slashed forward and back.

Jesus, someone said, her palms pressed flat against the

window as she tried to increase the friction against him, suddenly her head almost struck the window as he came, his mouth wide as he froze then jabbed softly.

She gave him a moment and when he pulled away she walked to the man in the chair, sitting astride him as her hips continued to gyrate.

The couple kissed as he grabbed her buttocks pulling her onto him, a few moments passed as they clung together, then it was clear they were coming their heads rolling back as they held tightly together.

They pulled apart and the three stood together, yes it was clear they were communicating with someone, they watched together, occasionally embracing before clapping and waving.

Suddenly, the lights in our room flicked on, our friend cringed as he realised what he had done, we sat there, three of us on the sofa in full view, we even had glasses and slices of our pizza in our hands. Wanting to dissolve I ran and flicked the light switch, too late, the three of them were watching, smiles on their faces.

The next day I returned from work, a handwritten letter awaited me, stuck in the letter box, an invitation, to join them by putting on our lights!

The Hitchhiker

I drove by him first, the young man at the side of the road, he was heading where I was but to pick him up would be frowned upon surely, even dangerous? I had chores first in any case, if he was still there when I passed again I would stop and check whether he was a psycho.

Sure, enough later he was still there, his enthusiastic waves now quashed as he sat on his bags, the sign leant against his legs. I pulled up beside him, he was young, a student, trying to save cash, hop in I told him, deciding he was innocent enough.

We travelled across the country chatting about nothing, it was nice to have him with me. I spent too much time alone, his attitude impressed me, young and free, he had big plans for his life, not yet soured by reality. Only a few years older I had already discovered that life loved to toss plans, already the man of my dreams had become a nightmare, hence the long drive away from him.

We stopped at a kiosk at the road side, grabbing a bite to eat as I stretched my legs, I tossed a blanket on the field at the side of us and laid across it, relaxing for a while. He lingered at the car, on his phone, of course, I had just seemed to miss the generation that were permanently attached to it, owning one, but checking it rarely, no one likely to call.

The minutes passed and as I looked up I caught him snapping a pic discreetly, I frowned, hated being photographed.

I rose to my feet, slightly annoyed but not showing it packed the blanket and headed back to the car. It was time to go, I had hours of driving ahead of me. We set off and I clicked the radio on, letting it blast for a while as we travelled ignoring each other.

He sang along carefree to the cheesy pop songs, his joy infectious my mouth began to mouth along, my voice whispering not quite confident enough to sing along. The engine suddenly stalled and I panicked, pulling in to the side. I flicked the key round again, the engine growled but then nothing, I tried again, nothing.

I looked across at him, willing him to tell me to flip the hood so he could fix it, but he stared back bewildered, useless. I banged my hands against the dashboard in frustration. He didn't speak, sensing it was probably safer, and stayed strapped in the car while I got out pacing around it and slapping it a few times for good measure.

Eventually he got out and tried to calm me, he tried his phone, like mine, no service. I kicked the car a few times for good measure, his reasoning was beginning to piss me off, no it would not be 'fine.'

I wished I had never bothered with him, it was getting dark and we were in the middle of nowhere. As I shouted he made the mistake of trying to hug me, I pushed him away. He returned holding me tighter, I wanted to walk, he wanted to sleep in the car, idiot, I thought as I pulled away, setting off into the darkness.

He grabbed me again and pressed me against him, suddenly his hands were everywhere, dragging me back towards the car, I struggled against him, my hands desperate for the freedom to slap him.

He leaned against me pressing me towards the car, my rage

subsided. He leaned his face towards me and he kissed my mouth roughly, astounded I tried again to push me away, half-heartedly nipping at his arms as they held around me.

I fought to turn my face away but desire was crushing me and as my mouth opened involuntarily, he thrust his tongue into me.

He lifted me by the butt and slammed me down onto the bonnet of the car, his hands pressing mine flat out against me, he kissed my lips and neck, his hands released me and quickly reached for my dress, ripping it open.

My hands drew up and I pushed my arms flat against his chest, trying to push him away from me, but my tongue gave me away as I forced it into him, biting his lips with my tongue, eventually my hands surrendered and I wrapped them around his shoulders, pulling him close to me.

One of his hands lowered and he shuffled around, his organ freed, he drove it towards me, my knickers forced aside as he pushed into me.

I clenched my eyes closed, shutting out the fact that we were in the open as he thrashed against me, my butt rose and lifted from the car as I drew my arms around him and writhed close to him, it hit the car as he crashed down forcing himself further.

His mouth pressed against my neck, pain wrenched through me as he sucked drawing blood to the surface, I cried out in pleasure as the sweet pain escalated, he pulled my legs up and over him as he wrenched me to the edge of the car.

Standing against me, his legs planted firmly to the ground, to increase the pressure of his thrusts. I watched astonished at the concentration on his face as he neared climax, his jaw clenched, eyes boring into me.

My head rocked as it hit me, rising like a fireball within, my mouth threw open and I was groaning wildly. As I came I rode my hips in circles willing him to join me, he did, his body bending as with a final grind he shouted and held me crushed against him.

He pulled away and lifted me away from the bonnet, crushing my body to him, "we sleep in the car" he told me, his hands passing across my breasts once more, I couldn't resist, my body ached for him still.

He took my hand and led me to the back seat, following me in, I struggled to pull my dress around me but he stopped me, his hands pushing it further apart as he took my nipples into his mouth, teasing his tongue around them.

He lay me back against the seat and lowered his head to my groin, already too sensitive I pathetically tried to object but he persevered, until the pain turned to pleasure and I felt wet against him.

The intensity shocked me to core, I let myself go, in all honesty it was irresistible, my moaning increased in intensity and tone and I held his head against me, driving him close.

He pulled away and me over onto him, his penis erect, pressed into me, I gasped with pleasure as he filled me. Riding him dramatically, I kissed passionately, sucking his neck, his ears, his head lolled back, his groans joining my own, my pelvis angled so that my clit was crushed against him and I lifted and fell, my pressure increasing as I neared orgasm.

I pulled his head to face me, staring into his eyes as he came, his arms crushed me to him, his body shaking. I shuddered as I came, sweat dripping from me as we rocked together.

We remained frozen together and he reached for the blanket pulling it around us, I rested my neck against him, no rush to leave, we were stuck together for the night, we would make the most of it.

The Nurse

She avoided eye contact today as she had entered the ward, last night I had pissed her off, grabbing her arse as she passed by me, she had not been impressed, a weeks' worth of flirting out the window. Today she looked as hot as ever, uniform a little too tight, her curves crying out for attention.

She wondered by later and I caught her eye, I knew she couldn't stay mad forever and as I smiled, she shook her head, still annoying but unable to disguise the smile in her eyes or the crease at the edge of her lips.

Visiting time arrived and my friends joined me, drawing annoyed glances from the nurse's station as they laughed a little too loudly surrounding the bed.

One of them had slipped the nurse his number the night before, she had tossed it straight into the bin, slapping him down with a sarcastic remark. They knew I wanted her but had joked I had no chance, a known fantasy, patients and nurses but not a reality.

I lay on the bed, looked down and there she was leaning over me, her mouth around my penis, the curtains drawn around us, her dress rose to reveal stockings and suspenders, I groaned as I throbbed into her, she looked up to me licking her lips and returning to my dick, licking its tip.

I jumped suddenly and cracked my eyes open, I was dreaming, of course, I laughed, a good dream, under the sheets my penis pressed against the thin sheets.

She stood at the foot of the bed, looking down at me, my eyes flickered, I wondered if I was still sleeping, but I was awake, I cringed as I noticed my dick holding the sheets above me. She stepped forward and drew her hands across the sheets towards it, as she reached it I gasped.

She held it in her hands over the sheets, wrapping her fingers around it, staring at me seductively, her hands pulled the zip on her neck down, her breasts revealed squeezing over her red bra, I groaned, her hands quickened.

She leaned towards me, my hands grabbed for her, her nipples peeked out over red lace and I fingered them roughly before forcing them into my mouth, my tongue flicked greedily as they pierced forwards engorged.

Her hand crawled under the sheets and as I felt her hands on my naked penis I almost came, ramming upwards against her, she pushed her breasts against me to silence me, but it just made the pleasure increase and I reached down between her legs, my hand cupping her, fingers running roughly over her clit, I heard her groan as she fell into me.

I had to have her, but the ward, other patients, it was impossible.

She lowered her head to me and enclosed her mouth over my penis, I held my hand to my mouth to stop myself screaming out as she sucked, the dream becoming reality.

She pulled away and pushed her bra down, releasing her breasts and squeezed them over me, using them to jerk me roughly, my penis appeared between the nipples throbbing as it burst through.
Her tongue there to greet it, licking it softly before it was dragged away again. The breasts bobbled before me, my eyes

widened I couldn't hold off much longer.

I wanted to touch her, I freed my penis from her grasp and reached my head to her, snogging her deeply, her hand took over with my penis and she reached between my legs cupping my balls tightly.

I reached up her skirt and fondled her, moisture seeped through her nickers as she writhed, I pierced my finger through the edge and inside her, her legs bent as she lowered towards me, grinding her hips as she rode, I pushed more fingers through flicking her clit as another finger joined the first, her breath hot against my cheek.

The pressure to ejaculate grew, I searched her eyes for a sign that she was close, I ached for her to sit astride me, but knew it was too much to ask, the sounds of patients snoring surrounded us. Footsteps entered the ward and our groans silenced, but we couldn't pull our fingers away, they continued to probe silently, rushing to finish.

Her face lit up and she sunk against me, her legs almost collapsing as she came, a moan escaped me and she thrust her fingers into me, I bit against them to stifle my screams as I shot forward and came against her hand as it yanked up and down against me. Our eyes lingered over one another as we revelled in the orgasm, our lips met and we kissed slowly, as the fire passed.

The sheet pulled over me and my hand withdrew from her, I lowered back to the bed as she pushed her breasts away, straightening her skirt as she pulled herself together. She pulled the curtain aside and slipped through silently as I lay on the bed, grinning wildly.

The Friend

I was a shoulder to cry on for her and she had been using me a lot lately, since school always just friends, as I had been for most of the girls, the class joker. How could she not see what everyone else did, he was a complete jerk to her, nailing, or attempting to nail everything that moved behind her back.

He was a fool, she was better than any of them, Adele, sweet, beautiful, why had she gone from bad to worse in relationships? Like them all she went for the bad guy.

We planned our night, she would stay with me, her phone was banished. We had a movie picked out, popcorn and chocolates, tomorrow she would return, I knew despite her denials but tonight she was mine.

She leaned her head against me as we watched the movie draped on the sofa, how could she not know how I felt, that her touch drove me nuts as I resisted every second to stop myself holding her, to hold my hands to her face as I kissed her softly.

She laughed as she watched, the film one of our favourites, I missed most of it, instead I watched her, her eyes shining as she laughed at all the wrong bits, her hand dipping continuously into the popcorn.

My smile mirrored hers, I loved her laugh, in fact I loved everything about her. I had to get her out of my head, I knew that as she stumbled through relationships, I remained single, others paled against her.

She was drinking too much and so was I, we flirted

innocently. Her phone was banned, I knew from experience that once she was drunk enough she would make a call and be swept away.

She draped her legs across me on the sofa and I massaged her feet casually, she lay back smiling, I considered pushing my hands up to her thighs, but there was too much to lose, it wasn't worth the risk, or was it?

I considered my options as I pushed my hands against her calves, circling my fingers round her knees, her hand dropped and stopped me, she stared into my eyes, leant in and kissed me.

Confusion reigned was this friendly, I daren't kiss her back if we were going to do this it had to be her fault. She held her lips against mine and I pressed against them hesitantly, I physically forced my back against the sofa away from her. I ached for her.

Her body shifted in and she placed her hands around my shoulders and pressed her body against me, it was too much, I grabbed her kissing her back passionately, our kiss lingered, I was on fire. I pulled her legs around me I wanted to feel her whole body.

My lips dropped to her neck as I ravished her, her eyes were fixed close, her head lolling back. I stood lifting her with me and carried her to the bedroom.

I dropped her on the bed, she lay, staring up at me, perfection, I leaned over her and began to remove her clothing, I wanted to take in every part of her, I had dreamed for so long of this body, watched it change over the years till it reached utter perfection.

As each part of her was revealed I ran my hands, then lips over it, checking out her reaction with each movement, she lay softly moaning, her eyes staring. I returned to her lips kissing and laid beside her, she embraced me tightly, her hands helping me strip my own clothes off.

We rolled together on the bed, our breaths hot against each other, her lips lowered to my neck, her kisses driving me crazy with desire, her hands enclosed me, dragging my penis roughly, lower still they flitted across my stomach before settling on my penis, soft kisses first teasing its edge.

I reached down to stop her as her mouth enclosed me, my body throbbed with desire, she sensed I was close to the edge and pulled away from me. I pulled her body flat against me, holding her still, running my hands down her back and to her arse, so perfect and round. Even frozen her body against me drove me wild.

I flipped her round, separating her legs roughly as I pushed my face to her clit, I teased it gently with my tongue, my fingers pushing inside her. Her back arched, blood rushed to her cheeks and her clit bulged against me. My nose pressed against it as I drove my tongue into her.

Endlessly I probed, all my fantasies coming true, her body shivered, her hands held my head firmly against her she moaned, soft sighs interceded with cries of pleasure as she came.

She threw her hands to the side of her bead as her groin arched up towards me, I sucked feeling her come against me, lapping it up. As she relaxed, her breath softened and I rose beside her, spooning her against me.

Her eyes closed she lay there in silence, I kissed her neck holding her close. My hands held her breasts, my thumbs circling her nipples, moments passed, the tension thick, her hands reached around and she felt for me, a smile pulled at the edges of her lips as her hands enclosed my thick penis.

I twisted her round to face me, kissing her lips softly, she stared lovingly into my eyes, no hesitation, I edged onto her our bodies pressed together as I pushed inside her, her legs wrapped tightly around me as she gripped her body towards me, her sighs rising once more.

Locked together our kisses escalated, our bodies rolled together, I ground myself deeper inside her, my hands clenching her buttocks ever closer to me. I pulled my lips away as we stared, searching each other for a sign of the pleasure peaking.

Endlessly we ground until finally her eyes squeezed closed as she came, her body shuddering as she squeezed, her eyes opened, the pleasure revealed and it wrenched me over the edge and I joined her, counting the seconds as we rocked together. As it subsided I couldn't pull away and we held each other close, both unwilling to let go.

Morning came, we lay together still, her eyes were closed and her breath rose and fell gently. I had awoken periodically through the night, expecting to find her gone, but she had remained, her arms wrapped around me.

Her eyes flickered open and we stared, each as unsure as the other, I wanted her to stay there forever but how did she feel, I had no idea. In answer, she leaned in and kissed me, her hands across my face.

The Voyeur

I crouched in space, soon the room would fill and I would be watching in silence, it had taken time, so many times I had tried to get the hole in the perfect position, only to sit waiting and discover my view was wrong, the hole in the wrong place, too low, too high, now I was sure it was right.

The couple returned to their room, they were bickering, typical, night after night I had sat by the wall jerking my hand over myself to the sounds of their love making, now I could see the bed, perfectly framed why weren't they on it.

The radio flicked on, she sat on the bed her head in her hands, his legs strode by intermittently, He shouted, the door slammed. Moments passed she remained alone.

I grew excited anyway as I watched her, I had glanced across at them many times as they had breakfast, the perfect couple, once I had seen him reach for her under the table, her face glowing as he'd teased her, I'd rushed to my room when they had left, releasing my penis as soon as I had entered my room so that I could come to their groans, they hadn't disappointed, their screams of pleasure had wracked through me.

She stood, lifting her dress over her head as she undressed, my eyes lit up, my hands in place. Her breasts fell from her bra as she unclipped it, hands reaching behind her back. She stood then, in little white nickers, grabbed something from the desk and lay back on to the bed.

A phone, her fingers skipped across it as she wrote, telling him to come back I hoped, he would find her laying there, he wouldn't be able to resist, who would.

My mind wondered, I fantasised about joining her, she might fall asleep as the light lowered and I could slip into the room, she might think I was him if I quickly took her, my body blocking her eyes, she would love it she would moan for me.

As my imagination played out the scene I rubbed my hands over myself, I should do it I thought, my pace quickening. I could push my head between her legs, rip off those nickers with my teeth and shove my tongue inside her, she would rub her hands through my hair, she would notice the difference but wouldn't care, she would scream as I licked, her wetness dripping down my chin.

I stopped myself, my orgasm threatening, I had waited too long for this night I wouldn't waste it on a fantasy.

Finally, he returned, they spoke, I strained to hear, yes, he was sorry, yes, she would forget about it. She stood and they embraced, his hands rubbed over her back as they kissed, slipping into the top of her knickers as he squeezed her buttocks.

She unfastened his belt, pushing his jeans down as he unbuttoned his shirt and discarded it. His body was even better than he had expected, his shirt had hidden the rips in his chest, no wonder she had been screaming, he imagined his own hands over running over the mans' chest, drawing near to his dick as it rose towards him.

The woman sat on the end of the bed, the man kneeled before her, her eyes were closed, I couldn't make out what he was doing, just saw his hands moving forwards and back, his head leaned against her, I resisted the urge to touch myself, I had to watch first I told myself, I had to last.

Moans began to escape her mouth, I could imagine being her, having him leaning over sucking my dick, my mouth would match hers I'd be gagging for him to be faster, deeper. I couldn't resist my dick was throbbing, in my mind he was rubbing his mouth over it licking his its head,

I grabbed myself and jerked once, twice, I came, the semen shooting out in an arch as I clenched my teeth to silence myself. My body shuddered, too fast I scolded myself.

They fell together on the bed, rolling as he lay above her, his dick now hard pushed against her, she rolled on top of him, laughing as she held his arms down, I could see her arse, naked now, hovering over him.

My body stirred, it would be ok, the shame that usually followed my orgasms was on hold, I relaxed and settled. The woman stood and left the room, the man was left laid there, she was getting drinks, he touched himself as she paced, she sat on a chair beside him out of view.

He continued, his legs bent as he jerked his penis with his hand, it continued to stiffen, now huge. I compared us running my hands across myself, yes, I could compare, easily, my own dick now just as stiff against me, I smiled.

She appeared in view, joining him on the bed, she sat astride him, over his face, my eyes bulged. His tongue shot up driving into her as he took his hips into his hands, holding her above him lifting and pulling, her eyes were squeezed close, she drove her hips around her thigh muscles tight as her legs tensed, I could taste her, I licked my lips at the thought.

She dropped forward, her mouth spreading wide as she clenched it over him. I squeezed my eyes closed I could be either of them, I wanted to be both.

Their increasing moans forced my eyes open, I wished I was filming, I'd look into it, to be able to watch again and again, oh I moaned the thought pushing me near.

His hand reached down and stopped her, yes, I begged, fuck her, ram into her tight pussy, he would I knew it, heard the bed pounding against the wall night after night. He pulled her round, held her body tight against him as he pinned her to the bed, his arse tightened as he pushed himself into her, driving intensely forward.

Her arms were wrapped around his shoulders. They began to cry out, words muffled, begs I thought, she was begging for him to fuck her harder. I would, I thought stealing the words, I would fuck your brains out.

I grabbed for myself desperately, she would be screaming soon, I was astounding her, driving deeper with each thrust, I began to shake as I watched him, speeding up, his groans eclipsed hers, I was imagining him grinding into me now, his mouth biting my shoulders in desperation as he began to ejaculate, shooting into me.

I pushed my shirt into my mouth, I couldn't let them hear me, but I couldn't remain quiet, they were coming, I could tell, with a final shove he froze there while she made the most of his rigidity, driving her hips up towards him, I burst, my wrist slapping against my stomach as I tossed myself desperately.

The Strip Club

We were there for the groom, but all just as eager, like a bunch of kids in a candy store, our excitement clear. We cheered as she hit the stage, prancing around in heels, spinning around the pole, her legs lifting and spreading, a glimpse of her arse as she spun. Glasses raised we toasted her.

Waitresses tread gracefully between us, topless, their pert breasts bobbing, nipples sprung to attention, we lavished them with attention, helping ourselves to the drinks from their trays as we folded money into the tops of their stockings, the only touch allowed, security mixed among them, eyeing the crowds checking behaviour.

A woman approached our table and offered private lap-dances, those of us in agreement cheered while others shrunk back in embarrassment, 6 of us agreed, we'd share three dancers and were shuffled off into a private room. We pooled our money and agreed terms drunkenly.

We paid for more than just dances and took our chairs, eagerly waiting in anticipation. The first one entered, a naughty schoolgirl, she twisted before us, flicking her skirt back to reveal her nakedness as she writhed bending to her toes and dropping her pelvis to the ground.

She danced before us slowly unfastening and opening her shirt, revealing naked breasts, she threw it off and stood over the groom, pushing her tits into his mouth as we cheered, jealously.

He sucked her greedily rubbing his hands over her, his hands raised and she scolded him, security came into view and the rules were clear, no hands.

As we watched another woman entered a French maid, tickling our necks with feathers as she frolicked around, she stood in the centre and began to undress, her dress dropped to reveal her crotch less knickers and peephole bra, she writhed her body around suggestively and we yearned to touch her, our dicks rising.

They lingered between us leaning over us in turn and allowing us to kiss their breasts, our hands pressed against our chairs, we had been warned another touch and the show would be over.

The women came together in the middle of us and embraced, taking turns to lick and suck the breasts of the woman before her, as they kissed I felt my dick straining against my jeans rubbed my hand against it, I wasn't warned, this was clearly allowed so I pushed my hand into my hands into my jeans and rubbed myself against it.

A quick glance to the side assured me my friends were the same, their shoulders scrunching as they rubbed.

One of the women dropped to her knees and the other stood above her, now naked the woman's tongue flicked across the clit of the other and her hands pressed her head towards her, her tongue flickered in and out as the standing woman moaned.

A third woman entered, dressed in leather, mask in place she headed for the groom, pulling his chair to the centre, she took his hands behind him, securing them in place with leather.

We clapped along as she rubbed her body against him, he objected weakly as she undid his trousers, pulling his penis from the hole and leaving it throbbing there. She turned and threw a whip across the arse of the standing woman, who groaned loudly, the pressure against her clit increased as her arse was pulled closer.

Her face flush she began to moan as her pleasure escalated, the whip crashed down again stifling the sounds. The woman came as she bit her lip, struggling to contain the pleasure within her, her arse clenched as her body shuddered. Finally released she dropped to the floor.

The woman in leather ordered her to her feet and pulled out a strap on dildo, she wrapped it around the woman's waist and ordered the schoolgirl to her knees, slapping the whip across her arse she manoeuvred her in front of the groom, she lifted his penis and pushed it into her mouth, taking it deeply, he moaned in pleasure, my dick throbbed,

I freed it from my trousers to pump it gently imagining lips around me, suddenly a whip thrashed across my thighs and the pain ripped through me. My hand dropped as I paused, my friends jeered and laughed around me.

The woman with the dildo crept towards the one on her knees and pushed it into her, their bodies draped together, as it thrust in and out. The groom strained against his binds as she sucked incessantly, the pressure of the dildo pushing her closer.

The woman on her knees began to orgasm, her cries rising as the groom throbbed and ejaculated over her, it dripped from her face as she came, her hands held against him squeezing out his last drop as she licked him up.

Screw the whip I was about to come. As the couple continued

to writhe against each other, I jerked my hand against myself, the whip thrashed again but it just heightened my pleasure, the women stared as I came, my voice shouting out as I jerked harder finally ceasing as it passed.

I shrugged as the men's voices came into focus once more, taking the piss of me. I couldn't care less, I had had my money's worth, time for the night to continue.

The First Time

I peered over my elbow at him as my head lay across the desk, he was left handed so his arm looped awkwardly around his book as he wrote, his eyes met my stare and I pulled away. Finally, the bell rung, we were free, he draped his arm around me as we stumbled from class.

My body held stiffly against him, my awkwardness clear, we had been dating for weeks but I still couldn't relax around him, his touch jolted me.

As we walked towards the exit I could feel eyes piercing into me, there astonishment undisguised as they continued to flirt, my presence irrelevant, but we were and I held his hand proudly.

We parted with a kiss, his hand lingered over my face as I tore myself away from him. Tonight, was the night, his parents were away and my alibi was already set.

My bed was full of discarded outfits when my friends arrived, panic had set in and nothing fit right. They laughed and joked as they settled on casual, almost as excited as I was to hear all about it, I wouldn't be clothed for long they joked and I shushed them desperately, my mum was next door if she had a hint of what was about to happen she would kill me.

I dressed and we stumbled out of the house together, alibi reinforced as I kissed her goodbye with a wave.

I knocked on the door and he answered, his hair flopped across his eyes and I pushed it aside as he greeted me with a kiss.

In his arms I was putty, my stomach fluttered at the slightest touch. We headed for the kitchen and he grabbed bits from everywhere, he needed a sandwich, snacks and drinks, he threw it all onto the tray and we headed to his room.

I looked around as he ate, taking in the posters on his walls of bodies I could never live up too, I glanced at him nervously, he was so far above me I could hardly take his attentions seriously at first, but he'd pursued till I relented.

All doubt of his intentions went out of the window when he looked at me, my yearning for him was reflected in his eyes and when we kissed I felt his passion, his penis had pressed against me as we'd kissed and I'd ignored it amused, he had tried to manoeuvre my hands over it often, but I had resisted.

Each step we took was an advance in my experience, I felt foolish beside him not sure what to do but trying to fake it, kissing was easy I'd practiced with friends before perfecting with one of their brothers, she'd laughed as we discussed it, he had followed me around for weeks after wanting to teach me the next steps.

He finished his food and pulled e beside him on the bed, the laptop resting on his knees as he flicked through YouTube, laughing at videos, I couldn't concentrate.

He held my hand as we watched, put the laptop on my lap and turned his face towards me, he ran his fingers across my bare stomach, smiling as I inhaled. My eyes fixed at the screen, attempting coolness, but as his fingers lingered they fluttered and closed.

His hands continued to linger and eventually rose upwards, flitting to the edge of my top and reaching under it, his eyes continued to stare at me as they pushed over my breasts, my nipples thickened as the blood rushed to them and I stiffened as I felt pleasure rush through me.

I drew his head towards me, no longer able to keep from squirming under his touch, his tongue pressed into me and I accepted it greedily, the distraction from his touch essential, disguising my groans.

Our kisses were interrupted as he pulled my top over my head and he stared down at me, his hands continuing to search. I turned my head away, but he pulled my chin round to face him, kissing me softly his hands at the side of my face.

As we kissed a hand dropped and I felt him releasing my buttons, I held my breath as he pulled them under and away from me and I tried to keep his eyes to mine as I realised I lay almost naked before him.

He stepped away from me and undressed quickly then laid back beside me, as he held me he whispered in my ear, I was beautiful he loved me, his voice swished around but I couldn't absorb it, my focus was only on keeping my heart from exploding and remembering to breathe as his hands neared my underwear and his fingers brushed over it.

He kissed me again to distract them being pulled away, I'm naked I thought repeatedly, silently cringing. The thought swept aside when he touched me and I had to pull away from his lips to allow my moans to escape as pleasure washed over me, he smiled, pressing further.

He pulled my legs apart and brushed his fingers across my thighs, I ached for him, nervousness and pleasure combined, beside me his penis throbbed and he pushed it to my hands, helping set the pace as my hands pressed against it awkwardly, under my hand it grew, and his eyes glowed back at me.

His finger pushed into me and my tightness surrounded it, I wondered how anything bigger could fit but as he played I felt myself loosen and he asked me again if he was ready, my pace quickened on him as I assured him it was without words.

He hovered over me, lowering himself gently my legs spread wide, his tip entered me and I pulled away in fear, he kissed me gently his lips reassuring as he lowered, almost there he drew his hips around in circles and moans escaped his lips as he concentrated.

Slowly deepening, my pleasure escalated and I lifted my lips to join him, his hands pressed around my butt as he pushed further and I groaned feeling the fullness of him within me. His pace quickened as he pressed, his kisses deepening.

I couldn't contain the sounds within me, my voice releasing nonsensical words in the gaps of his kisses, he pushed his face to my neck, languishing kisses across it as my voice rose.

Finally, I gasped as my pleasure peaked and the orgasm I had read so much about ripped through me, beyond any expectation it thundered through me and I screamed out in pleasure.

Somehow through it I noticed that he too was feeling it and the knowledge pulled me further to ecstasy, we writhed together clutching each second, until it passed and we trembled, locked together on the bed.

The Lift

The lift stopped suddenly, lights out, shit I thought.

A voice behind me, a man, I hadn't even paid attention to whether the lift was occupied when I'd hopped into it, head in my book as usual. Now, he brushed my shoulder as he swept by, he apologised, he was looking for the buttons. Another voice followed his, another man. Buttons brushed over, one of them helpfully advised that we were stuck, genius, I thought.

One of the men asked who was there, they spoke together, giving their names and seemingly sharing a handshake. I considered remaining silent and shrinking into the walls, but remembering one of them had already brushed against me I offered them my details, cringing inwardly.

After an hour, my hopes of a quick resolution were abandoned, they had both sank to the floor earlier abandoning any thoughts of the state of the floor, and I had remained standing, stubbornly in my heels but now they pressed against my toes and I gave up, slipping my toes free and removing my jacket.

I laid it on the floor and leaned against the back wall. In blackness we sat, they chatted by either side of me, I bit my tongue, offering titbits of information when asked but otherwise staying out of it.

I leaned my head against the wall and drifted in and out of sleep, hours seemed to have passed and still nothing from the outside. I lifted my head suddenly awakening and realising I had laid on someone's knee, I jerked up and apologised, from the other corner I heard gently snores.

A hand reached forward and touched the side of my head, its ok a voice assured me. I pushed back against the wall, forcing myself to wake up.

He laughed and spoke to me quietly, we had been there for at least five hours he told me, it was the middle of the night, I snored. I groaned inwardly, I couldn't wait for the lift to start so that I could escape facing forwards so they would never have to see me.

He offered me a drink and I took it gratefully, he worked the floor above me. I grunted as my head fell forward once more and I had fell straight in to a snore, he laughed as I cringed. He reached out and pulled me towards him, leaning my head on his shoulder, sleep he told me, it's not a problem.

He smelt good, I shook my head and forced the thought away, I didn't know what he looked like. I couldn't sleep but I lay there against him. His hand drew around my shoulder, I froze willing myself not to flinch, his hand stroked me softly.

Time passed, I snoozed, I awoke to them both snoring, I tried to pull upright without waking him but he woke so I leaned back in. My hand rested against his lap and I noticed a bulge in his trousers, as he snored I tried to pull away but has hand beside me rested over it gently. I listened, was he still snoring, yes, he was asleep.

My fingers moved slightly under his, the bulge in his trousers stiffened, amused I continued, stroking harder. His fingers stepped across to my lap and his hand rested on my groin, the snores had stopped, had he been pretending? I froze, turning my face to his, listening to him breathing, his breath felt hot against my cheek.

I breathed him in, his lips drew towards me and settled on

mine, a brief kiss, silent. My hand touched his cheek and I pulled him back to me, kissing him back, my tongue flicked across his lips and he reached his out entwining it with mine.

We were so quiet, the man beside us snored a few feet away, I wanted to talk but couldn't. His hand hit my bare leg and continued, travelling up my skirt, I sighed as he forced my legs apart, gently massaging my thighs.

I bit my own lip to stop myself crying out, his head lowered to my neck as barely touching he pressed his lips against me travelling to my ears and pulling them gently with his teeth closed over the lobes.

The pressure in my hand increased as I held him firmly, my body was shaking as I anticipated his hand travelling further and as he reached my clit I rammed my mouth into his neck to stop myself crying out.

I released his penis through his zipper, it strained towards upwards to freedom as my hand wrapped around it and a moan escaped his lips, I silenced him with a hand across his mouth and we both paused, waiting for a sign that we had disturbed him, he continued to snore, louder and reassured our movements continued.

I rubbed my hands across his balls, pleased at his response as his body stiffened. My clitoris throbbed as the blood filled it, slowly he drew his fingers towards my vagina our breath grew quicker, if he woke it would be obvious, we sounded like we had been for a run.

Our lips met each other's hungrily, our bodies leaning together, pauses in his snores froze us but as they returned we let loose, his finger pushed into me and I pulled my legs together in shock.

I tried to hold him there, if he continued I wouldn't be able to contain myself, the man would awaken and I would die.

His penis throbbed in my hands, he pushed my legs apart again and forced his fingers into me, carried away now our kisses deepened and the pace of my wrist increased. Despite our desperate attempts to stifle them our moans increased.

I held his arm as he pushed his fingers into me, encouraging his movement, I listened for snores, there weren't any, I held him beside me, he caught the reason and listened too.

Nothing, then a pig like grunt and snore escaped and we hastened, I could not hold any longer as I held my mouth against his neck and clenched my mouth as the orgasm shook through me, he struggled to push his mouth against mine as he joined me, his organ releasing as his body trembled then relaxed. Our mouths raised and we kissed softly, our bodies relaxing.

Our kisses gave way and I quickly adjusted my skirt, embarrassment washing over me, I drew my body straight, pulling away from him and heard him cleaning up and rearranging himself. I wiped my hands on my top, die, die, die, I thought.

Perfectly timed a light suddenly flickered and the lift headed downwards. I panicked, standing and throwing my jacket on, the snoring stopped and both men stood. I stepped forward, right to the doors, I would bolt as soon as they opened.

The floor drew close and the lift settled, fixed in place, the doors crept open, I bolted, resisting the temptation to run as I fled the building.

Almost out I felt a hand on mine and the man pulled me back, hey you forgot your bag he said, as he passed it over to me, I turned, cheeks roaring red, was this the man who snored, or the one with the magic fingers I realised I had no idea. A second man followed close behind him, raising his hand as he waved and departed.

The Boss

He breezed into my office, barking instructions that I struggled to note as he swept out again, I pushed my chair back and rose to follow him. He didn't make eye contact, barely knew my name, but I adored him, would hang on his every word, whether I was paid too or not.

Throughout the day, he grew more annoyed as I struggled to keep up with him, he screamed as he discovered his lunch was wrong and he finally told me to get the hell out when I presented the wrong papers to him. I shrunk out of his office, trying desperately to contain myself, drawing glances of pity from staff around me, as I grabbed my coat and escaped into the lift.

Second job, I really didn't need the day job, only kept it to be close to him, but after the day I had I doubted if I would return, he grew meaner by the day as the pressure increased and there seemed no end to it. I pulled the mask across my face to complete my outfit, the leather spread skin tight across my body, accentuating every curve, in this I wouldn't be shouted at, I was in charge.

I entered my office and looked down over the balcony, the slaves cowered there on their knees awaiting collection, to my astonishment there he was, my boss by day crawling around expectantly.

I strode down the stairs, my heels crashing against the concrete as I reached him, brushing the others aside I released his chain from the wall and pulled him beside me into the waiting dungeon.

I ordered him round the room as I explained the rules, he was not to raise his eyes to me, if he did he would be punished, he was to observe my every command without question if he did he would be rewarded. He agreed with a nod, but as his head raised a little too high I brought my whip down on to him, thrashing it against his arse, bare it pressed towards it.

Annoyed at the expression of pleasure I whipped again and he cowered, biting his lip. I lowered myself to the chair, forcing him to kneel before me as I stretched my legs up and on to his back, I scraped my legs against him as he kneeled, I grabbed a magazine, flicking through it in silence, he was being very good holding still and in silence.

As a reward, I allowed him to uncurl, clicking my fingers giving him permission to worship, he turned his head towards me, his pleasure clear as he held the bottom of my leg, rubbing his hands across my shoes he brought his lips to my ankle kissing it passionately as he stroked.

His head bowed he begged permission to release my foot and I allowed it, he slowly pulled off the shoe, his hand drawing tentatively across its base, his eyes narrowed as he drew it towards him, his body shaking as he took the toe into his mouth, swooning as he kissed it gently. His hands flitted from the shoe to the foot, till I noticed the shoe was drawn towards him, rubbing against him.

Furious I stood and ordered him to replace the shoe, his shoulders rocked as he obeyed, I pushed my heel against his shoulder, ordering him to lay in the floor, his body hunched so I drew my whip down upon it ordering it to straighten, legs spread.

I stood between his legs my foot drawing the skin of his balls across the floor, several inches before me, his face clenched as he felt the pressure, I lifted my second foot and pressed the heel against him the heel threatening the balls as the sole pushed the penis towards him.

He writhed silently, his concentration evident, determined his pleasure not show but hardly able to contain it.

I smiled as I towered over him, his humiliation growing as I teased. As it became too much for him too bare to contain the pleasure I withdrew from him, ordering him to rise again to his knees and dragged him again around the room, correcting his posture with a tug, he tensed, his muscles bulging with the tension of his efforts.

I pulled him to his feet, slapped a bound around his wrists and hoisted them up, securing the chain to the wall, as he stretched there, his feet ground to the floor. I walked around him, his body throbbed as I scraped my nails against him, I clipped metal pegs to his nipples, smiling as he groaned in pain.

The moans louder as I pulled, as he got carried away I strode behind him and whipped his ass violently, my shoulder drawing back for maximum effect, his penis strained upwards as I whipped again, I reached through between his legs and gripped his balls, my nails almost ripping through his skin as I squeezed, he rocked towards me and I pulled away again inflicting a strike against him.

I backed away leaving him there and then walked before him, striding around as he stared, his eyes glowing. I headed back and released him, ordering him to the floor, he kissed my feet at my instruction.

He had been good, I told him so, if he continued he could

come, but only at my say so, he nodded eagerly, his penis strengthened. I sat before him, watching, tugging occasionally on the nipple clamps, I straightened my leg and allowed him to take off my shoes one by one he did so, stroking them as he lay them side by side beside him.

I pushed my bare foot against his penis, he held it against him his hips pushing involuntarily towards him, he stared up at me, seeking permission, I nodded in agreement, he pulled the other foot to him and I stretched it under his balls, pushing upwards to nip them against him.

His back crouched as his pleasure grew, he brought a foot to his mouth and began sucking the toes intensely, I pulled away, I had not given permission and he knew it, I struck my hand across his face. And he pushed his head and shoulders to the floor begging my forgiveness, I pushed both feet against his back and made him wait there.

Eventually I released him, patted his head to offer my forgiveness and he rose again, again my foot pushed between his legs and gently he held it against him rubbing softly, his groans increased and his eyes drew to me seeking permission, I watched as hesitantly lifted my foot, replacing my shoe and pushing his hands over it, he bent and kissed it as my foot pressed against him.

His body rocked as he came, his body collapsing in pleasure as he relaxed. I clicked my fingers and through a towel to him, commanding that he clean me and looked in disgust as he did.

He cowered, he would remain here for me to deal with him later, as requested, it would be a long night.

The Sex Club

I had been here before, tentatively dipped my toe into this world, it was fascinating and addictive, watching turned me on, but too much and it wasn't enough anymore, this time I didn't want to be on the outskirts I wanted to be the attraction.

I had dreamed of the room for weeks and had watched many times as the men queued, waiting for permission to enter, five at a time, one orgasm allowed only, the women changed hourly, entering fresh and excited and leaving exhausted. I knew it was crazy, but I yearned to be one of them and tonight I would be. I watched the woman before me, her time ending.

At last, my turn. I entered the room, two men remained who she had not had the chance to use, three more joined them and the clock began. I lay on the counter as instructed, quickly they surrounded me, hands everywhere, immediately my stomach clenched, the yearning peaked.

My legs were spread, there was no need for foreplay I was already wet, No.1 had already waited patiently with my predecessor, he was ready to fuck me, he entered driving in deeply, my mouth widened as he pressed.

My breasts were surrounded by tongues, my hands reached out to find a penis each, long and hard, I grabbed my hands around them, pumping quickly, they were already hard, pushing against me, I brought one of them towards my mouth, licking the shaft greedily.

My mouth took over him and my hand took another, four now pressed towards me throbbing and probing me roughly.

Above me a body shook as the first man came, holding me firmly as he drove into me, he fell forward and we kissed as he came, the penises pushed aside as I searched in his eyes for the moment. Once it passed, he was discarded and another replaced him fresh meat he watched from the edge of the wall.

As he left No.2 drove into me and my legs relaxed against him, his drive was less desperate and his hands rubbed across my clitoris as he worked, my body shook, he was good at that, my hands jerked faster on the penises against me, perhaps hinting to the man that I wanted him to fuck me deeper, he smiled as he saw my head thrashing side to side.

He refused to quicken so I drew my attention away from him, taking no.3 into my mouth and riding it deeply, his stomach tensed, we made eye contact as he writhed against me.

He pulled my mouth away as he took himself into his own hands, jerking wildly as I licked his shaft, he directed himself towards my breasts as he ejaculated, I pulled my hands towards the mess, rubbing the two penises against my breasts as I rubbed them into it.

As I watched the pleasure on their faces mine peaked and the man before me finally screwed hardly into me, I cried out as I began to orgasm, his fingers rubbing incessantly against me as he stretched it out, before finally he came, bringing me to the edge with him.

The man against the wall wasted no time as he pulled him aside and became no.4 as he pushed himself inside me. I didn't notice the faces of anyone who entered, but it remained five, those who had climaxed quickly replaced without drama. No.4 was fast, he pushed himself against me, no use for hands his face concentrated, he was already so close.

No.5 beside hims' face began to harden and I looked down and noticed that no.4 had him in his hands, I assisted reaching under and placing my finger in the edge of his anus, their lips met and they snogged.

My eyes were dragged away by no.6 as he pushed himself into my mouth, my pleasure began to rise again and I rocked my hips into it. Two more men watched, I urged them to closer as they touched themselves tentatively, there pleasure clear but patient.

Suddenly no.5 began to climax, as he did I pushed my finger in deeper, no.4 spurned on by his moaning, joined him, thrashing into me as they came together, their eyes fixed. No.6 commanded my attention as he too shot into me his arse trembling against my hands.

My hips twisted as the man abandoned it, enticing a replacement. No.7 had been waiting patiently, he took his place inside me, no.8 beside me his dick waiting for the attention of my mouth, I obliged again sucking deeply.

A timer sounded as the final three men entered the room. I could hardly accept the time had almost passed 10 minutes left, five men I had to have them all, my body ached, my vagina tightened as the soreness escalated but it escalated my sensations.

I was able to move now and I did, temporarily pausing them as I twisted to my front, no.7 drove straight back in from behind reaching round to my clit as he coaxed my orgasm from me, as I began to come I screamed out, pushing the dicks in my vagina and mouth to come simultaneously I lapped them up, sucking and pressing as we rocked together.

As the orgasm continued to rack through me unabated no.8

slipped under me, lying flat as I lowered myself onto his body kissing him deeply, each twist felt like my last as the pleasure rose, my moans rose ecstatically as I felt him pressed against me.

Three minutes remained and I begged him to last, oblivious to the two men that remained, their penises readies as they stared. I flailed around and found one of them, pushing him into my mouth greedily as I writhed, suddenly the pressure in me doubled as the final man pressed into my arse. I was no longer in control of my rhythm as he forced us round together against the man on the counter.

I screamed out, yes as my orgasm escalated further, bracing myself for the final burst and crash. No.8 withdrew from my mouth as he came, pushing himself against my chest as my breast bounced against them.

Once he withdrew my arms collapsed, I surrendered to their pace as they pushed into me, at last each man froze and then pulsated rapidly against me, I kissed the neck of the man below as he climaxed, his eyes wide.

I was coming again, my body pinned between them shuddered as they rocked, each of them screaming out and holding us desperately together. We lay together as the timer clicked to nothing, relaxing as at last the pleasure waned and satisfaction settled.

The Gym

I was more interested in the trainer than the training, hence the reason I was here, he was in high demand but few wanted his attention so badly that they were willing to show up for a workout at 6am on a Sunday morning.

No one else had in fact, not even the trainer and I wondered if I had my days mixed up, the class was tough but, I thought, catching a glimpse of my reflection in the mirror, worth it.

A few minutes past…. 6.10, I could have crawled back to bed but whist here I might as well make the most of it, I jumped on to the treadmill for a quick warm up, attached my ear plugs and lost myself in the music.

The door swung open and a man entered, not my trainer but a very good arse nonetheless, I hadn't seen him before, probably a fellow member, watched as he laid himself out under the weight bench and proceeded to grunt loudly as he hiked the weights up.

We ignored each other, him on the weights me at the bars, I lifted myself and tucked my chin over the bar, dropped and did a few set sets of pullups, endorphins rushed through me, my favourite bit. I pushed myself, determined to drive my body as hard as the class would have and timing myself from one station to the next.

I caught his eyes in the mirror, watching me, I paid him no attention, I barely needed the trainer, the workout set in my memory I had attended it so often.

Once my alarm sounded finally, I let my body fall to the floor, took a long drink of water and enjoyed my stretch, breathing slowly as I contorted my muscles methodically.

He waited till I had finished to approach me and introduce himself, he owned the gym, this morning's class had been cancelled the night before, an email had been sent out, it seemed I was the only one who hadn't received it. He asked how I liked the gym, whether I enjoyed the classes, his eyes draping over my body and told me it certainly looked like it was working.

I smiled, could this hot guy be flirting with me? I could hardly be appealing, my body covered in sweat now, hair pulled back tightly and not a touch of makeup. I was not left longer to wander, he walked to me, rose his hand to my face to brush my hair aside and crashed his lips against mine.

His body was as sweaty as mine was, his dick visible through the fabric of his shorts, the muscles across his thighs, chest and arms, pumped and tense. I pressed myself against them, letting my hands drop to hold his firm arse and pulling his body closer to me.

He kissed me greedily and ran his hands across my back and forced them down into my shorts, clasping my bare arse against his fingers.

His lips began to descend, sucking against my neck and the top of my chest. My hands pulled against his clothing, adrenaline ripping through my body as I fought to release the Lycra from his, once his top was naked, I ran my hands across it, pushing downwards until his shorts dropped over his knees. His dick pushed forwards towards my embrace, I enclosed my fingers around it, massaging it roughly.

His mouth dropped to my breasts, his hands ripped my top off and he rammed his tongue around my nipples, sucking greedily, wrapping his arms around me, he lifted me till my hands grabbed the bars above and I hung there desperately as he ripped off my shorts and shoved his dick forward and into me. My legs wrapped tightly around him, his hands against my arse took my weight and he ground himself in and out of me.

I held the bar to balance us, swinging lightly as he forced me out forwards and back against him. Our mouths pressed together, tongues wrestling wildly. My breath heightened as the buzz rushed over me, I tensed my arms and legs forcing myself closer to him, my groans escalated as I rushed towards my climax.

He ripped me from the bar above me, his legs struggling to hold us any longer and carried me, his dick still within me, to the weight bench and lowered me down onto it.

He pressed his body against mine, inhaling sharply, his dick withdrawing almost completely and then crashed it back down and into me. He crushed me against the bench as he fucked me harder and harder until I screamed out in ecstasy, my body shuddering against him.

He persisted, driving down on me as I came and he joined me, releasing himself as his voice joined mine and squeezing his body against me, we kissed, blissfully enjoying the plateau, until finally he collapsed against me, his head resting across my chest. Our heart rates settled, I jokingly thanked him for the impressive cardio workout, an unexpected benefit.

He peeled his body away from me, then, by the hand pulled me up towards him and held me there, running his hands across my body, mirrors surrounded us, it was hard to avoid our reflection, I didn't bother, he looked good on me, his arse firmly stood against his thick legs.

He dragged me around wedged against him, dropping briefly to collect our clothing and led me off still crushing me, towards the showers.

We sighed as our bodies tore apart and the cool water sprayed down upon us, he grabbed the soap from me, squeezing it into his own hands and spreading it across the length of my body. I closed my eyes and let the water run down my face as he rubbed my body, pushing my legs apart slightly to rub soap around every crevice.

The bathroom door swung open and we froze, time for the next class, voices rushed in, he shook his head, gave me a kiss and scurried a towel covering his head, out of the changing room.

The Park

The dog wasn't listening, I had made the mistake of letting it free from its lead to play catch, but it had other ideas, delighting in letting me almost grab it before darting away, its tail wagging excitedly. If it had been my dog I would have given up, but it wasn't, ridiculously I had thought I could earn myself some easy money, walking dogs between classes.

As it disappeared again I collapsed onto the ground coughing and spluttering, wondering how the hell I had gotten so unfit.

I closed my eyes against the sun, wishing I had brought some treats and wondering what I should do next. I heard footsteps, my eyes flashed open and a shadow fell across my body. A man stood before me, I heard whimpering, I jumped to my feet, crying out in pleasure as I realised he had saved me, the dog panting contentedly in his arms.

I quickly secured its lead round its neck and he dropped it down to the floor, where it flopped, exhausted now onto its belly.

He introduced himself and I thanked him, he had seen me chasing it whilst he'd been out on his run, he sat down beside me on the grass and I secured the dogs lead around a tree. The sun was almost ready for setting, the park deserted, if I hadn't found him soon I would have had no chance, I was incredibly grateful. He asked me, his brows high if there was a reward, I looked confused but then smiled as realisation of what he was referring to, set in.

I wrapped my arms around him and pulled him down with me to the floor. His body pressed over me, I laid flat against the grass as he brought his head to mine, his lips were hot against me, searching, he ran them down my neck and against my chest.

His hands reached up into my top and he released my nipples over my bra, squeezing them between his fingers. I glanced around as his lips left my face and satisfied we were alone still, pressed my fingers towards his shorts and walked them down within them.

His dick was hard and throbbing, I held my hand around it, swiping it up and down gently and letting my other hand wrap around his balls and squeezing gently. His mouth pulled away from me and I watched the pleasure spread across his face, he glanced side to side, reached into my skirt and whisked my nickers away from me.

His body dropped and he lay beside me, his fingers lingered around my clit as he stroked it gently, intently watching my face.

My thrill was evident, his fingers were probing me, his touch maddening, I lifted my hips, desperate for him to enter me. He smiled as he did, forcing one, two the three fingers inside me and letting his palm remain against my clit.

I bit my lip to silence myself, I could scream, but with my luck someone would come running to my rescue, I panted instead, struggling to steady my breathing.

His body pressed towards me, his dick shuddered under my touch and it was obvious he was eager to push himself inside me, reluctant though, we were in the middle of a field.

As our hands continued their work our kisses became more

desperate. I couldn't stand it, and started to beg him to fuck me, my clit was swelled beyond recognition, my body was wretched with yearning, his no doubt felt the same.

His body moved over me, I shoved my clothing aside and ripped his shorts down, before grabbing his dick and pulling him into me.

He rammed inside, his dick hitting the spot completely, I enclosed my legs around him dragging him firmly against me and my hands rose inside his shirt as I rubbed his back and shoulders, with my fingertips. His mouth squeezed against my shoulders, his teeth pressing hard against me, he was desperately trying to stifle the screams rising inside him, a muffled cry, the only sound allowed to escape.

His arse pumped wildly, I threw my head back and began to moan, he slapped his palm across my lips, urgently trying to quieten me. We were both becoming less concerned with our surroundings though, obsessed completely with our own pleasure.

As I climaxed I couldn't care less if anyone was listening, watching or joining in for that matter, I cried out in ecstasy, biting his finger to push his hand away from me, whimpering and groaning in pleasure.

He followed, bursting forward and pinning against me, his muffled cries now outdoing my screams as he released himself blissfully inside me. Our bodies rattled together as our breaths settled, he slid from me and we quickly rearranged our own clothing, laying side by silence in silence and I realised I didn't even know his name.

I sat my body forward, the dog was sleeping soundly, I grabbed his lead, releasing it from the tree, I pulled him towards me but he stared, refusing to move alongside me and gazing at the man still sat on the floor.

I Grabbed his hand instead, pulling him up beside me, the dog followed us, tail wagging madly, it seemed the dog liked him as much as I had and insisted we walk together back to his home.

The Snow

There was nothing quite like it, the feeling of plummeting down the slopes, complete freedom, abandonment, all concerns swept aside, I only wished the hills could go on forever. The slopes levelled, the rush was over, instead of silence, crowded voices. I sped off seeking solace once more.

I had come here to escape, I should have been somewhere near naked on a beach, on honeymoon, instead I had travelled to as far as I could in the opposite direction, hot to cold, married to single. My friends had assured me I had had a lucky escape, discovering his infidelity before rather than after the ceremony, why then did I feel so incredibly unlucky.

I had launched my phone out in to the snow the day before, sick of his incessant calls and messages, only to find myself searching for it late into the night, digging around in the snow, I had found it but it wouldn't turn on and was currently drying out in a towel bale. Google had advised me to store it in bowl of dried peas, unfortunately I was on holiday in a ski lodge, there were no peas available.

One of our guides had watched me, instructed, then ordered me inside, I had refused of course, then cried for hours wishing I had listened to him, as my body had slowly thawed. He hovered around me now, probably worried I was going to throw myself off one of the cliffs, he had no need for concern, but I had enough of hiding now and wanted to go home.

I decided to leave the group, all couples I had known as soon as I had arrived I had made a mistake, their eagerness to please each other was depressing, I cringed at every loving word.

I let them know I was leaving and would see them back later at the lodge and headed off towards the lifts to hit a final slope.

He appeared beside me whilst I waited for the lift to scoop me up and into the hills, I assured him I was fine, annoyed to have him bothering me, he insisted on joining me and I had no option as he was bundled into the chair beside me.

I glared at him, who the hell did he think he was, I ripped into him with my words, once I had finished I realised it had not been him who had deserved the lashing and turned away feeling guilty about the harshness of my words, he reached out and turned my chin back towards him smiling.

His lips crushed against mine, I tried to push him away, half-heartedly though, his breath lingered hotly across my face. He hovered inches away from me, the choice was mine pull him back or push him away.

I gave up trying to resist, I needed a distraction, anything to take away my pain. I dragged him closer to me, our lips pressed together, tongues clashing, our bodies leaned in towards each other, we could barely feel though, the only bare skin the circle of our face.

He pulled away from me, we were approaching the top of the hillside, he readied his skis as did I and a second later we were roaring down the hillside. Adrenaline cursed through my body, he was ahead, I was chasing him, bending my body and tilting as we scuttled down the mountain. He veered off the track and I followed him, the terrain was rougher and I struggled to follow him, his abilities so much stronger than mine.

He looked behind at me, laughing, the slope was softening I drove my skis against the ground to keep my speed up, wondering where we would end up.

We were miles off track, a building emerged not far from us, a cabin, he pulled alongside it, a plume of snow drove from his skis as he twisted himself to a halt. I copied him, he grabbed me around the waist, dropping down with me to the floor.

As our bodies pressed together, we struggled awkwardly to get our skis off, freed at last we released them and headed up the steps, and pushed in through the open door. The cabin was practically abandoned, a few emergency supplies were all that remained on the floor, I was desperately trying to hold my body against him but it was almost comical.

Once my hands were free of gloves it started to get easier, I pulled at his and once they were free we worked on each-other's coats. The bulk of our padding was peeled off finally, and he ran his hands over the curve of my body, pushing in through the layers, but reluctant to unclothe me completely.

As my body heated up from inside, the cold became irrelevant, I grasped at his pants, desperate to partially expose him.

Our lips worked desperately against one another, his hands reached in to my jumper and as their coldness hit my hot breasts I moaned in pleasure, my hands reaching down to steal the warmth from his arse. I reached in further, twisting my hands until I had his dick, massaging firmly through my fingers, it was stiff and solid, I yearned to feel it pushing inside me.

The cold hit me as he ripped my trousers off but I didn't care,

I pulled him with me as I fell upon the floor. He lowered himself on to me, piercing straight into my vagina and his warmth flooded through me as I gasped for him to give it to me hard. He pummelled his body against me, I screamed blissfully, driving my hips forward and against him.

There was no thought of lengthening out the experience, we drove desperately towards the climax our hips pushing wildly in circles, until we reached our goal. I was whimpering as we came, gripping him tightly, his mouth pressed to my neck as his groans made way for him to suck and grope at my breasts again.

He reached to a stack of blankets and he wrapped them tightly around us, rolling across the floor until our breaths settled and our kisses landed more softly. We talked, I told him the reason for my misery, I had five days left, he would be happy to take my mind off my woes. For now, we had to get out of the cold though, so we got dressed and headed back into the snow.

The Lake

I swam around gracefully, glad to have escaped the madness of the camp, the lake was off limits to the students, as a chaperone I could spend my free time wherever I chose. I chose to spend it as far away from them as possible, the summer was almost over, I had put my time in to secure my place and couldn't wait to be surrounded by adults rather than children.

I heard a splash behind me, a body had plummeted from the rocks above and didn't emerge, I swam towards it, hoping it wasn't one of the spotty teenagers who had taken to following me. As I neared a body pierced up through the surface, forcing his hand over his head to push the water away and shaking to free his mass of curls.

His eyes opened and he spotted me, realising who it was I tried to swim away as if I hadn't seen him, he spotted me though and cut through the water to join me. I had spent the summer with him but we had hardly spoken a word, he seemed to prefer the adoring company of the teenage girls, who followed him all day hanging on his every word.

He touched my shoulder as I tried to swim away from him, his eyes pierced into mine, clearly, he was not used to not being swooned over and he stared at me confused when I ignored him and swam away from him back towards the rocks.

I lulled against them, waiting for him to disappear so I could get on with my break. I watched as he climbed back up along the rocks, he looked down at me and waved, again I ignored him, closing my eyes and leaning against the shore.

His body was decent, I had to admit but he had arrived before me and his reputation was well known, he had slept with half the staff, my room-mate included and she had not had a nice word to say about him, so I had steered clear.

I worried briefly that he was pushing it as he climbed higher, I couldn't understand how anyone could find it fun to do anything so risky, I doubted anyone would bother without an audience, the urge to show off being the driving force.

He shot down towards me as he pushed himself off the rocks, splashing the water out fiercely, I figured that must have hurt. He didn't emerge, I figured he was trying to be dramatic so made no move towards him, as the seconds passed though I began to get concerned.

I was pissed off, where the hell was he, I dove forwards and swam frantically towards the point of his impact, pushing under the water and searching my eyes through the depth of the lake.

I couldn't see him, I thrashed back up through the surface, pulling the air inside me as I prepared to push back down to search. My eyes caught a flash of movement against the rock, he was there leaning against the rocks and waving, I swam furiously towards him.

Once my feet touched the surface of the pool I let my voice rip into him, he had done it on purpose to scare me. He smiled, thrilled at my response.

I would have loved to smack him in the face, but I was sure he would love that, still the desire won out and I strode towards him, my hand raised and he caught it before it made contact, holding it tightly and grabbing my other, before it had chance to take its turn.

He held my hands against him, under the water, driving my body towards him. I could still yell though so I did as I struggled to get my hands free, he shut me up my pressing his mouth to mine as I attempted to pull away he wrapped his arms around my back, taking my wrists up with him.

As his mouth covered mine greedily I surrendered to them, reluctantly opening my lips to allow access to his tongue and returning mine just as forcefully.

He held me still, debating whether I would still try to hit him, but as my body pressed in closer and I began to moan, he released me, using his arms instead to grab my arse and rip my hips closer. My hands held his shoulders tightly, it had been too long, I had denied myself unnecessarily, this feeling was too good to escape.

I dropped my hands to his arse, pushing his shorts down and grinding his nakedness against me, his dick was solid, my room-mate had not mentioned the size of it, thick and long. I ran my hands over it, enclosing his balls in my fist.

He stared at me, he had expected a kiss, maybe a fondle, the others had joked that I was frigid, before his eyes I had transformed into a whore. I pushed him backwards towards shallower water, once enough of his body was exposed I dropped to my knees, ramming his dick into my mouth.

I sucked deeply, driving him to the back of my throat, he held his hands against my shoulder, struggling to keep balance and lifting his hips up towards me.

I pushed his arse cheeks apart with my fingers, driving my finger into him, he tried to protest but soon realised his pleasure had escalated and rocked along as I dropped my attention to his balls, I ran my tongue across them, gripping the skin softly with my teeth and stretching them out towards me.

My hands worked his dick, I grasped it firmly, my fingers tight and forced them up and over it, jerking rapidly at the peak and lowering down again slowly before repeating.

His balls were swelling and I took his testicles into my mouth individually sucking them hard until the pressure almost hurt. He was about to ejaculate, he warned me with a shove, I pulled away from him, holding my fingers over his dick until his breath was restored. We pushed shallower, his arse sat against the shore now and I sat over him, dragging my bikini to the side and pushing my vagina on to his dick.

He kissed my lips desperately, his hands frantically searched my body until he found my tits and he squeezed them gently, allowing them to drop out from my top. I ground my vagina onto him, driving my clit against his groin as my hands pressed him down against the shore.

He warned me again he was close to coming and I forbade it, my pace quickening as I force my climax close, he rammed his head against my chest in concentration, finally putting his experience to work.

I felt the flush raise within me, I was ready and told him so desperately, my desire for him from nowhere now absurd. Yes…yes… I screamed as it hit me, scratching my nails down his back as I plateaued.

He was more than ready, allowing his hips to rise from the shore as he ground his body up and against me and he yelled as he released himself into me, his body shuddering in ecstasy.

We collapsed against each other, his lips still searching mine. I pulled my groin away from him and readjusted my clothing, settled a final kiss on his lips and turned away, walking off up the rocks and back to work.

The Office

I knew he wanted me, he was always around, my intern. I hoped he would return soon, I had sent him along to my home, where my wife would provide him with my cases, I had unexpectedly been called to offices abroad. He couldn't join me, it was a shame, it was his last day, I had waited patiently this last month knowing I couldn't have him, I would never get involved with anyone at work.

The clock ticked by five, his employment was over, his reference had already been submitted to his next placement, everything was now above board. I dismissed my staff and sat waiting for him, he walked into the office and I instructed him to secure the doors.

His arse pushed tightly against the seams of his trousers, his chest was firm, his posture confident, the whole office knew he was gay, no one knew I was, I had taken the easier life, more acceptable amongst my generation, these days it barely mattered at all.

He knew though, he had sensed my attraction somehow, and had made his feelings known, weeks ago in the lift I had almost kissed him, his breath next to mine had been intoxicating as he had fussed over the collar of my shirt, he had let me know, that he knew by brushing his arm past my groin, my dick had been straining against my trousers, I had had to pull my suitcase in front of me to disguise it.

I thanked him for his work, wished him luck and passed him a copy of his reference, he was free to leave.
I opened my suitcase, removed my tie and stood in front of my mirror, he took it from me as I knew he would and

wrapped it round my neck, before tying it expertly.

His face was inches from mine but I resisted the urge to lean in to him, his breath fell upon me and mine quickened, I felt myself dick rising and pressing forwards towards his.

He dropped my tie and stood in front of me, his hands brushed forward and he traced the edges of my penis with his fingers, I froze, his face stared expectantly, I gave my hands my permission to reach for him.

His eyes widened as my hand pressed over his dick, then closed as I ran them across it, dropping his zip and reaching in to release it. His eyes closed and a soft moan escaped his lips as his body leaned in towards me and his lips rested gently against mine.

His dick stood solidly, pulsating against my touch and I opened my mouth to allow him to push his tongue into me, mine joined his and we thrashed around violently, his hands rising and tearing my tie back off as he pushed my jacket to the ground and struggled with my shirt buttons.

My hand remained against his dick, rocking it against my wrist, whilst he struggled to undress us both. I undid the top button of his trousers and allowed his trousers to fall to the floor.

My dick strained towards his touch and as he enclosed his hands over it I groaned in anticipation, his head dropped towards it and I watched in the mirror as my face lit up and he enclosed his mouth around it, pushing me into him and pressurising my balls with his fist.

I pulled him back up to me and took his place, my lips pressing over him as he struggled to remain standing against me, I drove his legs apart and as his butt cheeks separated I drove my finger into him, checking he would be able to accept me, he almost screamed in pleasure and I smiled satisfactorily as I sucked his balls and pulled him back up towards me.

I turned his body away from me, wrapping my arms around him and shuffled him over to my desk, I bent him over it, we both faced the mirror and as I pulled his hips back towards me I drove my dick into his arse, enjoying the resistance it offered against it.

He was gasping in pleasure, his eyes piercing into mine as he stared at my reflection in the mirror. I watched as he shuddered in pleasure as I forced myself deeper into him against the desk. My hands reached round and I pulled him away from the edge of the desk as I took his dick into my hands and jerked it violently against me,

I was about to come, I ground my teeth to postpone the inevitable, but his face in the mirror pushed me over the edge, his body was flailing across the desk in ecstasy and as he shuddered and yelled out I felt his semen splatter over my hands and across my desk. I grabbed his hips ground him stiffly against me and surrendered to the inevitable ecstasy.

Seconds passed slowly, we hurriedly caught up to our breaths, I pulled my hips back and allowed my dick to fall from him, before stepping into my bathroom to get fresh.

I returned and retrieved all my clothing, dragging my clothes back on as he dressed silently. I stood in front of my mirror to secure my tie and again he helped me, fastening it and tucking it down into my jacket, his hands touched the sides of my face and he kissed me softly before he left.

The Hotel

She had been in to my room every morning, to dust around and make the bed, usually I left her to it, nipping out for a quick walk, but today I had no work to do and hadn't bothered with the alarm. She had been surprised by the sight of me laid naked upon the bed, but not deterred, apologising politely and striding off in to the bathroom.

I considered dragging the sheets back over me, but considered the odds of persuading her to join me, if there was no chance she would surely have spotted me and left. I allowed my thoughts to wonder as I laid there sensing my dick throbbing as I laid back against the pillow, closing my eyes. I had noticed her tits over the past few days, they were hard to miss, pressed up firmly upon her chest.

It was rare to find a hotel with maids in traditional uniform, they almost looked as if they were in fancy dress, all that was missing was fish net stockings, I would be easy to insert the vision of those into my head.

I heard her re-enter the room, her footsteps paused briefly then continued, heading over to the desk. I heard the bin being emptied and some fussing over the items, cans cluttering as the duster ran across it.

I decided to push my luck further, placing my hand over my dick and rubbing it gently, the silence was deafening around me and I flashed my eyes open wondering if she had left. She stood leaned against the desk watching me, her eyes full of desire, I raised my eyebrows in question, she smiled, bent to drop her nickers beneath her skirt and strolled over in her heels to join me.

Disbelief settled over me, I wondered if she would be expecting me to pay, I could not possibly be this lucky and I didn't have any money. My dick was thrilled though, and forced any questions out of my head.

She placed a knee beside me, through her second leg over me and dropped her groin down in to my lap, her hands reached down for me and she dragged my dick up before dropping and forcing it inside her.

I gasped in pleasure, reaching my hands forward and pulling her top down her chest, her breasts were huge, fake and glorious, her perfect nipples piercing towards me, I forced my body up to take them in my mouth, wrapping my tongue around them desperately. She threw her head back whimpering softly, her hands forcing her tits towards me and grabbing me closer by the head.

Her hands dropped beneath her skirt, her mouth widening joyously as they worked, I reached beneath her skirt, expecting to find her fingers against her clit but instead found her fist wrapped around a massive dick.

Her eyes flashed to mine, her time to question, a tentative smile teased against the corner of her lips, it dawned on me that my dick was pressed in to her arsehole, but as my hips circled involuntarily I realised it just didn't give a shit.

I drove my hips up higher, wrapping my hands around hers and jerking her dick roughly, she moaned in appreciation, shifting her hands to let me take over, I worked it as if it were my own, teasing slowly and jerking it violently.

Her lips dropped to mine, we kissed passionately, her hands

reached down to my arse as she pulled me up tighter against her and reached round to force themselves into my arse. The pleasure ripped through me, I pushed her lips away to ram my groans against her tits.

Her dick was throbbing wildly, her face was contorted in bliss. As her cum shot out and splashed across her tits, she screamed wildly and I pressed my lips across them, greedily lapping it up.

Her arse bounced over me, wrenching my dick up with it and as I ejaculated in to her, she forced me back and bounced her tits over my face, grinding deeply and squeezing me in. Once she had settled her breath, she lay nervously against me, her body pressed naked against my skin. I stroked her hair from her face with my hands as she lay there, then lifted her gently up, and lay her silently beside me.

She had to go back to work, I told her she didn't have to bother making my bed. She crashed a pillow against my head and I launched it after her as she walked off, laughing. I wouldn't see her the next day, would be checking out early for my flight, I left her some chocolate and wine on my bed with my number, in the hope she would see me again.

The Cinema

My boyfriend had been acting like an arsehole, I was sick of listening to him whining, he was leaving to work away for a while, he wasn't looking forward to it but it was hardly my fault, tonight would be our last night together for a month.

He had expected a perfect evening, instead I had left our apartment slamming the door behind me after he had begged for me to join him. He was being ridiculous I had classes and a part time job and had no intention of sitting around in the hotel of town out in the sticks whilst he worked ten-hour days.

I didn't know what was wrong with him lately, we had spent our first year apart when he went to college and I had reluctantly followed him, attending the same college, even the same course. Now that he had graduated and was working he had changed completely, did he really expect me to drop everything to slot in with his life? Apparently so.

I had decided that rather than walk the streets or sit in a bar, wafting off single guys I could let the time pass by whilst enjoying one of my favourite old films. I grabbed a drink and a basket of popcorn and headed in to the almost empty screening.

There were a couple in the front row, I sat at the back, just as the film was about to start a man entered and sat right beside me. To say I was annoyed was an understatement, there were over 100 seats free, I considered moving but settled with an intentional glare, to which he responded with a cocky smile.

I looked away, but could feel his eyes on me still, I tried to concentrate on the film and put him out of my mind. A few minutes later he leaned in to me, offering a chocolate, I shooed him away without a glance but he persevered, waving the tray in front of me. I turned my head to him, a smile was still plastered dumbly across his face, I forced my condemnation out in a whisper, but he ignored it.

His shoulder pressed in against me, I sank away, moving as close as possible to the opposite arm of the chair as possible, his arm rested on our joint arm rest, moving ever closer before dropping on to my lap.

I refused to give him the satisfaction of walking away, so sat stubbornly beside him, my body stiff as a board. His fingers began to walk to my knee and swiftly pushed underneath my skirt.

I was furious but shockingly thrilled, I stole a sideward glance at him which he spotted, his smile broadening and I felt a tug at the sides of my mouth, he was probably my age, maybe a little younger, his hand continued to walk towards me and as it pressed towards the inside of my thighs I parted my legs slightly, shocking myself.

His fingers pressed up and skimmed against the edge of my underwear, I sighed audibly, laying my head back and closing my eyes. I wondered myself what the hell I was playing at but the feelings washing over me were just too good to deny.

He reached in, his finger pushing against my clit and rubbing gently, I let my body move slowly towards him, my shoulder pressed against his, my hand slipping under the arm of the chair and resting against his lap.

He used his other hand to move my hand across his groin, his zip was already open, I pressed my fingers into the gap, his dick was stiff and hard awaiting my contact. I took it into my hands, wrapping my fingers around it and pulling it out gently. His head stared forwards, eyes fixed to the screen, mine joined him as our fingers probed against one another.

His fingers were driving me crazy, my body shook softly and is his fingers pushed into me, I gritted my teeth together to deter the escape of my moans.

He worked around me, his thumbs against my clit, his fingers forcing in and around me, it was getting difficult to concentrate, to keep silent. I could hear his breathing, my fingers worked slowly around his dick, but firmly and tightly I held him.

The film was very quiet, I wished we were watching an action thriller, that could disguise our actions but the characters spoke in hushed conversations, I held my breath as my passion escalated, desperate for a background track to cover me.

He had abandoned the film, his eyes now pressed closed as his head pushed back against the headrest. Feeling brave I pushed his fingers aside and dropped knees first in front of him, his eyes scanned the room in panic, then fell back down to me.

I took his dick into my mouth, feeling brave now, no strangers in my eye sight, I let my tongue wrap around it, licking its edges as I dropped and unfastening his top button, to allow his trousers to open further and my hands to push in and wrap around his balls. I closed my lips tightly as I draped over him, ramming in deeply into my mouth and towards the back of my throat.

His hands grasped the arms of the chair tightly, his knuckles turning white with the effort. His body shuddered and he struggled to contain his groans, his hand moved to my head, I looked up to his face, his eyes pleading, he was about to ejaculate.

I sucked harder, licked longer and as his balls bulged against my hands I felt him release inside me, his semen shooting directly down my throat, his expression was ecstatic, his eyes squeezed closed, his jaw set solid, he did well, not a sound escaped his throat.

I crept back up towards him, he turned to me, wrapped his arms around me and kissed me slowly. The sound of kissing is hard to disguise, I pushed away from him, sinking back into my seat and dreading the couple below turning to investigate the sounds of our kissing. His hands returned to me, with more purpose now, his fingers working hard to find their targets and once he found my hotspots, he lingered roughly, working hard to satisfy me.

I wasn't sure I could be as quiet he was, already on the way to my climax, I felt like screaming out, my concern for our company was diminishing, I just needed to feel my orgasm. Low moans escaped me, I was about to come, my hips ground towards him and as it hit, I collapsed against the seat, my body shaking in ecstasy.

He pushed until, my breathing settled, ensuring I was completely satisfied, then pulled his fingers away, straightening my underwear as he went and flattening my skirt down. I couldn't look at him, he adjusted his trousers, re fastening his zip and took my hand.

I leaned against his shoulder, he pressed his fingers to my cheeks and gently stroked my face. The intimacy between us was strong, but shouldn't be, once my feelings of joy had settled, the shame set it.

The film was ending, I had missed most of it, I turned to him, planted a kiss firmly on his lips and told him goodbye. I gathered my belongings and left, resisting the urge to glance behind me.

The Club

I grabbed a glass of water from the bar, I had danced for hours and was desperate for a break, my friends were around, lost in the crowds, one of my favourite songs came on, I downed my water and headed back to the dance floor. It was heaving I pushed my way through the crowds, my body swaying to the music.

He had been hovering around me for the past few hours, never approaching but eyes stuck to me. He was perfect, his fringe falling across his dark eyes, his body was solid, his chest straining against his black T shirt.

I moved closer, wondering if he would scoot away, he didn't, his body gently swelling to the beat. I had waited long enough for him to approach me, it was time to take matters in my own hands.

I stood before him, placed my hands on his waist and moved in closer until my body pressed against him, thankfully he yielded, dropping his arms around my body. The crowds around us melted away as our lips met, our bodies stopped swaying as the electricity flooded through me.

Our eyes locked together, our lips searched eagerly, our tongues tasting as they took turns patiently reaching into each other's mouths.

His hands were pressed against my arse, pressing me tightly towards him, I could feel his dick pressed against me, I wanted it closer. We edged outwards away from the crowds, he led, I followed eagerly our lips still pressed together.

There was nowhere in here that offered the solitude our bodies craved, our eyes searched for privacy, the tables were packed. Against the wall now, he pushed his body against mine, I had my hands up his shirt, massaging the muscles of his back as he pressed against me.

We headed to the bathrooms, ignoring the girls who gawped at us as they stared into the mirrors and pushed ourselves into one of the stalls. His lips fell to my neck, kissing it passionately whilst I ripped his trousers open and grabbed his dick with my hands. He reached to my skirt hiking it up around my waist, and shoved my underwear aside as he forced his dick into me.

His hands pushed the fabric from my top as his mouth lowered till they reached my nipples and he sucked them gently, feeling them piercing against his tongue. I pulled his shirt up to feel his bare skin next to me, my hands squeezed down to his arse as I grabbed and ripped him closer to me.

We ignored the voices around us, no one else mattered our eyes locked to one another as he ground his hips against me, I lifted my foot to the stall, his fingertips pressed against my arse as he held me tightly against him, our kisses grew more passionate as I pulled him forever deeper inside me. The sensations overwhelmed me I was floating in ecstasy.

I collapsed against him as I came, my voice screaming out in pleasure and he grunted, pumping deep as he burst into me, his face joyous, his eyes on fire. Our kisses slowed as we rocked together, our surroundings coming back in to focus. His mouth pressed against me softly now, his eyes wafting across my body.

He kissed my nipples before tucking them away and pulled

his dick from me, slipping it back in to his trousers and smoothed my skirt down. His arms wrapped back around me and our kisses continued.

I released the lock on the stall and we pushed back into the bathroom, again ignoring the women around us. Back in the club we swayed our way back through the crowds heading towards the dance floor, he steered me around it though towards the exit instead, desperate to be inside me again, we bundled ourselves into the nearest taxi and headed off to his home.

The Rain

Typically for a festival, the rain flowed, nobody cared, it was an unusually sizzling summer night, the rain was a welcome relief from the hot sun that had shone down on us all day. I waved my hands along with the rest of the crowds to the music blasting from the stage, our bodies crushed together.

Hands were upon me as we danced together, whose they were, was irrelevant we all danced, grabbing alternate bodies to swing around with.

The set finished and as we separated, steady hands remained, pressed against my hips, fingers reaching forward to press against my bare stomach. I look behind me, he was hot, his eyes bore into me and his mouth pressed forwards towards mine, I turned my body towards him, a handsome stranger as our kiss deepened and the rain slashed down harder against us.

My eyes scanned the crowd, my friends had departed, this stage was closed now, we pressed our bodies together, our mouths searched necks, lips brushing against ears and chests. Festival staff descended on us, clearing the area, we edged away, our lips abandoning one another as he took my hand and led me away. It was dark now, we headed towards the line of trees and tucked in behind them.

I didn't know his name, he didn't know mine, I wanted to know every inch of his body though and as I pushed his shirt up, he tore it over his head and threw it to his side, mine followed, he struggled with my bra clasp, I reached my arms back to help him.

Naked now, our chests pressed together, the rain continued to wash against us, he licked the drops from my nipples, sucking until they pierced desperately forwards and grasping his hands around them.

He unfastened my denim shorts, they were soggy, stuck stiffly to my body, he peeled them down and with them travelled my underwear, his hands traced across the outline of my arse and he reached between my legs, forcing my thighs apart as he forced his fingers inside me. I struggled with his jeans, unable to discard them completely, but wrenched his dick free and held it firmly in my hands, massaging it gently.

My knees dropped to the floor and his hands fell from me, I shoved the jeans down his knees and reached my mouth towards him, staring up at him as he stared back desperately.

My tongue teased the edge his penis and I licked it from tip to shaft, drawing my fingers down after my tongue and working him slowly inside me, until he throbbed against the back of my throat, I held his balls in my hand and as they swelled my mouth dropped to them as I sucked each separately, drawing it deeply into my mouth as the skin stretched against him.

He held my hair in chunks and pulled me away from him, lowering his body to mine and laying me down against the wet dress, he worked his tongue against my lips, lowering to my neck and as his fingers wrapped around my breasts, his tongue edged across my stomach and to my groin. His body shifted, I opened my eyes the rain splashed down upon me and his mouth reached my groin.

His tongue tickled across my clit, his hands pushed my thighs apart and he pressed his nose to my clit as his tongue reached inside me, twisting in circles.

He pressed hard against me and my hips rose to greet him, grinding harder as the intensity of my passion peaked.

I reached down and held his head against me, my body twisting in ecstasy, the rain pounded down on me, sending shockwaves through my nipples and his hands rose to caress me as I came, screaming in pleasure against him.

His body pressed against me as he worked his way back up my body, my fingers searched his body, I ran them across his back, down to his arse and I squeezed his cheeks in my palms, leading his dick towards me. His mouth returned to my lips, his tongue forced in to me as his dick lowered and as it pushed in to me, I rose my legs and wrapped them around him.

Our bodies ground together as my arse pressed into the wet grass all around me, the rain continued to crash around us, the wind howled through the trees, and thunder joined it crashing through the clouds as the lightening illuminated us briefly. I caught his eyes and he stared as he drove his body down and into me, my hips thrashing forward to meet him.

My clit drove against him as our bodies shuddered together, the rain intensified everything, my groans crashed with the wind around the trees and his moaning joined it, as they escaped our lips crashing together. I held my head in my hands as his climax neared and it hit, it hit me too, wrenching out of me as our bodies ground against each other, our eyes locked.

His body fell against me, his cheek laid against my chest and I stroked his hair away from his eyes as we lay together, enjoying the rain falling upon us. Eventually he pulled his body from me and dropped to my side, laying back against the grass next to me.

We laid there, hand in hand until our breaths settled and then he kissed me again and helped me to my feet. We dressed in silence, it was quite a struggle, soaked as they were, denim had not been the best idea.

We walked hand in hand back towards the crowds and he left me at my tent with a deep snog goodbye and a touch to my face, I crawled into the tent where my friends were waited, their faces full of expectation waiting to hear all about the man they had left me with.

The Boat

It was a rare night off for me, my nights were usually spent in the bowels of the ship, entertaining the crowds, I wondered on the deck, the sun had just set and I looked out across the ocean, which stretched for miles in front of us. I thought of the film the titanic as I looked out, the romance rather than the disaster aspect, boats held no fear for me, I had been travelling on them most of my life.

I wondered around, the odd couple strolled hand in hand, most of the guests were below though, enjoying the theatre, casinos and concert hall, I grabbed myself a deck chair and laid back, looking up into the clouds. The soft lulling of the ship was so relaxing, I wished I could sleep up here, I sipped my wine leisurely, enjoying the peace and quiet.

He strode by in his uniform, not quite the captain, but not far behind, his hands leaned against the railings of the ship as he looked out to sea, he hadn't noticed me, I left him to his thoughts, laying back and closing my eyes.

I felt him scrape a chair up beside me, as my eyes flicked open I caught him staring down at me, he had drawn in to check I was alright.

 He apologised for startling me and introduced himself, shaking my hand, he asked if I was enjoying my trip, I told him I worked on here, he confessed he knew I did, had watched my show almost every night. I was flattered, and I recalled that I had seen him before, in the audience, several times.

He took a chair beside me and we sat in silence together, I

couldn't help but feel it was romantic, we hadn't touched and had barely spoken together, he was handsome though, I couldn't fail to notice, I let my mind fantasise, imagined us walking together and his lips joining mine as he held me tight against the ships railing, looking out into the ocean.

I wrenched myself from my thoughts as I realised he was talking to me, his hand was reaching down to mine, he wanted me to go for a walk. I flashed my eyes a few times to make sure I had awoken, and let him take my hand and pull me up towards him.

We strolled to the edge of the ship, my hair blowing freely in the wind, his hand held mine as we chatted about our journeys, as we leaned against the ships railings he turned to face me.

I held my breath, his face hovered in front of mine and as he reached his hands to the side of my face his mouth pulled closer and he kissed me, slowly allowing his lips to brush over mine.

My body leaned in towards him, silence enveloped us, the waves crashing against the side of the ship the only sound. Our bodies pressed towards each other, my arms rose and I held him against me, his dropped to my waist as he crushed me tightly against him.

His tongue wrestled against mine, the movie moment had passed and we pushed beyond it, our mouths searching passionately across our necks and shoulders. He asked where my cabin was, we determined his was closer and he took me by the hand and dragged me towards it.

He ignored hands that stretched out to greet him as we pushed through the floors of the ship, grasping my hand tightly as we ran down the stairs together, his shift was over, he was supposed to meet and greet but I was the only thing on his mind, we were desperate to be alone together. We reached his cabin at last and he quickly unlocked his door and pushed me inside it.

Our hands grasped each other again as our kisses continued. He unfastened the zip at the back of my dress and pulled it over my hand, inhaling sharply as his eyes took in my body, he pushed himself against it, running his hands across my bare back and discarding my bra quickly. His hands forced down my underwear and I stepped out of it as he pushed me down on to his bed.

He watched me lying naked as he pushed his jacket off, hanging it and his hat on a hood at the end of his bed, his shirt followed and his trousers dropped to the floor, he pulled his underwear off, his dick stood proudly to attention and I smiled at him, eyebrows raised, he stepped forward to join me, his arms wrapping around my body tightly as he tucked in beside me.

We shifted around the bed as we kissed each other, taking turns on top as we traced our tongues over each other, he licked my thighs as his fingers pressed towards me and spread my skin with his fingers before sliding them in to me, his eyes staring continuously at the expression on my face. I shuddered against him as he pressed his fingers in to me and took his penis into my hands, rolling my palm softly across it.

He stole his body away as he leaned across me and brought his lips down to my vagina, dragging his tongue across my clit and I tried to distract him away as the intensity of pleasure rocketed, sending it in to convulsions.

He sensed my urgency and rose to me, driving his penis into me in response to my desperate requests. We froze against each other as he let my heart settle briefly, only for his kisses to drive it into a frenzy again.

I wrapped my arms around his arse and dragged my feet up to help me, he ground his hips into me, I rose my arms to push myself away from the headboard and force my stance against him, he rammed me closer.

I screamed in ecstasy, my climax hitting in waves as he bound effortlessly against me. I gasped to catch my breath, letting my hands fall to his head, he wrapped his arms around me and wrenched us over, leaving himself flat against the bed as I laid over him.

I sat above him, my hips winding slowly as I enjoyed the pleasure on his face, his hands pressed up to my breasts as he held each in handfuls, circling his fingers around my nipples. He was close, his brows knitted, his mouth opening gently.

I pulled my body up and off him, rising from my knees and flattening my feet against the bed. I squatted down over him, squeezing the length of his penis in my vagina as I let it drive in and out of me.

His eyes closed as he lay tossing his head against the bed, his hands fell to my waist and then to my his as he dragged me over him, taking over the control of my pace and grinding me close to him, my clit pressed against his groin and I felt butterflies.

I worked with him allowing his strong arms to have me where he wanted me, my muscles surrendering, I pushed back to my knees, let my hands drop to his sides and pushed myself closer to him, his hands moved to my arse as he pulled me up and down against him.

His moans escaped him, his head thrashed as he writhed and as we rocked we came together, breathing heavily, groaning in ecstasy.

I fell to his side, our hands held tightly together, he kissed my lips softly and we lolled there together to the soft flow of the ship as it travelled on swiftly through the water.

Friends

I had not seen him since university, he had been my best friend for years, but a drunken night together had ended all that, I had told him how I felt, I shouldn't have, it had been the end of our relationship.

We were together now because of a mutual friend, his wedding, for either of us not to attend could have exposed us both.

He had a girlfriend, she draped across him, always by his side, I had hoped to steal him for a quiet word, it didn't look like I would get a chance, we were destined the three of us to be brought together.

We had avoided each other all night, it was becoming obvious, one of us always shifting from the group. He settled it finally, he and his girlfriend joining us at the table as we reminisced about old times.

It was easy to fall back into our friendship, the drink was helping, his girlfriend hung on to him still, I wondered if she knew about us, as her eyes met mine I knew she did, but she wasn't hostile, she was fun to be around actually, I had built her into a villain in my head, but was surprised to find myself liking her.

My sexuality had always been in the open, by the time I had finished school I was gay and proud of it, he was straight, I had always thought 100% straight, our friendship was just that, I had no attraction to him.
But that night he had kissed me and we had ended up in bed together, he had regretted it the next day, blamed me

completely, but it had been him who started it and he had avoided me since.

She dragged me up to dance, the girlfriend, her body rocked against me, I smiled she felt safe with me, yes, I was gay but grinding against me that will still turn me on. I loved women, my best friend knew I had experienced many sexual encounters with them, I just had no intention of being in a relationship with one. He watched us, dancing, desire in his eyes, she thought it was for her, I had a horrible feeling It was for me.

We drank, lots, before long it was just the three of us, her flirting with us both, she walked between us as we headed to our rooms, her hands on both our arses, I wondered what she was playing at.

It seems she got tired of making it obvious, and snogged us both, one by one in the lift and dragged us, wide mouthed into the room after her. I looked to him, he seemed as keen as she was, I knew he would regret it, as he had last time, but I was powerless to reject them.

We fell into their room, her hands were dragging our clothing off, we avoided eye contact, left everything to her. She took turns with us, first getting us naked, then stiffening our dicks with her hands, rubbing her hands all over our bodies and bringing her mouth to each of us, taking turns with her tongue,

I watched him as he stood behind her, his eyes hit mine finally as she sucked his dick. I resisted the urge to go to him, going to her instead, wrapping my hands around her body and lifting her to the bed.

She lay before us as our hands and tongues worked on her, her pussy was wet as we licked her, taking turns with our tongue, as our fingers hit her, she pushed our heads together and finally our mouths met and everything else faded into oblivion.

Our hands stayed with her, we rubbed her clit as we kissed and she stared at us kissing, taking both our dicks in her hands and wanking them whilst pushing them closer together.

His hands joined hers on mine and she transferred me over to him, his hand held me stiffly, his lips dropping to my neck and his arm wrapped around me and pulled me closer to him, she was moaning beneath us, her own hands shared between herself and him.

I watched in wonder as she orgasmed, her beautiful face lighting up as she stared wide mouthed at us and as her breath settled she grabbed my hands and placed them on his dick, lifting her legs away and settling at the top of the bed away from us.

She watched as our hands rocked against each other, we fell to the bed beneath her, her hands fell to our faces, she stroked us both lovingly. He had fucked me that first night, he turned me now, away from him and as his hands reached round to continue its work against my dick, he drove his own into my ass.

I screamed out in pleasure, my body reeling in ecstasy, his lips sucked at my neck as he ground into me. She lowered herself behind him, her arms wrapped around his chest and pushing her groin in towards him.

He came loudly, I felt his body shuddering with the effort he was using upon him, he gripped me desperately to him and as his hand ripped over my dick, my cum burst from it, shooting out freely across the bed.

We lay shattered against each other the three of us, I wondered what would happen next, once the realisation of what had happened set in. He withdrew his dick from me and laid on his back, I heard her roll her body against him.

Silence fell, I looked round, they were looking at each other, I tried to twist myself away. She held her hand to my shoulder and turned me towards them, I tried to keep distance, but she pulled me in towards her, leaving me leaning against him.

His eyes came to mine, they didn't flick away, his hand rose to my face and he stroked it and told me he was sorry. I leaned in and kissed him, "We broke up", she explained, "We are friends now, you are the one he is in love with, I came here to make him realise it."

The Steam Room

I laid my head back against the boards, he splashed water against the coal as he joined m, stepping on to the shelf behind me and laying his towel out then his body over it. I saw him looking down at me, closed my eyes and tried to ignore him.

I had watched him working out, his body was amazing but he knew it, he had tried to flirt but I had ignored him, he seemed far too high maintenance for me, looking at himself in the mirror more often than he looked at me. The door opened and the only other occupant left, we were left alone, he hummed annoyingly to himself.

I had been coming here for years, it was a well-known pick up place, I had never bothered though, I came here only to train. My body was looking good now, a few months ago I would have flinched if anybody had caught me half dressed, now I lay proudly in a bikini on a towel, the heat driving the aches in my muscles away.

I opened my eyes to see him leaning over the shelf towards me, making small talk, I ignored him, grabbed my towel and walked away. I stood under the shower and let the water wash my sweat away, he followed me, his skin brushing against mine as he squeezed his huge body under the head of the shower beside me.

I couldn't help but admire his body, his muscles rippled as he soaped his it, he caught me watching as he peeked his eyes open, I tore mine quickly away, his head was big enough.

I hung my towel out, not bothering drying and slipped in to the steam room, a mist hung thick, it was difficult to see the seating, I edged my way around to the back and took a seat on the top shelf, as far as I could tell the room was empty, I knew it wouldn't be long before he followed me.

I laid my body out, stashed away in the corner, he felt around for me and when he found my toes his hands crept over me, until his face fell in front of my face. I hadn't flinched from his touch, he took that as a good sign, I had intended him too, I didn't have time for conversation, apart from that I was up for anything.

His head leaned in towards me and I grabbed my hands around it and brought him closer to me, we kissed passionately, the steam now dripping from our bodies.

He ran his fingers across my body, we were alone but may not be for long, he tucked his fingers into my bikini top and released my nipples with a flick, his fingers played over them, then dropped to my stomach and as my legs spread he drove his fingers into me.

My back arched as my body pressed towards him, his fingers were thick and stiff, his bicep strained as he worked himself in and out of me.

I put my hands around his arse and pulled his dick in nearer to me, his butt cheeks were solid, I had noticed as he'd showered but to have my hands on them was heavenly. His dick hovered, I drew my hands around him, jerking my wrist as he throbbed against me, his moans flowed freely, I decided he was more than ready.

The steam was clearing, I could see the whole room now, someone could join us at any moment I wanted him inside me but we would have to be quick.

I pushed his arse to the shelf and as soon as he was seated I lifted my legs up and hovered my groin over him, he held his dick back for me and I parted the lips of my vagina as I settled myself down on to him. His dick was massive, it took several attempts for me to drop down onto him, but as my arse settled against his lap he was filling me completely, tip to shaft I drove myself over him, tightening my muscles around him.

His hands fell to my arse and he lifted me like a dead weight off and on to him, pounding me down firmly and pummelling his dick up and in to me. My heart pounded madly, sweat dripped from us both but we forced ourselves with all our effort to drive each other's bodies against one another.

I groaned as I headed straight for my climax and screamed when I reached it, grinding my body helplessly against his dick.

As I shuddered in ecstasy he lifted me, turned and settled me against the shelving, he pushed my legs open and plummeted his dick in to me. I held my arms desperately around his shoulders, slipping and sliding as I bounced before him, his butt cheeks pounded like rocks against me and as he finally came he shrieked out wildly crushing my body against him.

Once we caught our breaths he pulled his dick out of me, retrieved his shorts and plonked back down beside me, I quickly adjusted my clothing and the door opened and two figures stepped in.

He smiled down at me, that had been close, I pushed to my feet and quickly made my exit. I looked up into the water is the cold shower dripped down over me, my body still purring heavenly. He joined me and wrapped his arms around me, grabbing soap and swiftly rubbing it over my body, I sighed and withdrew from him quickly I was already aching for him again.

As I looked back I could see his dick stiffening, I watched as he rubbed soap across his chest, I dried myself in the girls changing room, forcing myself to continue to get dressed.

Outside he waited his foot leaning against the wall behind him, his vest barely covered his chest. I stared, he took my hand and dragged me towards him, I gave up he was impossible to resist.

The Interview

She was running through the standard questions, I knew I had impressed her so far, I knew I had barely had to speak to do that. The job wasn't that important to me, I had received offers already, from choices above this one, she intrigued me though, hot, confidant and in control.

I knew I was keeping her, her office had screwed up my appointment and she had assumed the fault was mine at first, glaring and more than willing to dismiss me, it had been her secretary though, the email sent confirmed that and though she had offered to stay behind to help deal with me she had let her go, along with the rest of the staff as 5 o'clock came and went.

She asked me blatantly if I had other offers, I confirmed that I had, she asked if I was likely to accept them over her, I told her I most likely would. She knew if she wanted me she would have to up the offer, she considered whether it was worth it. Apparently, she had decided I wasn't, she closed my folder and told me she had all she needed, the interview was finished.

I began to challenge her and she silenced me with a finger against her mouth, she typed for a few minutes, hit return and told me she had emailed her companies best offer, I could accept it or ignore it, in 24 hours she would presume my choice to be the latter. I stood to exit, she rose and shook my hand, lingering with it for longer than she had too.

She turned from me I followed her to the door, she held it open for me, but as I brushed past her my body pressed close and I paused before her.

She held me with her eyes, wondering, but then the door slammed closed with me still inside and her hands were against my chest as her lips pressed to mine. We bundled together towards her desk and she pressed my body against it as she forced herself closer to me, wrapping her arms around my shoulders.

I responded belatedly, shocked at her urgency, I held my hand to her arse, over her skirt and as we kissed I edged it upwards, grabbing and turning her and lifting her arse up to sit it in the desk. My hands pulled her jacket loose and I ripped her shirt open, she glared as the buttons ripped off and skipped across the room and did the same to my shirt, tugging it roughly.

I pressed my lips to her and shoved her back against the desk, dragging the edges of her nickers to one side, I pushed my trousers down, my dick had been ready since the moment she had sat down opposite me and it raged forwards now as I spread her legs and drove my body forward and shoved it deeply inside her.

She shuddered as I drove myself in to her, her teeth grinding to try to disguise the moans that were spilling from her mouth, her fingers clung to the edges of the desk as she tried to hold herself against me. I gripped her hips to help her, sliding on and off the desk and pummelling her body against me.

Moans escaped me, my arse tensed and I pumped wildly as I hovered near to my climax, she shook before me, her clit swelling, I let go of one of her hips to massage it, determined to have her begging for it. My hips continued to grind slowly against her until she did, screaming out for me to fuck her, her hands pulling her off the edge of the table towards me.

I obliged, abandoning her clit to fuck her as hard as I possibly could, she screamed as her orgasm hit and went on screaming till I was screaming with her, once our voices settled I pulled myself out of her and lifter her body up towards me. I pulled up my trousers and closed my shirt, with no buttons to fasten it, she laughed and offered the Sellotape.

She dropped from the desk to the floor and pulled her skirt down, she took off her own shirt and dropped it in to the bin, strolling over to her closet and grabbed another shirt and fastening it round her body smugly. I was tempted to rip that one open too, but her eyes warned me away and she eventually walked across to another closet and pulled out a new shirt for me, she unwrapped it from its packing and walked over to me, pushing my torn one off and wrapping it around me.

Once her fingers had secured each button she tucked its edges into my trousers, tracing her hands across my stomach and back as she did so. She turned me round to finish and tapped me on the arse, advising I was good to go. She opened the door again and I pushed through it, turning to see she had already let it close and was heading back to sort out her desk.

In the lift I opened the email, she had indeed upped her offer, it wouldn't have mattered if she hadn't, this place had become my first choice, I tapped respond and accepted, and could hardly wait to start working for her.

The Smoke Alarm

He knocked on the door, I checked who it was through the window, a tall and handsome fireman? It wasn't my birthday. I opened the door, he told me he was here to test the smoke alarm, I gawped at him wondering if this was a joke, it sounded like the opening script of a porn film. Of course, I would let him in, opening the door and pointing to where the first alarm was.

He held in his hand a white cane, I raised my eyebrows, he laughed and stepping into the hallway, used it to press up towards the tester button, its alarm rung out, all was well. I asked him if it was usual for firemen to visit houses in this way, he told me his team were visiting sporadically around the estate, I told him I thought it was my lucky day.

There was another alarm at the top of the stairs, I let him follow me, I was pleased I had chosen the clothes I had for the day, as my bare legs strode before him, short shorts and a tight vest top, I had just come in from sunbathing on the garden. Nine times out of ten I would be in jogging bottoms and a T shirt.

He reached the top of the stairs, reached out the cane and pressed the button, no alarm, all was not well, he turned his head to me and tutted. I smiled, taking a good look to ensure he was as hot as I thought he was and that the uniform hadn't played tricks on my eyes. He was decent enough, without the uniform he might not have been worth the effort, but the uniform made him more than doable.

I will have to come back he told me, I don't have any of that type of battery, that's ok I told him, I may have some, I headed in to my room and pretended to look through the drawers, there was not a hope in hell that I had, but I hoped he would come in to the room to join me.

I lingered for a few seconds, he popped his head around the door. I had taken the liberty of removing my clothing and lay butt naked on the bed, an expectant smile plastered across my face.

I wasn't sure if he would join me, I hoped he would but would not be upset if he didn't, I was moving to a new house the next day, I would never see him again either way, so I figured it was worth the risk. He stepped forward in to the room and closed the door behind him, he walked over to me and pulled my legs towards him, standing over me, he pushed his fingers inside me and told me he only had a few minutes.

I leaned up to him, determined to make the most of it, I dropped his trousers and reached my hands to him, his dick was solid, I wrapped my lips around it and drove it deeply against my throat. His hands leant against my shoulders as he pressed his dick towards me, groaning as I sucked him, then pushed me back against the bed and pulled himself over me.

He grabbed my legs and pulled them up around his hips and ground his dick into me, my hands reached around his arse to pull him deeper and I reached up under his shirt to feel the muscles of his shoulders as he held himself against me. Our lips crashed together as we snogged, his tongue driving into me as forcefully as his dick was.

I moaned in pleasure, he had warned there was no time to waste, so I let my climax grow naturally and as I moaned and writhed my body in pleasure he began to grind harder against me, his voice escaping in grunts as his bliss matched mine and we came together urgently, groaning as he collapsed his body against me.

Seconds later he withdrew from me and quickly redressed, I grabbed a gown to show him out, on his way he told me he would return the next day with batteries, I confessed to him I was moving and the alarms would be here but I wouldn't be, tonight then? He checked and I nodded, hoping he would still have his uniform on.

The Storm

I had cleared the area, the men were securing the shuttering, we had not had as much warning of the storm as I would have liked but had got everything done on the checklist, other than get ourselves out.

They joined me in the office and we called through to the mainland to let them know we were about to head out, we had left it too long though, the path wasn't clear, we would have to buckle down where we were.

We had no idea how long the storm would last, but at least there were provisions here for a few days and bunks, it was not the first time the island had been cut off and certainly wouldn't be the last.

I organised our rooms instead, it was highly likely the electric would cut off, candles were ready, there was nothing else to do. The guys helped themselves to drink, I headed off with a book, the winds howled around us and the rain poured down.

The lights suddenly switched off, I closed my book and felt for the candle, the guys had probably wondered off from theirs so I headed off to check on them.

As suspected they sat in the dark still, I didn't know them well, I lit their candles and proceeded to illuminate the rest of the area. We sat round the table, they were playing cards and asked me to join them. I grabbed a beer and we settled in for a long night.

I knew we shouldn't be drinking really, we were supposed to be on high alert, we were confidant we had done all we could though and it was too dangerous to go out at night no matter what happened.

I realised the guys were flirting with me, that was a surprise, their attention was usually on the waitresses who changed often, transient relationships. I supposed I would do when I was the only woman around, not that there was anything wrong with me, but they were young enough to be my children and certainly not my type.

They joked we should play strip poker and were surprised when I agreed, they were pissed, I was an excellent player, might as well have something decent to look at. Within an hour they were down to their underwear, I had only taken my socks and jumper off, they were beginning to realise it was not such a clever idea.

I laughed as the first man lost the next hand and clapped along with the other whilst he stripped his pants off.

The second man followed and they tried to convince me to continue playing, what more did they have to offer though, I asked them, they made an offer, it was tempting, I agreed to play on. I lost the next round and pulled my T shirt off, then the next, leaving me sat in my bra and nickers.

I took the game more seriously, winning the next two rounds and getting to watch them both masturbate for two minutes at a time.

I had to admit they were very enthusiastic, competing to achieve the best erection, they sat now minutes later, seemingly unable to stop touching themselves.

I dealt the next hand, one of the men lost and eagerly

continued the action on his own dick, I would have to think of another consequence, this seemed more of a prize than a punishment. I had to admit it was a prize for me too though, his face set in concentration as he enjoyed himself, his wrist flicking frantically as he tossed his own penis.

I lost the next hand, peeled off my bra and the next, purposely. As I set naked, one of the men made the first move, the other was keen to follow, determined not to get shut out.

Their hands were on my legs, moving up rapidly, I moved mine, one to each of them, as their fingers competed for my clit I took their dicks in my hand, stroking each roughly. They settled for sharing, one took my clit, the other drove his fingers inside me, they both brought their chairs forwards and let their lips loose on me.

Their lips met mine in turn, one stayed, one moved to my breasts, kissing them softly, my body was rocked with desire, the stiff dicks were ready and waiting for me, it was time to feel them inside.

I stood and threw my leg over one of them, sitting on top of him and guiding his dick in to me, my body pressed against him, driving my clit across his groin. The other man stood before me and I tore my lips from the man on the chair and accepted the dick he was pressing towards my mouth.

I sucked him deeply, my pace matching that of the dick within my vagina, both pumped themselves against me, desperately trying to quicken the pace. Hands were squeezing my breasts, moans began to escape me.

The man on the chair took his hands to my hips to force me down harder, he pressed me against him as he rolled his hips and as he began to pant I took the others dick out of my mouth, using my tongue to wash over it instead and grabbing the balls roughly with my hands.

They agreed to switch positions, I was not given a choice, the man before me took a seat and grabbed for me, lifting me on to him and driving his dick in to me. The man I had been fucking was now in my mouth, pushing my head swiftly over him and ramming his dick deep into my throat. All hands were on me, my body was on fire, I was well on my way to climax.

The man on the chair squeezed my arse as he held me, plummeting me up and down against him, I screamed out in pleasure as I came, forcing it out quickly to continue to allow the dick to press in and out of my mouth. He took it out though and pressed his own hands around it, I licked as he tossed himself and moaning, he ejaculated into my face. The other man followed him, driving his hips up and almost rising to his feet as he came, his body shuddering in ecstasy.

We plonked back down against the chair, I lifted myself off him and we dressed in silence, the candles flickered softly, it would have been quite a romantic setting if not for the fact that there were three of us, still it had been fun and we all searched for our clothing and got ourselves dressed, wondering how long the storm would last.

The Security Guard

I had peeled the store with my eyes before reaching for it, I knew where the cameras were, I had been here many times. This shop was one of my favourites, one of the cheapest in the mall, they had the odd nice pieces though and it was oh so easy to help myself to them.

I never hesitated, that would draw attention, I dressed immaculately, skirt suit, hair perfectly groomed, make up plastered, as I passed the stores mirrors I barely recognised my reflection, most used to see myself in t shirts and jogging pants.

I scraped a scarf into my bag, my mother's birthday was coming up, it would make a lovely present, I considered what else could go with it, deciding on some earrings and heading off round the store.

The ideal pair was in the display before me, I asked the assistant for a closer look as I pondered my decision over them, I distracted her by asking for a second tray and clipped my first choice off the cabinet, dropping it quickly into my bag. I told her I would think about it and return, thanking her I backed up, turned around and headed towards the exit of the store.

A man stood there in the exit, security, I considered he was there for me, but quickly bushed the thought away, there was no way, I smiled at him confidently and brushed by him. He stopped me though and my heart almost stopped as he held his hand over my elbow.

He asked to look in my bag, I refused and tried to wrestle

myself away from him, my response took him by surprise and I was free briefly, running as fast as I could towards the exit. He caught me within seconds and forced me with him out into the fire exit. We were in a corridor, on the outskirts of the shopping mall, for staff only, he was explaining to me that the police would be called, the store had compiled the evidence over weeks and had been waiting patiently for me to visit.

I struggled to get myself free from him, offering to pay for the things I had taken, anything, offering anything, my parents were going to kill me.

He held me more tightly against him, and asked me what I meant by anything. My body began to relax as I pressed myself softly towards him, anything, I repeated, driving my arse closer. His grip on me loosened, he ran his hands down my breasts.

Butterflies rushed through my body, I would have fucked him if he had asked anyway, and to get out of a police charge, I would happily let him do anything. He held me from behind, the fingers of one hand always gripping me, I reached my hand behind me and traced the outline of his dick to persuade him I was serious.

He held me against him as he pushed me towards the staircase and as I walked up the stairs his hands held me around my groin area, his fingers piercing forward to rub my clit through my clothing.

We got to the top of the staircase, which led only to a fire exit to the outside, he held me against the bannister and I faced forward looking over the stairs.

His hands reached into the top of my shirt and he pulled my

breasts over the edge of my bra, gripping them firmly and fingering my nipples. His hands pulled my skirt up till it was wrapped across my waist and he pushed my nickers down, I stepped out of them and spread my legs as he plunged his fingers inside me.

My hands reached around to him, I unfastened his trousers, reaching my hands in and pulling his dick out. He rammed it against me, dragging his palms against my clit as his fingers plunged in and out of me. His mouth was against my neck, kissing me roughly, we groaned together but then steps approached us and we froze in silence.

He pulled me away from the edge of the balcony, we held our breaths as the steps grew closer, his fingers continued to press though up against my clit, there were voices below us, more security guards chatting casually.

He slowly pulled his fingers out of me, I tried to softly pull away from him but he rammed them inside again, as I moaned, he brought a hand up and pressed it across my mouth. It was agonising, feeling his fingers against me the fear of being caught heightening my ecstasy.

I grabbed his dick in my hands, determined he should be suffering as I was, he rammed his mouth against my shoulder to silence himself as I tossed his dick in my hands, delighting as it shuddered and shook beneath me.

Our breathing must have been evident, every sound echoed on the barren staircase, it didn't draw their attention though and we heard their voices and footsteps fading as they scuttled off in to the distance.

He ripped his hand from my mouth and grabbed them solidly around my tits shoving me forwards again against the bannister and bending my body over it, my breasts hung down and he wrapped his hands around them before turning his attention to my arse.

He spread my legs, directed his dick towards my vagina and drew himself forward and rammed in to me. I cried out, I couldn't help it, he grasped his hands to my hips, ramming my body towards him.

My orgasm hit within seconds, my body shaking as he continued to grind himself into me, his hands reached round to rub softly against my clit as I gasped, enjoying the pleasure running through me. He shrieked as he came, pumping dramatically and then letting his body collapse over me. He wrapped his arms around me and straightened me up towards him.

We slowly readjusted out clothing, he was holding me still and I considered whether he would be calling the police anyway, I could make my own allegations now though and he must know it.

He let go of me though, turning me to him and kissing me softly. He released me and reluctantly told me I could go, I gave him a quick kiss on the lips and walked away from him, my pace quickening as I pushed through the doors.

The Camera

I watched her, she had checked in alone, I usually allocated this room to a couple, took care of my dick with my hands as they screwed. She was hot though, seeing her undress would be enough and I could fantasise about joining her while she was sleeping.

I had hidden the camera in the hotel room a week ago, my boss had screwed me with the night shifts, I had been ready to walk, if it was discovered I would be sacked but I no longer cared.

She peeled her clothes off in front of the mirror, her underwear remained, she grabbed a towel, I cursed wishing I had installed a second camera in the bathroom. She headed in to it and the shower and flicked the water on, I waited desperately for her to return, hoping that she would be wrapped in a towel.

The shower switched off, I could hear her drying herself and I was amazed when she walked back in to the room completely naked.

I took my dick in my hands, it was stiff already this was exactly what I had been waiting for. Her tits were as large and pert as I had expected, her pubic hair groomed neatly, as she turned I groaned as I saw her arse, high and solid. She was checking out her body in the mirror, she surely must be happy with it, she was perfection. I was desperate to come over her naked body, and hurried myself along to do so before she got dressed.

She lay on top of the bed covers though and I slowed my pace, maybe there was no rush after all, I sighed heavenly when her legs parted and when she pulled a vibrator out of her bag I clapped my hands in delight, it was like watching real life porn. She pushed the vibrator over her groin, flicking the switch on, her head pressed back against the pillow, my dick was throbbing, I didn't even need to touch it.

She pushed it inside her, dragging it in and out within minutes her body shaking, her fingers dropped to her clit and she pressed them over it, rubbing it softly. Her tits bounced as her body rocked, she pressed one of her hands over them, massaging her nipples until they pierced above her, I imagined my tongue on them, what I would love to be doing to her.

My hands had waited for as long as they were able, I let them dawdle over my dick, each touch pushing me closer to climax. Her hands dragged out the vibrator and she held it against her clit, groaning in pleasure now, her head tossing side to side. She shoved it back inside her and I grabbed my dick firmly in my hands, mirroring her pace as I imagined the muscles of her vagina pressing over me, my groans now co ordinating with hers.

As she rammed the vibrator in and out of herself her back arched, I grabbed my hands firmly around my dick, determined to follow her pace, hers quickened, as did mine and she screamed out in pleasure as she came, panting and gasping for breath.

My climax hit me as hers did and my cum shot across the room as we joined in my mind in ecstasy.

I laughed out loud, pleased with my decision to give the room to her, I had managed to watch three couples having sex over the past week and had thought each had been fantastic at the time, but this had been amazing, the best orgasm of my life.

I cleaned round myself quickly with a tissue, leaving my dick out ready for any more action, she took the vibrator out, a satisfied smile on her face. I watched anxiously wondering what would happen next, she set the vibrator beside her and shuffled lower against the bed, a naked nap I figured, I could live with that and waited patiently for her eyes to flash open again.

The First Date

I waited in the bar for him, we had spoken online so I knew what he looked like, or at least I hoped I did. I sighed in relief when he walked through the door, his profile was accurate, he was hot.

He walked over to me introduced himself and gave me a kiss. He bought me a drink at the bar and we took a seat, he couldn't keep his hands to himself, we had both laid our intentions out clearly.

He confirmed that he had booked us a hotel room, there was no reason to linger for much longer, we finished our drinks and I grabbed his hand as he led me from the bar. We snogged as we made our way through the streets to the hotel, he ran his hands across my body, obviously pleased with what he found, I found his dick hard, when I ran my hands across his trousers and could hardly wait to get my hands on it.

We rushed through the foyer and stepped into the lift, our bodies pressed together, our hands reaching round to rest on our arses. The lift had cameras, it was a shame, I was desperate to get my hands on him.

As soon as we were in the hotel room, we stripped, our hands working on our own clothes as well as each other's, we were naked by the time we fell to the bed, we would spend the night but urgently needed to get this desperation out of the way.

Weeks of flirting had led to this; his words had been enough to make me come as I'd masturbated on the phone to him. I had seen his dick before on pictures but they were no comparison to the real thing.

My head rushed to his dick, I took him into my mouth, ramming him against my throat as I sucked him, I held his balls in my hands, massaging them roughly. He pushed me away from him and twisted me round on to the bed, spreading my legs and shoving his face between them. His tongue reached inside me, I cried out in pleasure, holding his head tightly against me, his fingers pressed against my clit, rubbing me softly.

His pace slowed as I begged him to fuck me, it had been too long since I had had a real dick inside me, his body rose obligingly and he hovered over me, his lips pressing over mine, before ploughing down and into me.

I gasped in pleasure, my hands and feet grabbing him round the arse as he pressed himself in. He ground relentlessly, his jaw tense, I concentrated my gaze into his eyes staring as his climax neared, determined to wait for him.

His pace quickened, he pumped desperately and with a scream allowed himself to release into me, his eyes closed and I joined him, writhing beneath him as his pressure continued till I came.

My eyes flashed open as the fire in me settled, he was grinding slowly above me still and I wrapped my arms around him and pulled him in closer. His body settled beside me, our kisses continued as I had expected I couldn't get enough of him.

His hands explored my body, he tickled and pressed, searching for hot spots, my climax had come and gone, but lingered close still. His tongue joined in the exploration of me, he started at my toes, sucking each longingly, his hands advanced up my legs till his mouth followed, kissing my knees and pushing up my thighs.

My thighs were pushed apart gently, little kisses travelled up me, I yearned for them to settle in my groin but they bypassed it, running across my stomach and I inhaled sharply as he lingered, his hands travelling up to my breasts.

He clasped his teeth against my nipples, peaking my pleasure and pain, my clit was desperate to feel him again but he was ignoring it purposely aware he was driving me crazy.

He got as far as my neck, his kisses becoming more passionate, but his hands rose and turned me around and he started travelling down with his lips the opposite way. His hands pressed their way down first, rubbing against my back stiffly.

Once at my waist I rose my body towards him and he took the hint finally, reaching his hands under me and pressing against my clit. I cried out blissfully, whilst he pulled me up to my knees.

His head pushed in under me and I couldn't resist grinding my hips in tiny circles over his face, his tongue slid in and out of me, alternating with his fingers, clit to vagina, vagina to clit. I forced my mouth closed to silence me, determined not to give him a hint of my closeness, in fear he intended to tease me again, instead I concentrated till I came, screaming out of nowhere in utter ecstasy, ramming my body down against him.

Once it was over I collapsed next to him, allowing my body a few minutes recovery, then I pushed to my knees and moved down to his feet, my turn to start investigating.

The Ex

I spotted him across the bar, we hadn't seen each other for years, I considered splitting but decided against it, I was looking better than ever and he was not looking his best. He saw me and had the cheek to smile and wave, I ignored him and looked away, thankful that I had been served already and turned and walked away from him.

He had left me for a friend of mine, packed his bags when I found out and walked away, they were still together mutual friends had informed me, they deserved each other I had left them to it and moved away.

He walked over to me as I knew he would do, chatting casually as if nothing had happened, he asked if I was with anyone, I shook my head and failed to ask him the same.

I downed my drink, he offered me another, I nodded and waited for him to bring it back over to me. He was flirting, just as he used too, but now I could see through all his bull, I entertained him though just for revenge sake and decided she deserved to be hurt just as I had.

I hadn't expected him to try to stay faithful but nor had I expected him to be so enthusiastic to cheat, it dawned on me that she had probably not been his first affair, he had obviously cheated on her already.

I realised too late that it was not just revenge, I was enjoying myself far too much, as his lips met mine I felt the electricity flood through me, my old feelings, long forgotten rushing back across my body.

His excitement was clear when I told him I was staying in a hotel room, I was back visiting family for the weekend. I didn't need to invite him to join me, he followed me in silence from the bar, grabbing my hand as we headed down the street.

I wanted to hurt him, but it was more than that, I yearned for him, we had been together since we were kids and for years, I would never get over how he'd hurt me, but tried to convince myself this would benefit me and hurt him. I let him into my room, he closed the door behind him.

I took my coat off and he watched as I pulled my dress over my head, our sex lives had always been the one thing we had no problem with, even by the end and we hardly spoke but were still having sex every day.

He copied me, peeling his clothes off, his muscly chest had been replaced by a beer belly, I smiled but doubted he would know the reason, his arrogance was one thing that remained.

My body was hotter than it ever had been, I had taken to gym work in a big way, recently that had been the only thing that could get my juices flowing, men were on the back burner I was sick of getting hurt.

He came towards me, wrapping his arms around me as he pulled me close and unfastening my bra expertly, he pushed my nickers down and steered me towards the bed, removing his own underwear on his way. His mouth was on me, kissing me as he knew I liked it, long and hard, travelling to either side of my neck and sucking passionately.

I took his dick in my hands as he dropped beside me to the bed, as thick and hard as I remembered, his fingers came to me, we had discovered our sexuality together when we were teenagers, each being the others first, he knew me better than anybody else ever would.

I knew him too though and I used every trick I had learned, my fingers forcing into his anus as I pulled him against me.

He gasped in pleasure, he had clearly not experienced that for a while, it was coming back to him, the recognition spreading across his face. I dropped my face down to his penis, determined to remind him of all my old tricks. I worked with great concentration, driving his dick against my throat and pulling it out again to rub my tongue across it.

He had persuaded me to experiment with his balls when we were teenagers, we had tried everything and I worked on him as I knew he had most liked it.

I took each of his balls into my mouth, my teeth clenching teasingly around them as I pulled gently away, the skin stretched and he groaned out in pleasure, gently holding his hands against my head. My finger pushed deeper into his arsehole, he cried out, and pushed harder against it, grinding softly to push the way.

I headed back up against his body, determined to give him the fuck of his life, he stopped me though and flipped me round to the bed, I had almost forgotten how good he was with his tongue, he had learned as I had and knew just where to press and lick, it wasn't long till I was begging him to fuck me, my coldness long abandoned, I dragged his body towards me, desperate to have him inside me.

He hovered over me first, kissing my lips gently as he stared into my eyes, I tried to draw away to hide the love hidden deep within but it was impossible, he loved me too I could tell. His body pressed against me and his dick pierced in to my vagina. He held me tightly as he made love to me, my hands were caressing his body as we pulled each other as close as we possibly could do, connecting in every way.

We rocked together, moaning and groaning, my mind was flushed with memories I kept trying to push away. I had expected hot sex me in control, but that was not this, it was like old times, too much love and familiarity. I climaxed involuntarily, screaming and shuddering against him, he had timed it perfectly as always, allowing himself to release as I did and pressing his mouth to mine to stop himself shouting out.

I lay beneath him, our arms still wrapped around each other, he kissed me softly on the mouth and pulled away. He pushed himself off the bed and dressed, I lay shamefully realising everything had gone wrong, he leaned in to kiss me and I turned away, then watched as he turned around and left me again.

The Sun

We lounged on the beach together, it was so hot, I had intended to lay here all day with a magazine, my boyfriend napped in the shade of an umbrella but I had been determined to get a tan, he had told me I would have had enough in half an hour, my determination to prove him wrong was the only thing that made me stay here now.

I had managed just over an hour, enough to prove my point I figured, I peeled myself from the bed and grabbed the sun cream, quickly covered myself and grabbed a hat, I squeezed beside him under the umbrella and bent to kiss him. He opened his eyes and pulled me closer, I relaxed next to him. "Too hot" he asked me sarcastically, I shut him up with another kiss, grateful it was so easy to distract him.

His hand wrapped his arms and I dropped beside him onto his bed, his hands were getting a little carried away in their wondering and I wished we were in the privacy of our room, we were surrounded by families, hardly appropriate to get lovey.

I jumped up and pulled him to his feet, discarding my hat and dragged him towards the sea. We reached the shore hand in hand and stepped in to the sea together.

The sea provided a welcome relief from the heat, it rode to our waists before the heat settled and by the time it reached our chests it began to feel a little cold, we dove in and swam around to get warmed again and a few minutes later we were finally content.

I followed him as he swam towards the coves, he didn't mind

swimming, but his main aim in following me was to get his hands on me, odd bodies bobbed around in the sea around us but ventured further down the shore they lessened and it wasn't long before we felt completely alone. We travelled in land until our feet could reach the ground again and as we neared the rocks he wrapped his arms around me and carried me with him into the cove.

It was our first holiday together, the first opportunity we had to have sex whenever we wanted without trying to be quiet, or rush and we had taken every opportunity we could. He pressed me softly against the rocks, his hands squeezing my body close, I ran my hands down his body, he was hard to resist, even more so now, sun kissed with his hair lighter than ever.

We kissed slowly taking our time, his mouth teased across my face and neck and he bit softly at my ear lobes whilst his hands dropped to my breasts. He rubbed me gently, leaving my bikini intact but squeezing over my nipples till they hardened and pressed against the white material. He dropped his lips over them, sucking softly.

I pulled his lips back to mine and then let my mouth drop to his chest, treating his nipples as he had mine and letting my hands push into his shorts and grab his arse to pull it closer to me.

Our lips joined again as our bodies scraped against each other, he dragged my bikini bottoms to one side, we could touch and taste each other all we wanted in the privacy of our room, here we were happy with a quick fuck.

His hands grabbed around my arse and he drove his dick in to me, we wound our hips together, our tongues tangling greedily. Hands pressed against arses as we worked our bodies, my clit pressed against him and I released my tongue from him to let my moans escape me, he groaned along as our breaths quickened.

I looked out to sea, the sun shimmered across its surface, the view was heavenly, the feeling within me more so. I allowed the bliss to wash over me and pressed my head close to his. He pressed his lips to my shoulders as he came, determined not to shout out but moans escaping nonetheless. I joined him, screaming out unapologetically.

We toppled back in to the water as our breaths settled, readjusting our clothing and cooling ourselves down again. We swam back round to our beach and strode back out of the sea hand in hand, I figured I could take some more sun now.

The Housemates

I browsed the ads, my ideal scenario would be to share with people just like me, young professionals, still with my budget I couldn't be choosy, from a list of ten requirements I would have to abandon the last eight, circling those that matched budget and area left me with only two options.

The first was a rented room in a couple's house, perfect area minutes from work, the second a house share with two girls and a guy, a little further out but cheaper. I rang both and arranged to visit.

The couple first seemed a little uptight, the house rules had been printed and handed to me on arrival. I wasn't the neatest person and entertaining was off limits, I didn't have any friends here yet but hoped too at some point, it would be worse than living at home, even my parents had let me have friends round.

The second house seemed to have no rules, the shared spaces were a bit of a mess but the available room was a decent size, the guy who showed me round was a young professional but the smell of weed worried me somewhat, not enough to put me off though, I took the room on sight.

Once I met the female housemates I knew I had made the right decision, both were hot, off limits though, the male housemate assured me, I wasn't so sure having caught them both checking me out as they helped me move my stuff in.

We had a drink together that night and ordered a pizza, Daniel got stoned and became irrelevant, zoning out on the sofa, the girls Kate and Laura told me the house belonged to his parents and that that was the only reason they put up with him.

We left the living area and carried on drinking in my room, getting to know each other, whilst I unpacked my bags and boxes.

Katie was flirtatious from the offset, Laura more so the drunker she got, they sat either side of me on my bed as they laughed at the stuff my mum had packed for me. I had lived at home throughout my studies, now 23 I had left home for the first time and she had sent me with enough provisions to last me 6 months.

They joked it was sweet, they were older than me but not by much, but had moved out years ago. They asked if I had a girlfriend, I didn't, they were single too and would be happy to keep me company if I got lonely so far away from home.

They were joking but the thought involuntarily stiffened my dick and I was horrified looking down to see it, strained against my trousers.

When they saw it they took the piss, I laughed along with them but their hands on me didn't help, not quite touching it but tracing along the edges and across my legs. I didn't return their touch, sat frozen, but didn't utter a word to deter them, they looked at each other first in silent agreement and moved in closer to me.

Katie kissed me first and as she absorbed my attention I felt my trousers unfastened and hands on me, I moaned and moved my hands to her, wrapping them around her neck and pulling her in closer to me. Her hair smelt of strawberries, I held it in handfuls as a hand closed around my dick, I glanced down, there were four hands on me, I groaned in disbelief.

My clothes were pulled off gradually, I did my best with theirs but they hastened by helping me, I pushed Katie away from my lips to let my eyes take in their bodies as they writhed beside me. Lips pushed from toe and neck to dick and I stared wide eyed as they took turns with their mouths over me, sucking at my dick and balls, whilst their fingers fought for their share of me.

Katie moved Laura aside and sat upon me, the heat of her vagina spread through me, lighting my nerve endings till I threw my head back and moaned ecstatically, her hips ground as I lay forcing my hips up to meet her thrusts down to me. My hands reached for Laura, I pressed her lips on to me, feeling down her body till I met her groin and I forced my fingers into her, grinding my palm over her clit.

I didn't have a girlfriend but had had plenty of sex and used every ounce of self-control to force myself to wait. Katie was close, her mouth widening, I abandoned Laura for a moment to let her climax wash over me, her breath was deep her face flushed and as it hit she screamed, her body crashing down and collapsing over me.

Laura pushed her aside greedily, stealing her position over me, she pressed her body down against mine and we kissed as she ground over me. I let my joy flow freely through me, feeling her body with my hands and lips, her lips sucked my neck as her hips circled and I grasped her hips tightly to pummel her deeply on to me.

We climaxed seconds later, screaming out ecstatically. Her body collapsed on to mine as we fought to catch out breaths, she moved to my side and Katie joined us, clinging to the other side of me.

They told me they were impressed, their previous housemate had ejaculated as soon as they had put their hands on him, they confessed this had become a ritual for them, seducing new housemates, I wondered why anyone ever left. It's not an ongoing thing, they told me, just a one off that would never happen again.

Don't be so sure I told them, shoving my hands between their legs, they objected but failed to peel their bodies from me. Surrendering for the night at least, they put their hands back on me, surprised to find my dick standing proud and ready. We shall see, they assured me as they moved their heads in close to me.

Watching

Without doubt the biggest benefit of living in a flat is the view, we all have blinds but rarely use them, other than to black out the morning light, we sit at night looking over the city and the skies above it. The other blocks are far enough away to ensure our privacy, from the naked eye that is, so we relax, walking round our flats, doing and dressing as we like.

My flat is small, the windows open it, the flats that surround me and what is happening inside them is all the entertainment I need. The occupants are familiar, I have watched many of them for years but have never seen any of them in real life, when we spill like ants in to the streets. They are like soap opera characters to me – I turn my attention to them at different hours and times of the week.

Friday arrived, my favourite night of the week. Early evening, I watched the families first, arriving home from school and work, scurrying from room to room, arguments came and went, I sometimes wished I could hear them.

Little kids were amused for an hour before parents ushered them off to bed, so that they could relax finally with a drink. If only they could see what I see.

Teenagers desperate to be rid of their parents – humoured them for minutes, before planting themselves in front of blaring white screens locked in their rooms.

Elderly folks living alone linger in windows, staring at the streets beneath, hovering eagerly by the phone for weekly phone calls to be received. I watched as their joy floods through them as they pick up their phones, their grown-up children who were probably proud of themselves for giving half an hour of their precious time per week.

I could match make them, I knew more about their neighbours than they did, men and women sat lonely in separate flats, watching the same things on the TV.

It was almost 9, time for my first show, I topped up my drink and settled back with my binoculars on my balcony. I had hovered inside the first times, behind curtains until I had realised there was no need.

The light flicked on in apartment 24 – 9pm exactly. She walked in, as she had done for weeks. During the week a family lived here, as far as I could see they had no connection to her and when they returned on Sunday she would be gone, leaving no indication that she had been here.

She stripped as always, I could see her naked all weekend but had forced myself after a few weeks to watch her in slots, so as not to miss my other regular shows, this being my favourite, the arrival of her lover where she would greet him on her knees.

She bent before the window, angled sideways to me, brushed her hands across her breasts and turned to greet him as he came in. By the time he got across the room he was naked too, he stood before her, his dick protruding, she took it by the hands first and pushed him straight in to her. I focussed in on his face, his mouth opened, his eyes squeezed closed.

I widened out my view and put a hand in my lap as he pulled her up to him, their bodies pressed together as they kissed, till he turned her and bent her over in front of him. Her hands fell to the window sill as she pushed her groin towards him, he pushed himself purposefully in to her, grabbing her by the hips and driving his body forward to pummel roughly against her.

I placed my hands around my dick, imagining myself inside her and turned my binoculars to her face, her eyes were open staring directly at me, her mouth was moving, whispering words I couldn't hear but I verbalised for her, in my head she was begging me.

The rhythm of my stroke matched theirs as he pushed his dick in and out of her, slow at first then quickening, her teeth gritted trapping her words but it was clear her moans were escaping. I flicked to him, his face matched hers, his face was red his breath panting.

She climaxed first, shouting out, her legs almost collapsing, he wrenched her upwards pinning her in place as he continued to plough himself against her hips. His knuckles whitened as he came, clenching her hips and with a final thrust found his release. They would disappear now for an hour at least so I let my binoculars stray to my next show.

Floor 21, the husband had left just before nine, like clockwork. She had made a call to her neighbour below and as his light extinguished I waited for him to appear at her door. At half past nine he arrived, she had spent the past half an hour trying on clothes, which he would immediately peel from her.

He kissed her neck as she wrapped her body round him, he lifted her and carried her naked body to the bed, stripping off his own clothes before joining her. My dick throbbed now as I watched them, rubbing it more swiftly in my tightened fist. He leant over her body but pulled her round and onto him, she sat winding her hips as I watched them in profile.

His hands groped at her breasts as their lips and hips thrashed together, their eyes stared into each other but as they neared climax they closed, abandoning each other's lips, leaving their mouths free to moan. I grabbed a tissue when I realised they were close, forcing my pace to settle as I waited for them. I groaned, my hands shaking as I pushed to the brink of my release and as they ploughed together shouting out desperately, I imagined myself beneath her and my pleasure overflowed.

Rapidly I jerked my wrist and ejaculated, over the tissue and down on to the floor. Leaving them to collapse against each other I cleaned myself up, topped up my drink and got prepared for the next show.

The Guide

She returned to the main hall and collected the next party of guests, it was a beautiful hot, sunny day, visitor numbers were short, most preferring to spend time outdoors. She spent an hour with them, touring rooms and answering questions before leaving them to their own devices and returning to the hall to collect the next tour.

He waited alone, I had seen him wonder off from an earlier tour, perhaps it had been too crowded? We waited till the time advertised for the departure, when no one joined us we set off together and I asked him whether there was any part of the house, he particularly wanted to see, seen as though we were alone. His eyes stared at me without answer, an implication though?

He flirted as we walked, the mansion was old full of history, perfectly restored, he showed little interest in it, his eyes fixed firmly on me. I was not used to such attention, flattered, I blushed, if I knew how to I would have flirted back instead I babbled my words, struggling to keep to the script.

He was dressed smartly, I wondered what he was doing here, usually our guests were older women or couples, the men being dragged along usually, by their wives. He told me he had been here to give a quote for some restoration work and the owner had suggested he look round by joining a tour.

As we left the first floor, squeezing through the spiral staircase to the attic I felt his hands on me, holding my hips as we walked and as I stepped on to the landing his lips brushed the skin against the back of my neck and he kissed me softly and gently.

I inhaled deeply flooded with feeling but panic washing over me, the house was open anyone could see me and If they did I would be instantly fired, I loved this job and couldn't afford to lose it. He felt too good to stop though, I was seriously losing it, cheeks enflamed, the heat rushing through me. His arms wrapped around my waist and he pulled me in towards him.

I stepped forward and he moved with me, through a door to a room off the tour, strictly off limits to visitors and offering more privacy. The room was unfinished it would have one time have been a dressing room, no windows and no furnishings to lean upon.

He closed the door behind us and pushed me against the wall, his mouth joining mine as his tongue forced its way in to me. I was powerless to stop him, moaning as his hands pushed beneath my skirt, my own hands reaching down to unfasten his trousers and allow his dick to stand free.

He roughly unfastened my shirt, reaching in and thrashing his hands across my breasts, pulling them free, his mouth dropped and clamped across my nipples, stimulating each till they pierced again his licks. I struggled to quieten myself, the hairs across my body stood on end and with every touch I felt my resolve crumbling.

I pushed my hands under his shirt and ran them across his naked skin, his face left my breasts, his eyes stared at me as he lifted my leg and pushed forwards, driving his dick in to me. I lowered my hands to his butt, pulling him closer as he ground and circled his hips, his dick pushing in to me. He groaned, his brows tightening.

I heard footsteps on the stairs, a tour was following, we froze in silence as we heard voices closing in.

They stood feet from us, the tour guide giving a short statement before leaving them free to wonder. We stared at the door, it had no lock on it, it was marked private but anybody could open it.

Horrified I realised he was grounding again, picking up the pace and driving himself in to me. My eyes flashed in panic, his were electrified, yearning and desperate to release in to me. I pressed my mouth to his to stifle his groans, spurned on his tongue reached in to mine as he kissed me. I tried to push him away, my arms pushing against his chest, but it was useless, his weight was almost crushing me against the wall.

Any questions? I heard her ask and prayed that there wouldn't be, my own desire was threatening to spill as his groin continued to thrash against my clit. I surrendered to his tongue at least it stopped us moaning but as his hands wrapped around my arse and he dragged me further on to him, I felt one escape and quickly pressed my mouth against his neck to try to stifle it.

They were leaving, footsteps descended and the doors closed behind them, once they were gone I sighed with relief and he panted and groaned as he ploughed into me, ripping my climax from me as I whimpered in ecstasy. Within seconds he was coming too, scrunching his eyes closed and ramming his release in to me.

Our tangled bodies shuddered and he slowly let go of me, pulling his body away and turning to let me rearrange my clothing. We waited till we caught our breath and with a quick kiss goodbye I led him back to the room, the second tour had just left. Any questions? I asked him, returning to the script. What time do you finish work? He asked pulling my body back to him.

The Maître d'

I hated to complain but the room had evidently been cleaned before it had been given to me, the bed was unmade, the bins unemptied it surely must have been a mistake. I called down to reception and was soon joined by the maître d', he agreed with my assessment apologising profusely and led me to another room, opening it with a master key.

I looked around, pleased to see I had been upgraded, gave my approval and he left me, returning a few minutes later with my luggage and an updated key. I wondered if he had realised who I was, but quickly reasoned the thought away, if that had been the case the room would have been perfect in the first place.

I travelled the country inspecting hotels and their facilities, writing under a pen name and as far as I knew no one had ever connected the face with the name. This hotel was an unusual one for me, independent and smallish but with a renowned chef and increasingly good online reviews, a friend had recently had an impressive stay, which usually deterred me, my review could make or break a new hotel and once I had committed I always reviewed honestly.

The Maître d' managed the hotel, his parents owned it but left the day to day to him. I had read about him in my research, he was young and smart and handsome and was often mentioned for his personal service in the many reviews, most often left by women. I suspected he spent his days spent his days charming his guests rather than running the business, his celebrity drawing customers in.

He had spent years as the medias favourite bad boy, the rich rebellious teenager of A list celebrities. I took a hot shower and made my way to the restaurant, where dinner was excellent as I had heard, he milled around the guests, being charming and as I sat in the bar later he joined me.

I struggled to hide my journalistic tendencies, there were a million questions I wanted to ask him, but I forced myself to stay light, talking about the hotel as if I had no idea who he was, I found him funny and self-deprecating, nothing like the stories I read about him portrayed. He left me often, dealing with queries from staff, it seemed my original analysis of him was completely wrong, he seemed very hands on and was certainly putting the hours in.

I asked him what time he went home and he told me he lived here, in his own room at the hotel so that he could be around 24 hours a day. Our conversation grew increasingly flirtatious and I realised I had far too much to drink and better be on my way, he stared after me as I walked away from him, unable to resist a glance over my shoulder.

In my room, I took a shower to sober myself up and called room service, as well as needing to review it, I needed a soft drink and a coffee. Minutes later there was a knock at the door and he was stood there with a tray in his hands.

I let him in and he placed it on my table, I debated on whether I should hand him the tip, he smiled, mistaking my hesitation for something more and leaned in to give me a kiss. I intended to pull away from him, but instead melted against his lips, they were soft and bombarded me with a yearning that I hadn't quite felt before.

His hands wrapped around my body and my gown fell to my feet, he touched every part of me, his eyes hungrily taking me in. Ignition lit there was no stopping me, I rose on my tiptoes as I wrapped my arm around his neck and pulled his face towards me. He stroked me as we kissed, his touch electrifying, I couldn't understand why it was just something in his eyes.

My hands struggled to unfasten his clothing but he refused to let me in, instead dropping to his knees and prying apart my legs. His hands ran up the centre of my thighs and his lips kissed me gently following. As his fingers reached my groin I moaned for him, his fingers spread my lips and he pushed his tongue inside me, gently probing.

My legs struggled to stay standing and he directed me to the bed, before pushing my body down on to it. As my arse hit the bed he opened my legs spreading them out either side of me as his lips clamped over my clit. He sucked hardly at my clit as he pushed his fingers deeply into me, one, two then three, grinding in circles, the edges of his fingers hooked to probe every part of me.

I moaned in pleasure, my hands pressed against his head and reluctantly tried to pull him up to me. His fingers and tongue had no intention of moving, instead licking and rubbing incessantly.

I cried out, whimpering, my body now shaking, the plateau was so near but I was desperate for him to fuck me. I scratched his back as I realised it was too late, my climax hit and I rocked my hips up to him, my head thrashing side to side moaning and groaning.

I realised he had stepped away and looked up to him, he wiped his mouth with a napkin and leaned in to give me a kiss before telling me he had to go back to work and would see me the next morning. I allowed my breath to return before sitting back up and helping myself to my coffee.

An hour later I realised he wasn't coming back to me, it didn't matter, I was totally satisfied but had expected he would want me to return the favour. I poured my soft drink in a glass, but wanted ice so headed out to the corridor to visit the ice machine. I saw him standing before a door and dropped back behind the corner, he had a tray with room service and disappeared into the room before me.

I tiptoed past the room, quickly filling up my ice bucket but as I headed quickly back I couldn't help listening outside for a minute, sure enough the occupant was moaning, a females' voice only. I smiled, the reviews finally explained.

I was tempted as I typed to review the highlight of my day but stuck to generalities, five stars for the properties, five stars for the service.

Honeymooners

We had spent the past 48 hours locked together, only prying ourselves apart to catch our plane, after months of stressing the wedding had gone perfectly, but we had abandoned the reception at the earliest opportunity, desperate to be alone, wrapped in each other's arms in bed together.

We had barely surfaced since and three weeks of bliss awaited us in a villa on the beach in the Bahamas. Our hands could barely stand to be apart as we went through security, people stared but smiled knowingly when we told them we were on our honeymoon, perhaps remembering their own blissful newly wedded days.

We sat by side on the plane, we had treated ourselves to flights in business class, so had no one rammed beside us and toasted each other when we set off with glasses of Champaign. We kissed as we talked in hushed conversations, I had never imagined when he had walked into my life that we would end up like this.

He was my best friend as well as my lover, I couldn't wait to spend my life with him, telling him I loved him 100 times a day. By mid-flight and after a bottle of Champaign our kisses had deepened, we spread a blanket over ourselves to allow our hands to wonder, above clothes though, desperate to touch naked skin but too afraid.

It was a night flight, after dinner the lights were lowered but we had no intention of sleeping, all around us passengers slept and the hostesses kept away. I felt his hand began to travel up my skirt and this time didn't stop him, parting my legs instead and seeing the smile spread across his face.

He leaned in to kiss me and my tongue met his eagerly, he took my hand and laid it across his waist, his stomach was bare, his trousers were open so I pushed my fingers into the top of them, greeting the tip of his stiff dick. He closed his eyes and inhaled sharply as I ran my hands over him, allowing my fingers to crush him gently and with my second hand I cupped his balls.

We kept our movements small to avoid any bobbing of the blanket, our forced slow movements though were soon driving us insane. His palm pressed against my clit and rubbed methodically, his fingertip pressed inside me and pulled out gently. Our breaths were heavy, our kisses deepened, I was desperate to have him inside me.

I knew I was too turned on when I considered climbing on top of him, I was the conservative one but in this state, my desire topped everything, drawing the line though at arrest for indecent exposure, I quickly stuffed his penis back into his pants and dragged him down the aisle along with me to the bathroom.

I didn't glance to either side to see if anyone was watching us, my only thought was for his dick to be inside me, we squeezed inside and quickly pulled the lock across the door. The look in his eyes told me he was as desperate as I was, I lifted my skirt and shoved my nickers off and he dropped his trousers and took a seat.

I straddled my legs either side of him and dropped my groin to his, a groan escaped his lips and I pressed my mouth to his, trying desperately to stifle his moans but finding they had spread to me instead, groans escaping us both as I ground my hips ecstatically.

His hands released my breast from my dress and he massaged my nipples playfully, before dropping to my hips and grinding me up and down over him.

My breasts bounced and he slapped them against his face as I rolled my head back, pleasure flooding over me. My climax was near I told him in whispers, it was time to release himself in to me. His hands scraped across my now naked back and he kissed my neck wildly, sucking and teasing till I screamed out and he pressed his hand against my face.

I carried on bouncing till he was screaming almost as loud as I was, in the heat of the moment nothing else mattered and we let ourselves go, our bodies shivering, pressed together head to toe. He laughed at my face when I panicked about us leaving, it had been my idea he told me, grabbing me close for a final kiss.

He walked out first and told me all was clear, we hurried back to our seats and fell back under the blanket together. As he tried to kiss me again I waved him away, refusing to let him get me hot again, we would be at the hotel in a few hours he would just have to wait.

Like a drug though, the high passed too quickly and we couldn't help wanting each other again, our kisses spreading like wildfire across our mouths and necks.

The lights flashed on and we separated, the hostess woke all still snoozing ramming the trolley down towards us and serving us coffee, she passed me a bag with a wink and left us with a smile on her face.

I looked in the bag, wondering if the airline was giving us a wedding gift, I pulled out the pink material and almost died, stuffing it back in to the bag after realising it was my nickers, I must have left them in the loo I hadn't even noticed, my jaw dropped in horror, my husband just had a stupid proud smile plastered across his face.

The Audition

I pranced on stage ready to perform, the rest of the girls were undeniably taller than me, it was not as if we would be doing the cancan in a line though so I wasn't overly concerned. The choreographer ran us through the basic moves and we were called back one by one to perform, I gave it my all, nailing the moves and adding my own unique quirks.

Thirty girls stood on stage waiting anxiously for their numbers to be called, half were dropped, half invited to return the next day, thankfully I was one of the latter.

Desperation for work drove us all, we spent half our days auditioning for the following weeks work, but this job would last for months, hence the reason most of the dancers she knew had auditioned for it. Today we had been cut from 30, two days before there had been 200 of us.

They wanted five dancers so I thought I had a good chance, the producers left us with the choreographer for the next two hours we would learn the next day's dance, girls peeled away once they had picked it up, I stayed till the end determined to run through it till it was perfect.

I walked out of the studio with the choreographer, we bumped into a man by the door, he was introduced to me as one of the producers, I said hello and put my hand out to introduce myself, he referred to me by the number I had worn and asked if I wanted to join him in his office.

I knew I could hardly say no, my future was literally in his hands, but wondered if my agreeing would make my chances better or worse. He was attractive enough I thought to myself, it wasn't as if having sex with him (presuming that was what he wanted) would be a chore. He sat opposite me and asked me about the audition process, he acted professionally suggesting nothing untoward.

He came around from the desk, I held my breath, and was taken aback when he asked me about my toes, were my feet hurting after all the dancing and could he look at my toes. I slipped my shoes off, presuming he had a genuine professional interest as he took his feet in my hands I realised it was anything but, the joy in his face obvious.

He was oblivious to my stare though, his hands ran one each across my feet, as he dropped into their arches, he visible sighed and I forced myself not to smile as he glanced up at me. He asked if I minded, I told him to go right ahead, watching in fascination as he fingered my curves.

If this would get me the job it was no price to pay, I leaned back and enjoyed myself as he pressed and bent my toes, massaging them deeply in turn. Once his lips went to them I found it a little odd, I had been dancing on them for hours, they must have been covered in sweat, he didn't seem to mind though, his eyes were closed as he pushed my toes into his mouth.

I closed my eyes to avoid him staring up longingly at me, I could hear his groans and struggling to stop myself laughing out loud at him, that would certainly result in a no, so I let him get on with it, counting in my head to distract myself.
I heard him fiddling his clothes and flashed my eyes open to see what he was doing, expecting if his dick was out it would be heading towards my face or worse.

He stayed where he was though, his dick resting in his lap and dragged my feet over to rest on him, he worked them against him awkwardly at first, till I took over, if this was going to happen I would prefer it to happen quickly.

I pointed my toes and ran the arches of my feet down the edges of his dick, pulling his skin down with them and thrashing back to the tip again, his eyes widened as he stared and I moved one foot between his legs dragging up his balls. He groaned, rolling back his head and retuned his hands to me, leaving one foot on his balls and wrapping the other in his fist alongside his dick and dragging himself up and down against my toes.

As I massaged my toes against his balls I stared at him, his brow was knotted, his jaw clenched in concentration, he was so close and surprisingly I found myself turned on, it was his face, so handsome and so full of hunger, I just wished it was for me rather than for my toes.

He screamed out as he came, staring in fascination as he ejaculated over my feet, his body continued shuddering as he rubbed it into them and I tried not to cringe, telling myself it was good for my skin. His breath started to settle once it was all rubbed away and he slipped my shoes back on before he left me, returning to the other side of the desk.

He dismissed me with a nod of the head, I told him I would see him tomorrow. The next day he watched me from the stalls, I warmed up close to him, rubbing my feet at the edge of the stage first. He watched me hungrily and I could tell from his face that my position was secure.

Chaperones

The two of us ran along through the woods with the kids, this was work but didn't feel like it, the teenagers weren't much younger than us, they were on a school trip. Nathan and I were teachers, who had recently qualified, the others loved having us there, letting us do all the work while they sat doing nothing, but supervising, us as well as the kids.

We were taking a hike, I watched the girls hovering round him hanging off his every word, he was oblivious to them, just as I was to the boys, he told me hung around me. We were flirting and had been for days, we had only met at the start of the trip, teachers from two separate schools, classes converged.

The kids had to be in bed by ten, we entertained them till then, playing pool, cards and darts just as we would with our friends. Once they were all in their rooms we sat with the other teachers drinking coffee, they peeled off one by one leaving us alone.

We flirted, we had done all week, but it wasn't as if it was going anywhere, not whilst here anyway, we had no time off and were each sharing rooms with other teachers, he leaned in to kiss me, holding my face with his hands, his touch was soft his lips increasingly hard.

I was as hungry for him as he was for me but it was impossible, I jumped away from him hearing the creak of a door, no one was there, the house was old and rickety. He took my hand and led me through the kitchen and into the store room. I followed determined to only pursue the kisses.

There was no reason for anyone to wonder in here, it felt safer but marginally, certainly not safe enough to stand naked, his hands pulled at my clothing but I resisted, pushing his hands away. He settled for lifting my skirt and dropped to his knees before me. I groaned as his hands ran up my naked legs, my eyes fixed on the door, he pushed my nickers down over my hips and he pushed his fingers into me. My head told me I should stop him; my horniness overrode my thoughts.

My attention was ripped from the door to his action, my legs almost caved beneath me as his tongue tickled towards my clit, his fingers pressing in and out of me. I whimpered, my hands on his head as the fire rushed through me, his tongue was flicking endlessly, the pressure astounding me, my fears rapidly abandoned as I allowed my moans to escape.

The pressure intensified, my climax was nearing, I felt dizzy, giddy, adrenaline cursing through me, I screamed out as I came, bending my knees to force my groin to him, my hips circling erratically.

He stood before me and I leaned back against the shelving struggling to catch my breath, he kissed my breasts and unfastened the buttons of my shirt, I let him, delighting as his hands ran across my naked breasts. My face was hot and red, his lips returned to me and I kissed him hungrily, my hands reaching down to unfasten his trousers and pushing in to release his stiff dick.

He stared into my eyes as I took him in my hands, his dick was throbbing beneath my touch as I massaged and yanked at it, he moved closer and went to lift my legs but I dropped before him, determined to give to him what he had just given to me.

I opened my mouth and shoved his dick deeply in to me, ramming its tip against my throat and sucking greedily, my hands pushed his trousers away and I reached beneath him to grab and clasp his balls in my hands, kneading them lightly with my fingers, he moaned and I smiled up at him, I could see that I was driving him crazy.

I rose and stood before him, he turned me around and roughly pushed my body forwards, grabbing my hips and directed his dick towards me, pushing it into my vagina, which enclosed it tightly, squeezing as he pushed in and out. I planted my hands on the shelf below me, forcing my groin backwards to stand firm against him, he groaned as he ploughed into me.

I held my breath, the fire had reignited, flames lapping from my groin and stretching out over the rest of my body, my mouth opened as I whimpered, begging for more, his pumps were unrelenting, hunger growing as his climax neared. His moans grew louder as mine did, our bodies rocking together until he froze, his release imminent, I ground my hips against him desperate to join him.

It seemed he had used the pause to fill his lungs, revitalised he suddenly thrashed himself rapidly against me, his fingers bruising my skin, as he clung to my hips, the climax tore through me, I cried out in ecstasy, he rapidly joined me grunting continuously and shouting Yes as he came, before allowing his body to collapse over me.

We leant together breathing deeply, until he withdrew his dick from me, and helped me to my feet, he refastened my shirt as he kissed me, giving each nipple, a quick kiss first and then retrieved his trousers and yanked them back up his legs.

I found my nickers and quickly replaced them and each

ensured the other was fully dressed before we returned to the kitchen, which we were relieved to find was still empty.

We poured our cold coffees away and helped ourselves to more, chastising ourselves for getting carried away, we had each put our jobs at risk and agreed to stay away from each other for the rest of the week. It would be difficult; his eyes were already wondering over me and his lips pulled me as if magnetised back towards him.

Dogging

My husband and I pulled into the industrial estate and drove slowly around, we had not been to this location before but had heard that it could get quite busy. We neared the end of the estate and the flashing of headlights caught our attention, there were around ten cars parked in a circle, we joined them, my husband switching off the headlights and turning the engine off.

We hadn't missed anything, the centre of the circle remained empty, we waited, our eyes flitting around the neighbouring cars, anxious for the action to start. My husband put his arm around my shoulder and kissed me, his eyes were pinned open excitedly, we had been dogging for months and the excitement hadn't dimmed.

Anticipation spurred the adrenaline though us, no scenario was ever the same, on odd occasions we entertained ourselves alone in our own vehicle, we had had sex alone on the bonnet of our car whilst others watched us, sometimes others had joined in. We played it by ear, maintaining eye contact, and would silently communicate throughout the night to let the other know what they wanted, nothing was off limits.

His hands opened my shirt and I let him peel it over my shoulders, I hadn't bothered with a bra, my breasts hung freely and he wrapped his hands around them, I reached up and switched on the interior lights, illuminated we presumed that all eyes were on us. My husband played with my breasts, sending tingles through my body and stiffening my nipples.

Our lips pressed together, our tongues touching, other lights flashed on and we drew our faces away from one another to take in our surroundings.

Four cars were illuminated, a couple frolicked within each, breasts were teased and licked and faces looked out expectantly.

A car door opened and a couple stepped out, moving to the centre of the circle, a headlight flashed on and they were illuminated, a mattress had already been placed there and the woman dropped down to it, the man falling over her. They kissed whilst they fiddled with their clothing and within seconds he was inside her, his naked arse pumping as she wrapped her legs tightly round him.

My husband's hand pushed between my legs, I wasn't wearing knickers, my skirt was short, I merely had to open my legs to allow his fingers to push inside me, he found that I was already wet, my eyes were fixed on the source of my excitement. I lowered my windows, allowing the sounds of their excitement to join us, his trousers were already open, his hand on his stiff dick, I took over for him, massaging it slowly with my hands.

Another door opened and a man on his own stepped out, he headed towards the centre of the circle and as the first man finished and moved away, the second man lowered himself over her and began pumping his dick in to her. The man who she had come with, kneeled beside her, holding her hand as he watched her being fucked by the stranger, they kissed intermittently, till her moans drove him away and she thrashed her head, left to right as she came.

The man over her continued, desperately ploughing against her body, as he came I sighed audibly, I had been holding my breath waiting for him, once he relaxed I allowed my enjoyment to wash over me. The three individuals returned to their cars and my husband turned my face to him and nodded at me, I was ready, I opened my car door and we walked hand in hand to the middle of the ring.

It felt as if we were on a stage, lights shone towards us, we kissed and removed what was left of our clothing, I dropped to my knees as my husband shoved his dick towards my face and sucked slowly, carefully studying his face. I knew he was almost ready, his hands stopped me when he couldn't take any more, his cheeks were red, his breathing heavy.

I tore my lips from him and lay on my back before him, he lifted my legs and dove his face in to me, his tongue and fingers ravishing my clit and alternating as they pushed deep into my vagina. My hips circled and I cried out in pleasure, my head tossing to each side to look around me. Fuck me, I begged as his tongue worked over me, he rose his lips to my breasts, and he sucked as he rose his body to mount me.

His dick pushed into me and we allowed our feelings to run free, moaning and groaning as our hips ground together. My eyes flashed open as I heard another voice beside me, it was a woman, laying her body out next to me, the man with her laying his body over her. Her legs rose and she wrapped them around him, lifting her hips up to meet his.

Over me, my husband had slowed his pace, both our eyes were on them, wondering what would happen next. I made eye contact with the woman and she brought her face towards me, planting soft kisses on my face, she whispered her intentions to me.
I agreed with a nod and looked at my husband's face, I knew whatever I wanted he would agree too.

I pushed him from me and the woman did the same, we

pulled the men down to the mattress and switched places with each other, each boarding the others partner and pushing our lips back together. The men below us grabbed our breasts, pinning our bodies up as we ground our groins over them, her hand reached for me and I reciprocated, each circling our fingertips across the other's clits.

I screamed out as I stared at my husband's face, he was watching me, writhing in ecstasy, we let our eyes flit to the others beneath and beside us, eyes were closed, brows knitted and mouths opening as they silently whimpered. I tried to allow my eyes to take in the feast of naked bodies around me, in cars couples writhed, it was too much my body felt as if it were engulfed in flames. I was the first to climax, my body twisting in ecstasy as I screamed out, there were cries and moans all around me, the dick beneath me stiffened and hands roughly pulled my breasts as the stranger came, his hips rising to push him further in to me.

The woman fucking my husband had allowed her body to collapse over him, they were both shuddering, lips locked together, I allowed my body to do the same. My husband reached for me, he had risen to his feet and lifted me to mine, we headed back to the car, retrieving our clothing and allowed our breaths to settle as we watched the show continue around us.

The Peep Show

I sat on the chair in the centre of the room, windows surrounded me, shutters before them closed. There was no need to start before they opened, I waited patiently, adjusting and readjusting my clothes nervously. This was my first time in the peep booth, men would soon surround me, paying to watch me by the minute, most would be masked, all would masturbate.

The first blind started opening, it was time for the show to begin, I stood facing him, the music played and I rocked my hips to its rhythm, grinding towards the ground and bending my arse towards him. His timer clicked down, he had his hand on his dick, I whipped my bra off and rubbed my tits in front of him.

A second blind opened beside the first one, both men were masked and I danced before them, rubbing my hands across my body and peeling away my knickers, stockings and heels remained. I ignored the men around me, more blinds opened and I rested my arse against the chair and pushed my fingers into myself, allowing my head to roll back and closing my eyes as I began to enjoy myself.

Blinds behind me lifted and I tore my fingers away, realising I had to work all sides. I danced around erotically, my hands and fingers running across my body, the timer on the first booth was shrinking rapidly. His dick throbbed in his hands, so I gave him all my attention, bending my arse close to the glass and pushing my fingers in and out of myself. I pulled my arse cheeks open to improve his view and looked through my legs to gage how long he had left.

Seconds later he was coming, joy spread across his face. I let my body spread across the floor and continued ramming my fingers in to myself, lettering my other hand massage my breasts. My palm pressed against my clit and it dawned on me that I was no longer faking.

My eyes wondered around, I adjusted my angle to make sure everyone could see me and lost myself momentarily, crying out in ecstasy as my orgasm came, I looked around me and saw several of the men coming right along with me, I hovered on my plateau, allowing my moans to escalate.

My face was flush, my breathing heightened, I forced myself to my feet, taking stock of the faces that remained and faking my continued enjoyment as I waited for the heat to rise again. I shouldn't have let myself come I realised, I had gotten carried away, in future would force myself to wait. A close of my vagina held open seemed to satisfy the final face, I stood before him, holding the lips open and pushing my fingers over my swollen clit.

His dick throbbed in his hands and I watched fascinated by his face, fantasising that it would be so much easier if I could lay my lips over him. I allowed my mind to wonder what I could do to him, feeling the fire in me rising once again. The pleasure from my groin spread to my face, my fingers pressed in and I moaned as I spread them, feeling round desperately until I hit the hot points.

He ejaculated and I licked my own lips, new blinds were opening and I was more than ready to start again. I lingered with less pressure against my clit, distracting myself by dancing and letting my hands spread over my breasts.

I used the chair again, dropping down behind it and bouncing my arse against the floor, I stood before it and lifted one leg up, grinding my hips.

The sight of the men playing their dicks around me was driving me insane, the last timer would reach zero in five minutes, I forced myself to pace. I moved the chair and went to each booth individually, ramming my breasts then clit against the glass, their fingers pressed to it and I imagined them on me.

With two minutes to go, two booths remained one in front and one behind me, I pointed my feet out and dropped to a crouch, forcing my fingers in and out of myself, my vagina was visible from both angles, my clit hanging down as I traced my fingers over it. They were close, I was closer, I squeezed my eyes closed and let myself imagine they were both inside me.

A finger pressed into my mouth and I treated it like a dick, pushing it back towards my throat and lapping with my tongue all over it. I lifted and dropped my arse over my fingers, hips circling as my orgasm closed in. Seconds remained, I allowed it to hit, screaming out in ecstasy and thrashing my hands over my clit, the blinds began to close as I took my fingers from myself, laying my body flat on the floor and struggling to catch my breath.

The spotlights softened and my boss walked in, she had been impressed, it was time for me to take a break, later I would be joined by another girl, happy hour – two for one on drinks and girls.

The Fair

It wasn't unusual for girls to throw themselves at me, I worked the waltzer, standing before the cars and making them spin, I wore a vest, stretched tightly across my muscles and leaving my tattooed arms on full display.

I had no interest in the girls that stalked the fair, jumping from man to man desperately, it was the girls who resisted I most craved, the quietest ones who lingered at the back of the groups always turned out to be the best in bed.

I had one in mind for this evening, she showed little interest, her friends screaming as they spun whilst she sat stony faced. Her friends were loud, dressed scantily, pretending to cover parts of their body 'accidently' exposed. She wore shorts, not too short, there was no danger of her arse being exposed, she wore a vest top over it, but it offered no glimpse of a cleavage.

I stared at her as I span the car she was in, her eyes met mine once but were quickly pulled away, her screeching friends fought for my attention but I purposely ignored them. They followed my gaze and told their friend I was staring at her, she looked at me, allowed her eyes to run over me, head to toe, then ignored me and turned the other way. She departed the ride without a word and never approached it again.

My shift was over, I had kept an eye on her, her friends had peeled slowly away, unable to snag me they had pulled other staff, I could see them dotted around, their hands all over my colleagues. She stood alone playing one of the stall games, seemingly trying to win a cuddly toy, I walked over to her and offered to help, winking at the guy behind the counter to indicate he should walk away.

I slipped in to the booth and gave her some more balls, she concentrated trying to hit her target, she wanted a teddy for her brother she told me, I flirted, without her friends she seemed friendly, not flirty though, polite if anything. Still, it beat being ignored, I tried to stop flirting to allow my body language to match hers, she refused to give up, buying more and more balls.

I gave her a little leeway and allowed her to choose a prize, she was delighted jumping up and down, her smile was contagious and I smiled along with her, closing the booth and walking with her to the exit. She was supposed to be meeting her friends she told me, I knew they wouldn't be their I had seen them disappear into my friend's vans.

I waited with her, wondering whether I should invite her to wait in my van, I doubted she would agree so didn't bother, considering whether she was worth putting on the back burner till another day.

She told me she might be better leaving without them, I offered her a lift but she hesitated, wondering if she could trust me, I assured her I wouldn't touch her unless she wanted me too. She smiled at last allowing a soft smile to wash over her face.

I took the opportunity to draw myself closer to her, placing my hand on her chin and angling her face towards me, my lips pressed softly on hers, seconds scraped by as I waited for her response, then her lips moved with mine and she kissed me back. Our lips gently moved together, my hands reached around her and I pulled her body slowly towards me.

Her chest pressed against mine and I could hear her heart pounding, mine matched it, the kiss spreading like wildfire throughout me. I yearned to ravish her, but held myself back, if the kiss was all I would have tonight it would be enough for me, I let myself enjoy it, my tongue reaching in to her and hers copying me, thrashing roughly in and out of my mouth.

Her hands wrapped around my neck and she pulled me down to her, she rocked on her tip toes as our bodies moved together. She fell to her feet and clamped her mouth against my neck, sucking it slowly forcing a groan to escape my lips.

I struggled to keep my hands off her, determined not to blow it, my hands disobeyed my mind though dropping to her arse and grabbing it in handfuls.

Her fingers wondered under my top, fingertips spreading to my chest, I felt my dick stiffen and let her know, grinding myself towards her chest. I wanted to fuck her, but unusually wanted to see her again, the kiss was blowing my mind, I couldn't imagine how it would feel to be in her.

She was pushing me though, her groin was grinding against me, her body felt amazing I wanted to get her in my van so that I could spread my eyes and lips across it. I stepped towards it, as her hands pushed into the back of my jeans, spreading across my arse and reaching her fingers down towards my balls. She stepped backwards, our kisses deepening as I led her towards the van.

Her phone rang and I froze, she looked at the screen and realised it was her friends, they were looking for her, she agreed to meet them at the entrance in five minutes.

I tried to disguise my disappointment and asked her to visit me again, she agreed she would come tomorrow and let her lips wash over me again. We were near the entrance with minutes to spare, I was so desperate for her, I pushed my palm over her groin and rubbed till she moaned.

Her hands were desperately unfastening my jeans, we tucked behind a tree and I crushed her against it, three minutes remained, I unfastened her jeans and pushed them down to her knees, she kicked out of them, wrapped her arms around my neck and lifted her legs round my waist. My dick throbbed forwards and I rammed it inside her, two minutes remained our bodies ploughed together.

The kiss continued our mouths forcing towards each other, ravishing each other desperately, she moved her mouth to my neck to stifle her groans, she was coming, shivering and shaking grinding her hips on me. I came with a burst of my hips and shuddered against her, we were panting, grasping for breath and pried our bodies away.

Less than a minute remained, we dressed, our faces were bright red, she laughed and kissed me goodbye, running off to the entrance and promising to come see me the next day.

The First Time

I had worried for days before the first time she let me kiss her, whether I would be able to do it right, as it happened we discovered together that there was no wrong or right way. Our lips moved wherever it felt right too, slowly at first and then more quickly. Within days we had it perfected, taking the chance to kiss at every opportunity, besides the lockers in the corridors at school and stopping every few seconds as we walked home.

My parents knew I had a girlfriend but I avoided being with her in front of them, it was too hard to keep my lips off her and I would rather die than kiss her in front of them. Neither of us had been out with anyone before, neither of us had any interest, friends all around us were already sleeping together. I had been obsessed only with sports, she was the perfect student absorbed only in her work.

We had been partnered involuntarily on a science project, I had initially struggled to talk to her, each time I had my cheeks had flushed red, she was as shy as me which didn't help. It took us a month to get to know each other and now we were inseparable. Our friends found us adorable, constantly asking us questions and laughing as we blushed.

We had talked about sex, the furthest we had got had been touching each other, over our clothes, the first time she had touched me I had almost burst, when I had got home I had closed my eyes and masturbating, coming within seconds as I ran over the moments we had spent touching each other, laid together on her bed.

I worried whether I would be able to do it, just the thought of her having her hands on me almost forced me to involuntarily ejaculate. She was as nervous as I was, but we figured our kisses had to go somewhere, we were getting more desperate as the days passed, kisses just not quite enough.

Her parents would be out later, we planned to try it, I trusted her, if it worked, it worked if it didn't there would be plenty of opportunities to try again. She laid beside me on the bed and we let our kisses carry us away, she took off her top and I ran my hands above her bra, over her breasts.

My breath was heavy, I pushed my hands up her skirt, over her underwear I rubbed my hands over her and watched fascinated as her face reddened and her breath quickened. I reached in to her bra and released her nipples, they pierced towards me and I stared in wonder before dropping my mouth to them. She tried to touch me and I stopped her, my dick was throbbing I was about to burst, I left myself safe in my trousers as I continued to touch her.

I worked slowly, investigating her, I lifted her skirt and revealed her clitoris and vagina beneath it, it looked nothing like I expected and I stared in wonder at her reaction as I poked and prodded it. Her eyes were tightly closed, her mouth was open, nonsensical words escaping from it.

I pushed my finger in to her, she immediately moaned, moving her hand over mine to stop me but I persisted, pushing my finger in and out until she whimpered and shuddered beneath me. I wondered if she was coming, whether either us would know, she reached for my crotch, unfastened my zip and wrapped her hands around it. I panicked I was throbbing already, there was no way to hide it, if I came she would know straightaway.

She held her breath and suddenly screamed, her body

creasing forward, her face looked as if it was agony, it was ecstasy, I realised, it reflected my own, she was coming, groaning and panting beneath my hands. Her eyes flashed open and she looked at my dick, her hands moved faster, I moved my lips to hers to try to distract her, but she stopped me, determined to watch me as I had watched her.

I released myself, I tried to hold it but it was impossible, she smiled as she watched me, continuing to thrash her hands up and down my dick, I shouted out in pleasure, shocked at the intensity, I had masturbated hundreds of times but it had never felt anything like this.

We kissed, ignoring the mess I had made and laughed at the speed at which we both came, we hadn't had sex though, I apologised, thinking I had let her down, my mums out for hours, she told me, unfastening her bra and laying naked in bed beside me. We have plenty of time, she told me, stripping my clothes off and wrapping her arms back around me.

My dick trembled as her hands spread across my stomach, I agreed, surprised that I would be ready sooner than I thought to try again.

The Blind Date

I cursed my friends as I sat waiting for him, and myself for agreeing to this. My mother was bad enough trying to set me up, but this time it was my friends who had tried to convince me this man would be the man of my dreams.

I was almost 40, perfectly happy with my single life, no one around me was convinced. True it had become harder as I got older to get laid, clubs which had always been a safe bet to pull now seemed to be full of teenagers.

Holiday romances were my forte, I got away as often as I could and was always guaranteed to score. I would consider this date a success if I found Mr Right or Mr Right Now, most likely though, he would turn out to be a complete bore.

I looked good for my age, kept myself quite fit and had an excellent job that I loved, I had never wanted kids and my sisters and brothers had provided plenty of grandchildren for my parents, they insisted they just wanted me to be happy, couldn't understand that I was happy alone.

He walked in to greet me and I was pleasantly surprised, he was a little older than me with a decent body and dressed nice, he leaned in to greet me with a kiss on the cheek, he smelt good, I absorbed him with a deep breath. We ordered a bottle of wine and sat in a booth together.

I listened as he told me all about himself, he was divorced and had three children, who were all fully grown, he looked surprised when I told him I didn't have kids and worriedly asked me if I wanted any.

I assured him he could relax, I had never wanted kids, I was annoyed by his presumption that I would want to spend the rest of my life with him.

As he talked, he began to annoy me more and more, barely letting me get a word in and boasting continuously about himself. Mr Right was ruled out within ten minutes, he was far too arrogant, Mr Right Now, a maybe, he was attractive, I ignored his words and watched his mouth, checking if I had any desire to push mine to it.

There was nothing to lose, I started flirting and he responded positively, suddenly becoming more attractive, I asked him to mine for coffee and he said he would love too, paying the bill and following me out of the restaurant.

He kissed me outside as we waited for a taxi, his tongue thrashing desperately against mine, I was warming to him by the minute as he held me tightly against him. We sat together in the back of the taxi, our kisses continuing, I was oblivious to the driver and let his hands linger over my clothes. My hands held against his face as we kissed, his touch was soft and tender reeling me further and further in.

The taxi pulled up, he paid, exited and walked round to open the door for me, he followed me up the path to my house and I opened the front door. We burst into the house, slamming our bodies against the door to close it, I pushed off his jacket and unfastened the buttons on his shirt, his chest was muscular and solid, I leisurely spread my hands across it.

We took turns shifting our arms and legs around as we undressed each other, still in the hall at the bottom of the stairs, we stood naked thrashing together and I edged his body with me towards the living room.

He pushed me down to the sofa and dropped to his knees before me, descending with his lips from mine, across my neck and down to my chest, alternating between nipples he passionately kissed me, shooting shards of electricity across my body with every lick. My face was flush, my breath panting, I moaned softly as he kissed me, grinding my groin up towards him.

He yanked my feet out and dragged my groin towards him, settling it against his dick, which he angled downwards to the edge of my vagina and grinding his hips forward ploughed himself in to me. I cried out as I watched him pummelling. I laid back against the sofa and lifted my legs to wrap them around him, driving him closer and his chest folded down on to me, his lips crushing mine, his tongue piercing in.

His eyes watched my face intently as I began to whimper beneath him, I pulled my mouth from him to catch my breath and suddenly my climax exploded within me, my eyes squeezed closed and I held my breath, my jaw fixed, groans followed, relief the fire within me had peaked and was settling, I watched him closely expecting the same, his groin froze momentarily and he withdrew from me, taking his penis in his hands.

It dawned on me that we had no protection, I had forgot about it completely, he rubbed his dick across my body, ramming it against my breasts, his mouth opened and I squeezed my breasts against him with my hands, slipping my butt from the edge of the sofa and rested it on the floor.

Groans flooded through his lips as he watched and felt his dick, driving through my breasts, I lowered my tongue to kiss the tip as it thrashed up towards it. He screamed out as he came, ejaculating across my breasts and face, then let himself collapse, shuddering against me, his head resting against my neck.

Once our breaths had settled I grabbed us a gown and went to make the promised coffee, he wrapped his arms back round me as we waited for the kettle to boil and asked if he had to get dressed or could spend the night. I put the option of Mr Right back on the table, he had been an excellent Mr Right Now and showed potential in being something more.

The Cheat

He sulked as I confronted him, refusing to give me an answer, I knew from his response that what I heard was true, he had been seen with another girl, entering and later leaving her apartment. I grabbed his clothes in handfuls, pushing them into black garbage bags.

He attempted to stop me, grabbing me by the arms until I flung myself at him, thrashing my arms out and warning him to stay away from me.

Tears were streaming down my face but I refused to acknowledge them, preferring anger to heartbreak, I needed first to get him out of here, then I would let myself sob against my bed.

We had been together for just over a year, he had moved in here to be with me, it was my apartment, everything in it was mine apart from his clothes. I would throw them out of the window if he didn't take them with him.

He begged me to stop, crying and trying to apologise, he knew it was no good trying to deny it, his denials only fuelled my rage.

I went to the bathroom, throwing his toiletries into a bag, he tried to tell me he would pick everything up later, I told him I never wanted him to come back, I couldn't bear to see him, couldn't risk my stance against him softening.

My heart was in love, my head full of hate, my head would win, everybody knew about it, my friends and family would never accept me forgiving him.

Go, I told him, once all his stuff was bagged, he sat crying at the end of my bed, telling me he was sorry. I grabbed for him to pull him away, his arms held mine strongly and wrapped around me. I struggled, my fists pounding against his chest, he didn't utter a word, just crushing my arms against him.

I sobbed, realising I couldn't physically push him away, my voice protested still as the tears escaped me, his eyes were wet too, tears rolling down his face, they angered me, how dare he cry when this was all his fault. His lips brushed against mine and I turned my face, he held my jaw and dragged me back round to him.

His lips pressed against me, I held my jaw stiffly, refusing to return his kiss, his hands were spreading down my body. I was furious, what the hell did he think he was doing, he mistook my shaking in anger for passion, his mouth opening wider as he snogged me, his body pinning me against the wall, his dick piercing forward against me.

I struggled but he was oblivious, one arm flattening me against the wall, the other pushing between my legs, but as his mouth dropped to my neck and he sucked maddeningly against me, I felt the fire rise and urgently spread. I couldn't deny it I yearned for him, my body was defying me, crushing forwards against him.

My mouth stopped talking and met his lips, returning his kisses as passionately as him, my tongue forcing in his mouth to fight against his.
I pulled his shirt open, buttons flew off, in pops one at a time and my mouth flew to his chest, kisses spreading over him. He ripped open my top as I had his and pulled my skirt off, revealing my nickers which he ripped off.

He picked me up and I wrapped my legs around him, he carried me to the bed and dropped me on it, forcing himself down over me, spreading my legs whilst dropping his trousers and drove his dick in to me. I screamed out in pleasure, seeming electrified by his dick, he pummelled his body over me. His face set in grim concentration and as I climaxed he released himself, screaming as I was, before letting his body collapse against me.

I turned my head away as he tried to kiss me, I couldn't move, I was pinned beneath him, struggling to maintain my breathing, he knew it was over I could tell by the look in his face. He wouldn't ask me again to allow him to stay, the ball was in my court, I still loved him it was obvious, he told me he still loved me and knew he had fucked up, if I could forgive him it wouldn't happen again.

I looked coldly at him, he knew me well enough to know I would never forgive him, we had discussed it many times. He pulled his body away, kissing my mouth softly before he left and staring sadly into my eyes. I had always suspected he was too good looking for me, girls through themselves at him, even in front of me.

I pulled a sheet over my naked body and laid staring at the ceiling as he redressed. He was speaking, but I blanked out his words, forcing myself to be silent, before I conceded to him again. The door slammed, his key was on the table, he had gone as I had wanted, still I sobbed loudly, curling my body into a foetal position, lying on the bed.

I don't know how long I cried for, when I got up and dressed, it was dark outside, I grabbed my phone, I had missed too many calls to return, none I noticed form my now ex.

I took a long shower, relaxing as the water washed over me, I towelled myself dry and moisturised my face, looking in the mirror at my pallid skin and told myself not to cry anymore.

There was a knock at the door, I prayed that it not be him, it was my friends, armed with wine, pizza and DVDs, I hugged each of them, relieved and they laughed as I explained what had happened, happy that he had gone and I had no intention of letting him return.

The Whip

She walked towards me, dressed as I had arranged in PVC, her heels stopped before my face and I stared down at them, desperate to lick, she turned on her heels though, releasing the chain that fixed me to the wall by my neck and dragged me with her on my knees as she stomped around the room.

My eyes faced downwards as I crawled, my knees reddening as I moved along the concrete floor. I lifted my head slightly to look up to her and felt the whip crack down across my back, my spine arched down as I cowered away from it, but dynamite exploded within me and I bit my lip to stifle my moan.

My dick trembled, I froze in anticipation expecting more, I wasn't disappointed, she thrashed the whip across my arse and it tucked in to whisper against my balls.

I screamed, pleasure and pain washing over me, she dragged me to my feet and slapped me, open hand straight across the face. I begged for forgiveness, apologising profusely and as she pushed me to the floor, I curled into a ball. Knees, she screamed as she let the whip fall over me again, my shoulders stung, a thick red mark remained.

I squirmed, struggling to my knees, panting as I struggled to maintain my breathing, several minutes passed until she was satisfied of my obedience and she patted me on the head, eventually pleased. She pushed her foot forward and allowed me to lick her, I dropped my head, pushing my tongue out let it lick down the points of her heels, spreading to the front of the shoe, taking care not to touch her skin.

I moaned as I licked getting carried away, my eyes closed

reflectively as I waited for the whip to fall again, it hit my back, three times in a row, pain seared across my back and I cried out ecstatically, flinging my head back was a fatal mistake, she dragged me to my feet again. I stood before her looking down, my dick stood erect before me, she looked at it with disgust and ordered me to get rid of it.

I tried to push it under my legs, but it sprung back forwards, she drove the whip across the front of my legs and they buckled as I fell to the floor. With her foot, she knocked me to my back and I lay spread eagle across the floor, her feet kicked my legs apart and her heels stepped towards me, catching the skin of my balls and crushing them under her heels.

Her face was covered with a mask, I had no idea what she looked like, her voice was bitchy and commanding, she used it to degrade me, shouting out that I was useless and a fucking whore. Her foot pressed against my dick and she pressed both against my stomach, threatening to crush me but choosing to thrash the whip against my inner thighs instead.

The pain was agonising, I know I had ordered this but flirted with the option of using the safe word, I let my eyes run across my body, sure it would be covered in blood, thick red lines spread across my legs, but no blood lines, I was relieved and let my head relax back against the floor.

She ordered me to stand but her heels still pressed against my balls, I tried to reason with her, lifting my chest up, but she chastised me for speaking, again thrashing the whip, this time against my chest.

My dick throbbed and shuddered, I was convinced it was about to burst, as the pain increased the pleasure did and I was struggling to keep my dick under control.

She lifted her foot and I rushed to my knees, she walked behind me and whipped my butt, ordering me to lift it up. I felt cold metal against my arse and she drove a butt clamp into me, no easing it in just ramming it up and attaching it with a clamp against my balls. I twisted my groin, letting my arse, rip the clamp against my balls and she brought the whip over me again, driving the butt clamp deeper inside me.

She grabbed my chain and wrenched me across the floor, the pain and pleasure in my arse and on my ball's, was impossible to ignore, with each step I held my breath, desperate not to moan but it was impossible, my body was shuddering. She dragged me to a tiled room and I knew what was coming, I groaned in anticipation only to feel the whip drive over me again.

She settled me down to the floor, releasing the chain from my neck and forcing me to sit on the butt plug, the pressure from within flooded like electricity through me and she stood before me, releasing a panel on her suit, her groin exposed facing towards me. She crouched slightly and I rubbed my buttocks against the floor, my mouth open as I moaned.

A stream of hot water thrashed towards me, first slowly then coming in droves, she was pissing, I could taste it, grabbing it with my tongue as it slashed across my face.

There was no need to touch myself, like dynamite exploding my dick throbbed and I began to explode, lapping my tongue around my face as the piss, endlessly flowed.

It ran across my body as my ejaculate shot from me in an arch, I was screaming out in ecstasy, god she was good, worth every penny, my dick has softened but the pleasure continued along with the flow. It stopped and she shook herself over me, allowing me to enjoy every drop. Once it was over and my breath settled, I realised she had left me.

I inhaled deeply to absorb her odour, it was impressive, she must have held it for hours. I removed the clamp and pulled out the butt plug as I rose to my feet and peeled the chains off my body as I stepped into the shower and let the water wash over me. I exited into a changing room and redressed in my expensive suit, checking my reflection in the mirror as I put on my tie and headed out the door and back to work.

Public Loo

I walked through the park, looking for a pick up, I had read online that this was a good place but it seemed deserted and I wondered whether I was in the right place. I moved towards the light where there seemed to be more activity, couples strolled hand in hand, this was obviously not the right place, I headed back into the darkness.

I was out and proudly gay, years ago straight men had lingered in parks for gay encounters with strangers, that was not what I was doing, I was so damn bored, making out in public no longer shocked anyone, men kissed and made out in bars and clubs, where was the danger.

It was what I most loved about being gay, years ago when discovering another man was gay was a thrill, that led to mad frantic sex.

Lately I seemed to be surrounded by gay rather than straight men, getting married, adopting kids, all fine if that's what you wanted but for me being gay wasn't about loving another man, it was about being fucked, or fucking senseless up the ass. My gay friends had all become married men, just as dull as the straight ones, talking excitedly about putting their kids to bed.

A man lingered in the dark in the distance, this looked promising, I headed towards him, checking him out, he was younger than me but not obscenely so, dressed as I was, I made eye contact, trying to determine first if he was selling it. I had no intention of paying for it, if I had been I would have ordered one, as easily as ordering pizza to be delivered to me at my home.

I could tell his thoughts were the same, if he was selling it wouldn't have mattered what I looked like, but he was giving me the once over, checking me out head to toe. We approached each other warily, his eyes glanced towards the building before us and I nodded and followed as he made his way towards the loo.

I stepped in behind him and he faced away from me, perhaps making his preference clear, I hoped so. I stood behind him and ran my hands around his waist kissing his neck, he unfastened his trousers and reached round to unfasten mine, I appreciated we didn't have much time. His hand freed my dick, lifted it from my underwear and squeezing it whilst tugging it with his fist.

I copied him, mirroring his movements exactly, he had obviously been expecting this encounter, his dick stood proud, throbbing under my touch. His head turned to me and our lips pressed together, his rough chin ground against mine, making the hairs down my back stand on end, our tongues thrashed roughly against each other.

I pushed his trousers down to the floor and angled him downwards, letting his lips draw away from me and returning mine to his neck, before shoving his head further down towards the floor. His arse pressed towards me, my hands spread his butt cheeks as I drove my dick forward and into him. We both sighed initially in pleasure as I eased my way in.

He tensed and then relaxed as my balls dangled against his, the depth was set and he clenched his muscles around me, driving me out and then clutching me back.
I grabbed his hips as I ploughed him towards me, until the

pace was set and he took over, grunting as he pushed his arse towards and away from me.

My hands were free to give to him and he moaned as I did, clenching his balls in one hand and his dick in the other, I knew exactly how hard to push, squeezing and stopping just before the point at which I was hurting him. Thrashing and tossing my wrist. He was moaning so loudly, I worried someone would hear us, but instead of trying to hush him, allowed my voice to join in.

He screamed as his release hit him, shuddering and grunting as his semen flew out across the sinks, splashing the mirrors and slowly dripping down them, he was panting, struggling to catch his breath, but held his arse firmly for me to ram against. I screamed as loudly as he had, staring at my own face in the mirror as my jaw clenched and I climaxed, shooting myself in to him.

I fought to catch my breath and pulled my dick out of him, putting it back in to my pants as he bent down to retrieve his. Once he was dressed again he turned to me and asked how long I was in town, I had no intention of seeing him, a relationship was exactly what I wasn't looking for, so I fed him a line that I was leaving that night and let him lingeringly kiss me goodbye before walking away from him.

The Truck Stop

I had flirted with her for months, but then we all did, I suspected the staff were the diners main pull, it certainly wasn't the food, I had been driving for 12 hours straight, I just needed a quick bite and a good sleep. A coffee and a sandwich would do me, usually this place was packed but it was the middle of the night and there were only a few of us, fighting for the attention of the hot waitress.

The first time I had spoken to her, I had been flattered, she was flirting openly with me, it took a few more visits and keen observation to realise she was the same with everyone. The rest of the staff were the same, most likely to ensure we kept coming back. Her shirt was fastened only to the level of decency, her cleavage was visible over the top along with a good handful of breast.

She joined me, topping up my coffee and taking a seat opposite me, whilst asking how I was doing, we chatted for a few minutes before she moved on to the next trucker, who like I had been a few months ago, looked flattered at her attention. I read a paper as I ate, one by one the remaining customers left and I looked up to find myself alone, the waitress was in the kitchen, clearing off the plates, she chatted to the cook, her laughter peeling out.

She sat with me again, her shift was finishing, she wanted to know if I need anything else before she clocked off. I raised my eyebrows, figuring I might as well go for it, if she said no I would give this diner a miss in future and stop instead at the one ten minutes away.

"I wouldn't say no to a blowjob" I answered, expecting her to either laugh the suggestion off, or give me a slap.

"30 quid" she answered.

I looked at her shocked, she was a prostitute?

I didn't know how to answer, on one hand, I was disgusted that I had wasted so much time, on the other, tempted, I had never and would never pay for sex, but a blow job?

"Where" I asked.

"Your truck, 10 minutes," she answered.

I nodded, no wonder the food was crap, I had often wondered why they had so many waitresses and why they were all attractive, I guess I now knew the answer.

I went to the bathroom, cleaned myself up and went to my truck to wait for her, she followed me out, climbing up into the cab beside me, I let the blinds down over the windows and laid my seat back. If I was paying for it, I would leave her to it.

She unzipped my pants, she leant in to kiss me first but I deterred her, certain of where her mouth had been before, she took my dick out of my pants and dropped her head down to it.

I closed my eyes and relaxed, her mouth encased my dick, she shoved it deeply into her throat, applied intense suction and withdrew it, slowly, wrapping her tongue around the edges before repeating.
Her technique was perfection, with her second hand she massaged my balls, juggling the stones through the skin before stretching it with her fingertips.

She held my dick at its base, pulling it forwards as she continued to work with her tongue, I reached down to stroke her hair, it was long, curly and red, my favourite, the smell of strawberry shampoo wafted up from her. My breath became heavy and groans escaped me, I could easily have exploded straight away, but I intended to get my money's worth.

She alternated her pace, gaging my reaction with each and settling on slow and deep, I sighed and held my breath, wondering how much she would charge for full sex. I reached down for her breasts, lifting each out of its cup and rubbing her nipples between my thumb and forefinger.

My body shuddered, I wouldn't be able to hold on much longer, the volume of my groans was increasing, perhaps sensing this she quickened her pace, grinding her jaw over me, intensified the suction and licking more swiftly with her tongue, grabbing a hand around the base of my dick and jerked it roughly.

I pushed back further against my seat, holding my breath, I felt like sparks of electricity were shooting through me, meeting at my groin and screamed out in pleasure, driving my hips forward and ejaculating into her mouth as I came.

She sucked me threw it, pausing to swallow, before cleaning me up, tip to shaft with her tongue. I let go of her breasts, I hadn't realised my hands were still on them. She refastened her shirt and smiled at me, accepting the folded notes and telling me she hoped to see me again.

I watched her leave, more trucks had arrived whilst we were busy, more customers for her no doubt.
I climbed up to the bunk at the top of the cab, peeled my

clothes off and settled in for the night, wondering what I would have for breakfast.

Personal Shopper

He was undeniably handsome and incredibly rich, in my experience those characteristics always came with arrogance, but this guy was a complete jerk. I had spent several hours with him already, he was shopping for his girlfriend and was treating me like shit.

I scurried through the departments, trying as hard as I could to please him, but I was beginning to think he would never be satisfied, I was being berated at every selection.

He had so far rejected jewellery, handbags and accessories now it was the turn of lingerie and evening wear. Nothing I laid out for him was good enough, he snapped his fingers issuing new directions, tutting and shaking his head. I wished I could bin him off but I was on commission and couldn't afford to lose this sale, my rent was due and I barely had enough cash to pay it.

I smiled in agreement at his suggestion, scurrying off for more items to tempt him with. He was on the phone when I returned, with a beautiful evening gown, he looked at it, looked me up and down, told me to put it on and clicked me away. As I was leaving he threw a Basque at me, then looked away, returning his attention to his phone call.

I stepped into the dressing room and slipped off my clothes, this was highly unusual but not unheard of, though girls were usually hired to model rather than personal shoppers doing it. I left my own knickers on, strapped myself in to the Basque and slipped the dress over my head. I had to admit I looked hot.

I stepped back into the room to find him still on the phone, he stared at me while he talked, indicating with his fingers that I should twirl around. I did slowly, feeling incredibly nervous and telling myself he was judging the clothes, not me.

He came off the phone and walked towards me, nodding his head, he ran his hands down the dress and walked round me, telling me the dress was fine, I could take it off, he wanted to check out the underwear. I cringed, realising I had left my own nickers and hoping that at least the colour would match the Basque.

He unfastened the dress and I let it drop, bending down to pick it off the floor and hanging it back on the railing. He stared at me, his eyes looking over me and asked me to turn around, he nodded his head and moved closer to me, his hands ran down the Basque and as he stared into my eyes he dragged my knickers off, without saying a word.

I stood, shocked, he didn't look down, grabbed matching knickers from the rack and ordered me to put them on. I was torn between slapping him across the face and running into the changing room, but his eyes held mine and I obeyed mindlessly.

Once they were on he nodded and spoke one word – Perfect.

He stepped towards me and put his hands on my face, I panicked, holding my breath and he leaned in to kiss me. As his lips brushed gently against mine I felt as if I had been electrocuted, sparks shooting through me. His hand dropped to my waist and he pulled me towards his chest, time stood still, I melted into him, gently returning his kiss.

His hands lowered into the edge of my knickers, his fingertips stretching around the back of my arse, I was totally absorbed in his kiss, the fact that anyone could walk in at any time was irrelevant. His fingers walked towards my groin, resting on my clit and slowly massaging it.

I sighed audibly, forcing myself not to moan but wanting to cry out, my legs almost buckling beneath me.

He pulled away and walked towards the rack, he picked up the dress, some shoes and a necklace, placed them all into my hands and told me he wanted me to wear them tonight. I stared as he clicked his fingers and his assistant rushed in, they spoke for a few seconds then he left, without a second glance.

I put my uniform back on, the assistant took the items from me, including the Basque, when he returned he gave them to me in a bag and asked for my address, and told me a car would pick me up at 8.

I got ready, the outfit cost more than I earnt in a year, two even, I waited nervously, the car collected me and but he wasn't in it, we stopped outside a hotel and I was escorted inside. I was left in a suite, I wasn't surprised, but why the dress?

He walked in to join me and handed me a drink, he didn't speak to me, instead leaning in to kiss me again. It was if no time had passed since the first kiss, my cheeks flushed as the passion returned. He held me tightly running his hands across my body, settling them over my bum and squeezing me against him.

He lowered my zip and pushed my dress to the floor, the Basque followed, in less than a minute I was naked, shivering against him as he wrapped his hands around me and carried me to the bed. I lay silently, my body shaking with anticipation.

His lips started at my lips, licked across my neck and skipped over my chest before settling over my clit, I moaned as he hit it, his tongue lapping against it and as he persisted. I held my hand against his head, desperation flooding through me, I felt vulnerable, exposed. I moaned aloud, his fingers pushed in to me and I screamed out, thrashing my body around as I climaxed, suddenly.

He stood beside the bed, staring at me, I cringed, wondering what the hell he was playing at. He took his clothes off and lowered himself to lay beside me, his arms wrapped around me and as we kissed he manoeuvred his body over mine and drove his dick inside me. He worked slowly, his face set in concentration as he ground his hips, I stared at him, reaching my arms and legs around him and pulled him in closer to me.

His mouth enclosed mine, his tongue thrashed desperately around, my clit pressed around his groin as he ground, the fuse was relit, I was panting and gasping for breath, he remained in control, the only indication of his pleasure, his jaw stiffening.

I screamed out, scratching my hands down his back as I came, his thrusts deepened as I shuddered beneath him and his face relaxed as he released himself in to me, moaning gently and collapsing his body against mine. He lay with me for a moment, we had never spoken, I had no idea what was on his mind.

I wasn't about to find out, he pushed himself off the bed and put his clothes back on, I rose to follow him but he stopped me, telling me his plans had changed, he had to go on a business trip. I dressed once he had left and there was a knock on the door, dinner on a tray, Champaign and a note, he would be back in the morning and hoped I could wait for him.

Lonely Hearts

Each of them sat nervously in the bar, both had arrived early hoping a drink would settle their nerves, neither had seen the other yet. The meeting time arrived they edged back towards the entrance and realised with a laugh that both had been inside, they greeted each other with a kiss and pushed in to a booth.

They were both in their fifties, both divorced and single for a long time, they both claimed to have never used the dating site before, each knowing that they had but unwilling to discuss the disasters that they had endured.

They chatted, getting to know each other, Sarah had two children, both grown up and living away from home, Mark had one son, he and his mother had divorced when he was young. She searched for his fault, there was bound to be one, but saw no sign of it yet, she had arranged an escape but felt no need to use it, she sat back and allowed herself to relax.

He had been disappointed at first, the photograph on her profile had obviously been taken a few years before, she was attractive enough for her age but not his usual type, a little too bonny, friendly enough though. He flirted, if she didn't respond he would bin her off, if this date was going to go where he wanted it too (the bedroom) he didn't want to be wasting too much time.

She flirted back, when his hand rested on her lap she let it, she knew what he was after, luckily, she was after the same. He was quite dull, she had no intention of seeing him again, he would do for the night though, her friends were out with their husbands, she had no intention of going out on the pull alone.

They ordered more drinks, he asked if she wanted to eat, she told him she had already done so and invited him back to hers for coffee. He looked surprised, or faked it, as if that had not been his only intention as it was hers.

They kissed as they waited for the taxi together, both feeling the potential as their bodies pulled together, lips moving in sync. He was a good kisser, not too wet, not too piercing. Besides each other in the back seat they let their hands wonder. He followed her in to the house and she led him straight up to the bedroom, screw the coffee.

He had neither had to work as long, or spend so little money as he had with his usual blind dates, his dick was solid as he stood opposite her in the bedroom, watching as she stripped her clothes off, she was not the thinnest person he had slept with, but she was one of the most confidant, her breasts were impressive, natural, large and round, her nipples stood on end.

He took his clothes off, she thought he looked hot, he walked over to her and grabbed her breasts in his hands, roughly clenching his fingers around them before working his hands down across her stomach to her groin. She spread her legs, inviting him in, he obliged, pushing his fingers in to her.

She groaned as he walked her towards the bed, her face flushed and almost panting, she dropped on to the bed and he crawled on his knees over to her, letting his dick scrape against her stomach as he bypassed her crotch and crawled up to her head, ramming his dick into her face. She stuck her tongue out licking its length before grabbing it with her hands and pushing it deeply against the back of her throat.

She knew how good she was, she worked diligently, saving

one of her own hands to rub her clit as she sucked, massaging his balls with the other. He was moaning, his breath deepening, he noticed she was and looked round to see her playing with herself.

Loving her audacity, he pulled his dick temporarily out of her and shifted around on his knees to turn his body round, he shoved his dick back into her mouth and dropped his own to her clit, moving her fingers aside to take over, pushing and probing with his fingers and tongue.

They both drove their hips upwards, groaning but desperately yearning for more, he wondered whether to stop before he came, thinking at least he should give her a warning, she screamed out though, climaxing, her cum spilling towards his tongue, he lapped it up, kissing her clit as she began to relax and decided that as she had he could go for it. He cried out first, giving her a five second warning.

She made no move to stop him, instead pushing him deeper and grasping at his balls, he released with a shudder, gasping as she swallowed. He moved next to her, they both lay gasping on the bed. This was usually a suitable time to leave, both parties satisfied but he didn't feel like leaving and instead asked her if she wanted a coffee.

She would normally throw dates out at this point, he had given her the best orgasm she had had in years though and he was offering coffee, why not she answered as she watched him stride naked out of her door.

Breakfast

I pottered around the kitchen, the radio was on and I shuffled along to the beat as I made us breakfast, the sun beamed in through the window, it was going to be a beautiful day. I heard the bedroom door close and footsteps approaching, I greeted him with a kiss, my smile beaming.

We had been dating for a year, he had moved in with me the week before, we had taken a week off to organise our new lives together but had spent almost all of it in bed, we were like newlyweds, we couldn't keep our hands off each other. Today we were both going back to work, I had crawled out of bed an hour earlier only to have him join me in the shower.

The hot breakfast I had planned had gone out of the window, coffee and croissants were all we had time for, he grabbed me around the waist and kissed my neck as I poured coffee. I inhaled breathing him in, it had been difficult to draw myself away from him before, now smothered in aftershave he was irresistible.

I turned to return his kisses, abandoning the coffee cups and draping my arms around him as we kissed. He knew just how I liked it, applying pressure with his lips and gently entering his tongue, sliding it against my own, I swooned, like putty in his hands.

He lifted me, propping my buttocks against the counter, bringing my face opposite his own, usually our kisses involved him crouching and me balancing on tip toes, he was so tall, masculine, when I looked at him he took my breath away.

His mouth dropped to my neck, his lips lingering as he pushed his tongue against the crease that I created as my head looked down, to push my shyness away. He was excellent in bed, I tentatively followed, he had been my first, everything I knew now I learned from him. He was dominant, I was submissive, it worked for us both, I adored him.

He was hungry for me, always, now that we lived together there were no obstacles in our way, he could leave me shattered after hours of love making and minutes later I wanted more, the sight or smell of him was enough to ignite my passion for him, once he touched me, I needed more.

I was almost moaning as he kissed me, my hands reached and unfastened his trousers and he stared at me, shaking his head, I knew we were pushing it already, I couldn't help it, I needed him inside me, I also knew he couldn't resist. I released his penis and pushed my nickers to one side, luckily, I was wearing a skirt, I pulled him forward with my hands against his butt and drove his penis in to me.

I moaned as it reached in deeply, rolling my head back and closing my eyes, we could last for hours if we wanted too, but this one had to be fast. I wrapped my feet around him and rammed his body towards me, he was as keen as I was to do it quickly and ploughed his hips towards mine.

I kissed his neck, letting my tongue lick his ear lobes and dragging my jaw closed over them, I knew it drove him crazy, his breathing was heavy, he groaned, his eyes firmly closed and his jaw clenched as he concentrated, as quick as he wanted to be I knew he would never climax without me doing so first.

Her screams were raw, the tension building was staggering, he followed a second behind, her groaning and gasping for breath, the explosion hit and crushed over them both, screaming they came together, legs quaking, she leant her head against his chest and as he pulled his groin away she refastened his clothes and patted him on the arse as her body dropped back down to the floor.

He was rushing around, she poured their coffee into travel cups and threw their croissants in to paper bags. She followed him out of the house, locking the door and ramming her feet into flip flops, stuffing her heels in to her bag. She went to his car first, passing him his coffee and putting his croissant on the dashboard, she dropped on to his lap to give him a kiss goodbye, but as his arms wrapped around her again, she stopped him, pecking him on the cheek and hopping back out of the car.

Wife Swap

I flirted with her husband, she flirted with mine, it was always the same, we had seemingly happy marriages and didn't see each other very often. She always wanted to out-do me and I always wanted to out-do her. Our husbands didn't object, neither had been faithful to us although we hadn't revealed that to each other.

Her husband joined me as we collected drinks from the bar, his flirting was getting a little out of hand, he placed his hand against my butt as we pushed through the crowd, I ignored it assuming it was friendly or accidental. Once we reached the bar though he didn't remove it and shamelessly I let it linger there, leaning in close to listen to him talk.

He didn't seem in any rush to get served, his eyes staring hungrily at me, I grabbed the attention of the bar man instead, ordering our drinks whilst he continued to run his hands across the top of my legs. He whispered something to me that I felt sure I must have misheard, the music was blasting and I had nodded along before now, unable to hear him properly.

I leaned in closer and asked him to repeat himself, I was shocked, I had heard him right the first time, he was suggesting that he and my husband had discussed swapping wives for the night. I looked across at the table, my husband was flirting with my friend as he always did, there had never been any suggestion that we go further though.

I wondered if he was telling the truth, I was gobsmacked unable to answer, instead I grabbed half our drinks and stomped back to the table, leaving him to settle the bill.
I sat beside my husband, struggling to pull his attention away

from my friend and asked him straight, he smiled, told me he had been joking, my friend heard part of our conversation though and leaned in to ask what we were talking about.

Her husband joined her, the four of us stared at each other, wondering who would speak first. My friend looked to her husband, he explained what he had said to me, she laughed, presuming he was joking. I looked at her, she stared back open mouthed at me, neither of us knew what to say.

"We are up for it if you are?" said my husband, both men agreed, nodding to each other and turning to stare at us both.

I left it to my friend to answer, it seemed she was doing the same, I considered what my answer would be, her husband was more attractive than mine, richer and more confident, I wondered what was in it for her.

I guess it would be easy enough for her to feel the same, she didn't know what a prick my husband had become and in one night would not get to learn any of his habits.

"Hell, I would swap permanently" I answered, shocked that my thoughts were voiced out loud, rather than in my head as I had intended.

They all laughed along, presuming I was joking, my husband knew the truth though, for the past week we had been barely been talking, his latest affair with yet another secretary had been revealed and he was busy sucking.

To my shock my friend nodded in agreement and the three of them laughed, going straight in to sorting the terms. I went along with it, secretly worrying that it was a terrible idea, I downed the glass of wine before me and worried for the first time in years about what underwear I was wearing and when was the last time I shaved my legs.

My friend took my hand and led me away, we were apparently going to go to our rooms first, they would join us in half an hour, each taking the other's key. In the lift, an honest but brief review of our recent lives were shared. She felt the same as I did, sick of her husband who had done nothing but cheat on her, they stayed together for the sake of the kids but she had no love for him anymore.

We embraced before we left each other, vowing nothing would change and promising to speak honestly the next morning.

I rushed into my room, jumping in to the shower, dragging the shaver over my legs and under my arms and searching for my sexiest underwear and throwing a dress over them. My hair would do, make up had already been applied, I waited still unsure whether it was going to come, for a knock on the door.

It did and I answered it, shaking, he had a bottle of wine with him, thank god, I thought grabbing us both a glass and sitting on the bed without even thinking and pouring us both a glass. He joined me, sitting by my side and chatting first, I barely heard him, my thoughts consumed by what he would think of my body and what the rest of the night would bring.

He made the first move, a kiss, once his lips were on mine, I was no longer concerned, his mouth was hungry, his tongue greedily pushing its way in to me, his hands wrapped around me, pushing across my breasts, down my waist and finally up my skirt. I panicked for a second but then found myself getting swept away with him, his hunger contagious.

I unfastened the buttons on his shirt, reaching my hands in to brush against his bare chest, his stomach was flat, his back taut and muscly. I unfastened his trousers, struggling to push them down over his hips, as our bodies pressed down on to the bed.

I hardly noticed his hands as they unfastened my dress, he shrugged it off me, at the same time removing his own clothes, he laid me over him, reaching round and unfastening my bra and rubbing his hands over my chest. His hands pushed my nickers down and as I shrugged them over my ankles he opened my legs and drove his dick, already standing proud, into me.

My mouth opened, I pushed my shoulders back to sit over him, holding my hands against his chest as I ground my pelvis deeply. His face was set in bliss, his jaw tight, brows raised, he was groaning, his eyes boring into mine. My desire for him escalated, mirroring his desire for me, his hips ploughed up towards me and I rammed myself over him, feeling his dick filling me completely and his groin pressed up against my clit.

I screamed out, arching my back and shuddering as I came, creasing my face, body tense, I continued to roll my hips aching for him to come with me, his hands shots to my breasts and he pushed me further back, forcing me downwards solidly on to him.
His face drove me insane, his mouth wide as he shuddered and released himself in to me. Once it was over I collapsed my body on to him and he wrapped his arms around me, stroking my hair as my face lay against his chest. We slowly began to regain our composure and he told me how long he had wanted me, practically since the moment we met.

Seeing Red

Alex was aware she was losing it, this meeting was the latest in a string of negotiations, but with each step forward she was pushed three steps back, she had a job to do, her clients were depending on her but she was beginning to wonder if he was taking the piss and arguing for the sake of it.

Cameron was surprised that she had taken so long to blow, he had been digging and digging for weeks, he couldn't help himself, she was so damn hot when she screamed, he smiled, he knew that her points were fair and that he would concede eventually.

Alex smiled, she refused to give him the satisfaction of knowing that he had got to her, she took a deep breath and started again, imagining her boss was in the room with her. Alex laid out her points one by one, there were five of them, everything else was settled she didn't expect to get everything she wanted but she had to get something, otherwise the last five weeks of meetings would have been for nothing.

She laid out her first point, he agreed to concede but only if she dropped the second, she began to relax, finally she was getting somewhere. An hour later four points had been settled, only one remained, the most minor which to be fair, neither of their clients really cared about, the principal though was at stake, the score was two all, they both wanted to win.

They continued to negotiate, in past meetings when things had gotten so heated they had adjourned for the day, but today had to be the last, the office emptied around them until they were alone, free to let their voices raise.

When Cameron threatened to put the settled points back on the table she flew at him, she wanted to squeeze her hands around his neck but settled for shoving him, he fell back against the wall and reached out for her instinctively to stop himself from falling, instead she tumbled to the ground with him.

He crashed against the floor and she landed on top of him, for a moment they stared, tension filled the air, he sensed she wanted to kiss him, the yearning he felt for her was reflected in her eyes, but she was far too stubborn to concede first. He wanted to win as much as she did, but with her body pressed against his swelling dick he was left with no option.

She put her arms to the floor at each side of him to push herself to her feet but he grabbed her, holding his hands at the side of her face he pulled her face close to his and kissed her, slowly at first, she held her mouth stiff and tried to pull away from him. He persisted though forcing his tongue through the tight gap of her lips until she suddenly ripped away from him and he felt the force of her hand slap flat across his face.

He stared, stunned, maybe he had misread her, she looked like she wanted to kill him. Her cheeks glowed red, her breath hot against him and like a dragon she roared, pounding her knuckles down against his chest.

He grabbed her, holding her wrists tightly in his hands to stop her and pushed himself from beneath her, twisting her till she lay under him, he couldn't let go of her, he was sure that if he did she would punch him in the face.

He let her struggle, staring down at her and as her energy faded he pushed her arms beside her, he planned to pull quickly away from her but as he released her, her hands flew to the side of his head and he felt himself being dragged towards her.

For a moment, he thought she was going to bite him, but her mouth crashed against his and her tongue rammed inside him, shoving his aside as she drove it towards his throat.

Stunned he opened his mouth and let her in, he gasped as their tongues fought and she felt her hands dragging his shirt open and rubbing her palms against his naked skin. Her hands dragged down to his waist and he lifted slightly to allow her to unfasten his zip, he felt dazed, drunken absorbed completely by her kiss.

His dick was free, her hands were wrapped around it, she forced her fist up and down over him, he pulled his head away, freeing his mouth from her and reached down to drag her skirt up her legs. Within seconds, he had pulled her panties aside and a groan escaped him as he wrapped his hands around her arse and drove his dick deeply in to her.

She screamed, she had been doing so for hours, but now the sound was feral, desperate for relief, her eyes were closed, her head pressed against the floor, she lifted her legs and wrapped them stiffly around him. Her body shuddered, she was trembling, her clit throbbing against his skin, his dick ripped relentlessly into her, she curled her pelvis forward to greet it.

He stared as she writhed, aching for her to open her eyes, her mouth was wide, between screams she was panting, his heart felt like it was beating outside his chest, about to explode, he concentrated counting his pace in his head, as he struggled to stop himself igniting.

Her eyes flashed open and the flames of her passion engulfed him, he cried out, pummelling down over her, she grimaced and let go of an ear-piercing scream.

They rocked together as the orgasm hit, hands and bodies thrashing desperately together, mouths met again and they snogged on the peak and as it settled their bodies collapsed together.

He pulled away from her and they both discretely rearranged their clothes, as he held a hand out and helped her up to her feet. They stared at each other embarrassed, she wished she could leave but they still had the small matter of the contract to agree.

She returned to her seat opposite him and picked up her files, wondering if now he would agree.

The Open House

Vanessa had spent the day showing potential buyers around the property, the prospects for a sale were not looking great, her clients had been advised to lower the price but had stubbornly refused, convinced that someone would shell out for this place. They were in no rush though, they had already paid for and moved into their next place, they were happy to wait for the market to recover.

Luckily, she was being paid for her services hourly rather than by commission, so she entertained each visitor, fully aware that most of them were there to nosy rather than to buy, it broke the day up though and the house felt far too big and old to be alone in.

The weather wasn't helping, she was having to ask everyone to remove or cover their shoes and couldn't show anyone around the grounds, she had no intention of running around cleaning the floors once the house closed, she wanted to be out of there before it got dark.

She had one more appointment, he was already late he was an agent she had not seen before, viewing on behalf of an investor who lived abroad, she didn't think he would go for it, her hope was that he would make an offer which was not too insulting for her clients to consider.

The doorbell rang and she rushed to answer it, the man before her was drenched, she ushered him and passed him a towel, unfortunately the driveway was pretty long and she had been having to deal with unhappy arrivals all day. He slipped his shoes off on the mat and followed her into the entrance hall.

She fell straight into her prepared speech about the property and set off up the stairs, assuming he would follow her, he lingered way behind actually taking in the details, she let him catch up before she continued, pointing out the bedrooms and letting him wonder alone. He shouted out to her from the master suite and she joined him ready to answer his questions.

He was stood by the window, he turned to her and told her it was priced too high, though she agreed, she tried to justify the high price but he stopped her dropping an envelope into her hand and explaining it was his clients best offer. She opened it, it had obviously been typed up prior to his arrival and was a fair enough offer, below the asking price but not embarrassingly so.

She wondered why he had bothered with the viewing, but a hand on her waist was enough to answer her. She stepped back away from him, afraid suddenly that he was about to force himself on her. He held her hand though and pulled her back towards him.

"I'm not going to force you," he laughed as he saw her face, "I just thought of a better way to spend half an hour than walking around this place."

She stared, confused, wondering if he was serious. Apparently, he was, as well as confident, he shrugged his jacked off and hung it over the post of the bed, before unfastening and pulling off his shirt. Vanessa checked out his body, tempting as his offer was she was supposed to be at work.

He hung his shirt and pulled off his trousers, he looked good in the suit, but almost naked he looked amazing, she really shouldn't she thought but he was so tempting. He walked back towards her and kissed her and she knew she really had no choice.

She helped him strip her, unfastening the buttons of her suit as he peeled it away, in underwear they fell onto the bed together laughing. They played, each taking turns to role on top of the other as their tongues teased across each other's bodies, he held her beneath him pushing things a step further, unfastening her bra and dropping his lips to her nipples.

She moaned as he kissed her breasts, her nipples throbbed as his tongue wrapped across them and his hands pushed her nickers away, her palms pressing against her clit as it made its way. She left him to his work, pressing against the bed with her arms splayed out beside her, she breathed slowly, her eyes closed, he was very good with his tongue, he licked everywhere, lingering where she moaned most.

Her clitoris ached for him, just a little more, she thought as he rammed his tongue against it, she closed her fingers around the edge of the bed, stretching out as her toes curled, as the inevitable rush to the peak washed through her. He stopped and instead of the climax, frustration flooded through her, it seemed he thought it was his turn.

He grabbed her and rolled over to lay flat against the bed with her on top of him, pushing her head down and ramming his dick towards her face, it was only fair, she figured as she licked him, tip to shaft and over and beyond his balls. Her hands pressed over him, she spread his legs and kneeled between them, to allow her head to bob up and down over him, rubbing his dick to her throat.

He groaned as she sucked, his body hot and panting, almost, she thought, she drove her finger into his dick and he rolled back his head, crying out, his dick shuddering within her. At last he was as desperate as she was, she pushed her body up and dropped her vagina over his dick. She tensed the muscles of her vagina to drag him with her as her hips rolled, he held his hands over her breasts and squeezed as they groaned.

His hand dropped to her clit and he rubbed it with his fingers as she ground over him, she was breathing deeply, her teeth clenched, the eruption commenced and she thrashed herself against him erratically. He had been holding out for her, his body in ecstasy, she looked incredible writhing over him, breasts bouncing, but it was her eyes that held him, they were on fire.

They pummelled towards one another, he raised his hips as she thrashed herself against him, they cried out, each with their eyes closed, trembling and shuddering together, his chest pressed forwards and he wrapped his arms around her, fixing her close to him and encasing her lips under his. Their kisses slowed as their breaths settled and they lay beside each other wondering how the hell they had ended up in bed together.

The Conductor

She stumbled down the empty carriage to take a seat, this was the last train, filled with the inevitable drunks and creeps. He had already woken a couple of sleeping passengers, to ask here they were heading so that he could ensure they got off at the right stop. Few passengers remained now they were almost at the end of the line, he made his way towards the last passenger and asked to see her ticket.

She had been drinking a lot and said she didn't have her purse, he told her she shouldn't have got on the train without giving her details to the ticket office first so that they could bill her, she would need a ticket to exit the station though. He shook his head, there really wasn't anything he could do about it, he printed a ticket off for her and reached his hands into his pocket, to pay for the ticket out of his own money.

He passed her the ticket and she thanked him and asked what she could do for him in return, he looked down at her, her offer was tempting, her cleavage on full display and her skirt revealing bare knees. He shook his head though, she didn't owe him anything and walked away before he could change his mind closing the door firmly behind him as he stepped in to his cabin.

He took a seat, laid his head back and fell asleep thinking of her, he dreamt of her putting her hands on him, kneeling before him and sucking his dick. A tannoy announced their imminent arrival at the last station and he forced his eyes open, annoyed at the disturbance of his dream. Confusingly it seemed he was still dreaming though, he looked down to see a blond head hovering over him.

He groaned as he realised he wasn't having a dream, his hand dropped to stop her but then he absorbed the reality of what he was feeling. His spine was tingling, his groin was on fine, his dick was throbbing it was being rammed against her throat. He yearned to grab her and sit her on him, but there was no time, he had to be at the doors when the train pulled into the station.

He pushed his hips towards her, she took him out of her mouth and licked him, her eyes flashed up to him, and she said good morning, he reached out and grabbed her tits and pulled her back over him, his fingers squeezed her tits, she wrapped her hands around his balls.

Yes, he cried as she sucked him, massaging her fists around his balls, the explosion was crashing towards him, he cried out begging for more, she obliged squeezing her lips over him and as he ignited he held her head in place. He burst into her, his body trembling, his hips drove forward as he came into her, she gulped and swallowed, before sticking her tongue out and licking the remnants of his cum away.

She pulled away from him and pushed to her feet, ducking out of his cabin as the train pulled in to the station, he fastened his zip as he watched her walk away. He pushed to his feet with a smile on his face, placing his key into the lock to open the doors of the train.

He walked through the carriages making sure everyone was awoken, satisfied it was empty he disembarked and walked to the office, he signed out and exited the station but saw her lingering at the gate. He walked over to her, sure she had not expecting to see her again but he had to make sure she was ok.

She didn't have her bag she reminded him, she was hoping to

convince a taxi to take her home, convince the driver how he asked her with a smile on his face, she laughed, she had sucked enough dicks for the day. He signalled for her to follow him, the train ticket had only been cheap he figured the blow job cost would also cover the cost of a lift home.

Next Day Delivery

Her neighbour spilled the beans about her affair over coffee, Deborah had noticed a change in her lately, she usually hung around the house all day in a jogging suit but was currently wearing a short skirt and low top. It had started months ago, he was a delivery driver, she had come on to him when he delivered a parcel to her house, lately he had been dropping in almost every day.

Deborah was intrigued, her neighbour was her age, early forties and more overweight than she was, her husband was a complete arse hole, so she certainly didn't blame her for it, she just wanted to know what he looked like.

Deborah spent the next day in or around the front garden, waiting for the delivery man to arrive, when he did she was surprised, he was much younger than them, tall and skinny, his eyes averted when she looked at him, he looked scared to death.

He went in to her, ten minutes later he came out again, the parcel still in his hands, she stared at him, his face flushed red. Her neighbour had clearly instigated it, she wondered if he was any good and decided that rather than ask she would find out for herself.

She made the order online and paid extra for next day delivery, her husband would be at work, she even picked a time slot, to ensure her neighbour wouldn't be in. The thought of the next days' escapades thrilled her, that night she instigated sex with her husband for the first time in months, fantasising about what she hoped the delivery driver would soon be doing to her.

Once he had left for work, she scurried through her wardrobe wondering what to wear, she figured she had to be obvious so settled on nothing, she wrapped her body in a towel, that way if he rejected her, she could pretend he had disturbed her.

She was excited, she didn't feel guilty, she knew her husband had been screwing around for years and this was not her first affair, not that it would she intended this to turn into that, her neighbour could keep him, she just wanted to know if he was any good.

The van pulled up outside, she went to the door, when she answered he stared at her, he passed her the parcel, stuttering, she dropped the towel and took him by the hand. He followed eagerly and as soon as she slammed the door his hands were all over her.

He backed her up and lowered her body so that she was sat on the stairs, he opened her legs, kneeled a few steps below and stuck his tongue out towards her. She had planned to get straight into sex, rather than waste time in foreplay, but his tongue felt divine, lapping her clit and pushing in to her.

She laid her head back on the stairs and closed her eyes, his tongue was thrusting up against her clit, she sighed as it swelled, receiving head was rare for her, her husband never bothered, the lovers who had, made the obligatory pass by before sticking their dicks in. He was loving it though, his enthusiasm and enjoyment was evident, he was moaning along with her.

She could feel the moisture trickling within her, her heart was racing, fire spreading, her nipples had been ignored but stood solidly on her bouncing breasts as he rammed his fingers in to her and ploughed her against the step.

She began to groan, if he wasn't careful she would climax before even touching him. She reached for him, reluctantly pulled his face away and pulled his body up to her, he had already unfastened his trousers and had a huge throbbing dick in his hands, she smiled and directed it, with her hands on his hips towards her vagina.

His dick pressed in to her, filling her so tightly that she gasped, he ripped himself out and drove back in to her repeatedly, till she was screaming out to encourage him. Her hands grabbed his arse and she lifted her pelvis up towards him. Their lips met for the first time and they kissed, long and hard, tongues tangled.

Her body was shuddering, her climax neared, she wouldn't be able to walk for the rest of the day but she didn't care, the pain was exquisite, she circled her hips to accentuate it, pressing her clit against his groin. She screamed out as she came, thrashing her head side to side as she pushed away from his lips to concentrate and enjoy it.

Seemingly spurned on, he pumped vigorously into her, she cried out, riding the high and as he found his release, his body stiffened before he pulsated his pelvis and shuddered against her.

He fell over her, their breaths were hot and heavy, she winced as he pulled his dick out of her and he stood and got dressed leaving her gasping, legs spread wide on the stairs.

His demeanour had changed suddenly, he looked self-assured and confident, he passed her a hand-held screen and she signed for the delivery, he leant in to kiss her goodbye and let himself out of the door.

She stood up and dragged the towel back around her, she was hot and sweaty and headed up to have a shower. He had given a better performance that she could have imagined possible, she struggled to get up the stairs and wondered how her neighbour put up with a dick that size inside her almost daily, maybe she had stretched, but then wouldn't her husband have notice, maybe they were not sleeping together anymore, he would certainly be enough for her.

She knew she would be ordering again, but not every day, once a month would do she figured, it would give her something to look forward to, plus she needed time for the recovery.

Fresh Meat

The camp counsellors were close, there were six of them, three boys, three girls, they had slept with each other in all combinations, some discretely, some less so, two of them had become a couple, the others used each whenever they needed too.

They were working together for the summer, they amused and tolerated their visitors all day but their nights were their own, it was almost over. With a week to go a new girl was brought in to help and the boys stumbled over themselves to greet her.

Caroline was petite and blond, the girls took her to their room and helped her settle in, Stef, made it clear immediately which one of the boys belonged to her, but she was warned off them all. Stef had enjoyed her position as queen bee, she was the best looking of the three and knew it. Caroline told them she had a boyfriend and that they didn't need to worry about her, they backed off defensively, protesting that they didn't care.

She had met the boys first and all three had already flirted with her, apart from the three girls they had had no contact with females for weeks, she was fresh meat, they all wanted her. She smiled politely as she pretended to listen to the girls, she had already decided which boy she wanted, Stef would not be happy but at least the other two would be.

The seven of them finished work at the same time and headed back to their trailers, they lit a BBQ and sat around drinking, Stef's body was draped possessively on her boyfriend, but his eyes were on Caroline and she had already made it clear she was available to him.

Caroline didn't drink, by midnight the rest of the girls could barely walk, the two free boys had each sat with her, she had quickly deterred their interest, the fact that she didn't drink soon put them off her, they had suspected that her resolve would disappear once she had a drink, but sober it was obvious they had no chance with her.

They disappeared in twos and she sat alone, moments later Stef's boyfriend reappeared and she followed him away from the trailers and in to the trees. Out of the view he held her hand, deeper into the woods he stopped walking and turned to her. She put her arms around him and he kissed her, letting his mouth drop to her neck and clasping against her skin.

She let him suck her, a love bite on her neck the next day would have them all wondering, she held her hand against his dick, it was already stiff, she pulled her shirt off, she wasn't wearing a bra. He put his hands on her breasts and squeezed hard, dropping his mouth to them, licking her nipples and squeezing them softly with his teeth.

Their hands unfastened each other's jeans and they each wriggled to let them drop from her body, before pushing their groins close and letting them grind over one another over their underwear.

She had been teasing him all evening, licking her lips as she stared, even in front of the kids, he had put his hands on her arse as they had followed the kids back to camp and she hadn't stopped him, even letting him reach in between her legs to rub her clit.

He knew that his girlfriend would pass out as soon as her head hit the pillow, she always did when she drank, in front of everyone she acted like they were constantly at it when in fact she was quite frigid.

He kept her because the other boys wanted her, once camp was over he would never see her again, even though they lived quite close. He had also been discretely screwing the other girls whenever he had the chance, they kept it secret because they feared her.

He groaned as her hands pressed against his naked skin, she pulled his dick free and wrapped her hands around it, massaging it tip to balls. He copied her, brushing his fingers by her clit and driving his fingers in to her. They kissed as their fingers worked, their breath was heavy, his dick was throbbing, she jerked it stiffly, it was almost ready to push in to her.

His eyes closed and his jaw stiffened, he was too close, he turned her away from him and leaned her up against the tree. He ran his hands down her back and over her arse, it was perfect, pert and round, he brushed her hair aside and kissed her neck as he pressed himself against her. His hands wrapped around her, he enclosed her breasts in one and dropped his second down to her clit.

Her hips circled as she enjoyed him, his fingers pressed in to her, they were moist when he withdrew them and he used the wetness to further titillate her clit. She was ready for him, she was begging with whispers for him to fuck her, oh he would, he promised, he bent her body, pushed open her legs and rammed his dick forwards and in to her.

She held herself firmly against him, he planted his hands on her hips and ploughed his dick in and out of her. Within seconds she was screaming, he briefly worried that the others would hear her but rather than deter it thrilled him, it was too late to stop, he couldn't if he wanted too. He absorbed her screams, she was shouting yes repeatedly.

Her arse shook as she came, the intensity almost knocked her off her feet, she shook and his pace increased, until at last he was coming with her. They cried out together, their bodies felt as if they were engulfed in fire, the flames flashed from their groins to their heads and their toes, fixed together they rubbed through their peak and as it passed they collapsed, falling to the floor.

The Car Park

Trish reversed into the space in front of the empty unit, it was her last job of the day and she would have to work quickly, it was already getting dark, these miserable winter days limited her schedule, she needed the light. She took the external pictures first, taking advantage of the last moments of the light, they weren't perfect but using the flash as well they were adequate.

She inserted the key and opened the shutter doors, the industrial estate was eerily deserted, she closed the door behind her and got on with her work. The owner of the unit was advertising it for let and she was taking photographs for the website, she worked her way around its corners, taking pictures from all angles and by the time she had finished and stepped out it was dark.

She switched off the lights and re-shuttered the doors, she sat in her car and turned the key to start the engine but was met only by silence. She tried again, nothing, she grumbled to herself and slammed the door. She considered getting out and lifting the bonnet to see what was wrong, but what would be the point, she knew nothing about cars.

She picked up her phone, she would normally call her husband but she was miles away from home, it would take hours for him to get to her, she would have to call her recovery firm, she hated dealing with mechanics but really didn't have much choice.

She made the call, someone would be with her soon, how soon, she queried and grimaced when they told her it would be at least an hour, maybe more.
Fortunately, she had some snacks in the car, she helped herself

to chocolates and crisps and sat chomping as she waited. A car pulled into the estate and parked opposite her, she initially thought it could be the recovery firm, but realised quickly that she had only just got off the phone.

She locked the doors, panicked suddenly and picked up her phone, the headlights of the car were shining forward, but fortunately the car was a little to the left and not straight at her, she sunk into her seat hoping that the occupants hadn't seen her.

A second car arrived and parked beside her, she was relieved to see that one of the occupants was a woman, she felt safer and began to relax, perhaps one of these units was about to open, when a third car arrived she felt sure that was the case and carried on eating her chocolate. Two cars were opposite hers now, both headlights pierced in to the car next to her.

The internal lights were switched on and she could see the occupants clearly, a man and a woman in their 50s, they looked harmless. As she stared their faces pressed together and she suddenly realised what she was watching, she stared open mouthed and cringed as the doors of the car opened and the couple stood beside it and began to take each other's clothes off.

They were moving quickly; their hands were all over each other and within minutes the woman was being bent over the edge of the car bonnet.

He stood behind her, his arse was right beside her window, she tried not to look but it was impossible to look away, his arse was pumping against the woman before him and they were both screaming.
The occupants of the car opposite had so far been invisible to her, all she could see was the headlights of their cars, but as

she watched in horror their interior lights also illuminated.

A couple sat in each of the cars, their eyes were staring forward, the arse of the man beside her was clenching now, it was hairy and dimply, she couldn't see the man's face but this was clearly not the arse of a young man, skinny white legs held it up, and fat thighs wobbled before them.

Their screams were going through her, she wished they would hurry up and finish, the chocolate in her mouth was melting but she refused to let it slip down her throat, she felt sick, could feel the bile rising within her.

Opposite her, the passenger seat was now empty, its previous occupant was now bouncing on the lap of the man beside her, their car shook gently. She glanced to her side, the arse was still pumping, his body was bent completely over now, his legs were clearly struggling to hold him.

She swallowed and forced herself to look at the last car, piercing nipples at the front of two massive white tits stared back at her, they were pressed against the window, hands were wrapped around them. She turned her head intrigued as to where the head of its owner was and noticed it rammed against the top of the car, it appeared as if she was sat facing forwards and a man was behind her.

As disgusted as she was she reached for her glasses, the couple came sharply into view and she pushed her head back, regretting her perfect view but was still unable to tear her eyes away. She glanced between them, she didn't need to look to her side, she could sense and hear that his arse was still pumping next to her.

The three cars shook, she kept her eyes on the face of the men fucking the women before her. She could see their expressions clearly, they were ecstatic, about to ejaculate, she felt a tingle spread across her stomach. Both pairs of eyes were staring at the couple beside her, fire bellowed behind them, their jaws were stiff, she wished that the couple beside her would stop screaming so that she could hear their groans.

Her hand fell to her lap, her fingers pressed against her groin, her arousal shocked her, she barely had to apply any pressure for the fire to ignite within her, it was the expression on their faces, she let her mind imagine that she was the one who had inspired the hungry expressions in their eyes, that they were fucking her.

Her eyes were closed, her head had rolled backward, with a shock she realised that an orgasm was about to hit her, the sounds beside her had died away, her eyes flashed open and she realised that her car was flooded with light. A torch was shining in to illuminate her and the couple beside her were now sat in the car watching her.

In her mind, she knew she should stop but she was too close, she looked forwards and the men were now staring at her, the bodies of the women before them were trembling and she could hear their groans. Her mouth opened, she was panting, electricity bolted through her and as the men cried out and stiffened she came.

She thrashed her head to the side, closing her eyes, consumed by the tsunami of passion flooding through her, she was crying out in ecstasy, the orgasm had hit her from nowhere but refused to abate, it was if she was pinned there, she could barely breath and it finally settled and the embarrassment and shame took its place.

Her hand drifted from her clit, she had barely realised she had been touching herself, she straightened herself in her chair but refused to repeat the eye contact that she had made. It was dark, the torchlight had gone away.

A fourth vehicle pulled into the estate and stopped before her, one by one the other cars pulled away and relief flooded through her when she realised it was the mechanic from the recovery company knocking on her window.

A Brief Encounter

He followed her out of the property, he had been flirting with her but didn't know if it had worked, she had barely acknowledged him other than the look she had given him when she had arrived. They were at a house party, neither knew the host well, each had arrived with their partners who were now drunk and making their ways around the room dancing with anyone who would have them.

She had asked him if he wanted to join her for a cigarette, they were both sober, designated drivers and apparently the only smokers at the party. Her legs were amazing, her summer dress flirted just below her arse cheeks, he watched it as he walked, willing it to rise so that he could see even more of her.

She had seen him before but he hadn't recognised her, she worked behind the bar near his work, he was a good tipper and his girlfriend was a bitch. She stepped out on to the patio and lit a cigarette before turning to light his, he stared at her as the end of his cigarette glowed. She didn't attempt to pull from his stare, instead inhaling deeply as she looked back at him.

He was confused when she didn't pull away from him, she stood inches from his face and he tilted his head lightly as he looked at her. He drew closer and she surprisingly leant forwards and her lips pressed against his, he threw his cigarette to the floor and wrapped his arms around her, she returned his kiss, enthusiastically and they moved together to the side of the house and pressed against the wall.

Her hands were on his waist, they nudged around, he was fascinated to find that she had unfastened his zip, he gasped, his dick was in her hands before he knew it, he lifted her skirt and planted his hands against her arse, dragging her closer to him. I want you to fuck me, she whispered in his ear, but you need to be quick.

He was more than ready, his dick was already throbbing, her words almost finished him. He lifted her, she wrapped her arms around his neck and lifted her legs around his waist and he rammed his dick into her vagina as he pressed her against the wall.

He groaned, his body ached for her, her lips closed round his, she was attempting to silence him but her own moans were loader than his, she bit his lips and pleasure flooded through him. He wound his hips as he pummelled in to her, she was lifting herself up and down on to him, grinding her clit and clenching his dick.

Their bodies were shuddered, he was about to ejaculate, he stared in to her eyes, his were glowing from the fire within and he waited for the flames to ignite in her, as they did her jaw stiffened and he ploughed in and out of her, stiffening his groin and pounding her against the wall.

A loud groan escaped each of them until they pressed their mouths against each other's necks to shut themselves up, their bodies were shaking, orgasms ripped through them both and they let their groins pulsate as they enjoyed the peak eventually fall.

He lifted her and dropped her back to her feet, they adjusted their clothing and crept back to the back of the building, he passed her another cigarette and she lit them both, smiling this time and stepping away.

The back door opened, a few bodies poured out but ignored them, they were just letting some air in, they leant against the back wall, letting their hands touch as they ignored the rest of their cigarettes. He told her she looked familiar, she told him where she worked, he realised he had seen her before and smiled contentedly knowing that he would soon be able to see her again.

The Fitting

The men stood before him, he was annoyed that they had arrived so late, the shop was about to close but they had left it till the last minute. He dealt with the groom first, jotting down his measurements and then turning to each of his friends, they had already tried on the style of suits that they had chosen, to check that the width of the legs would fit, both men were short though, so their trousers would need shortening.

He turned the sign on the window around to indicate that the shop was closed and edged towards the door with them as they continued to talk. He was sure that they were trying to delay him and worried briefly that he was about to be robbed. As they got to the door the reason for their anxiety was revealed – a fourth man had opened the door and was edging into the shop.

Had he not been so handsome he would have turned him away, the groom apologised, the usher had arrived late. He rose his arms in frustration but agreed to fit the last man in, the rest of them would need to go though, his assistant had now left and he couldn't leave the men in the store alone. They agreed to wait in the pub across the road, he would only be a few minutes, they would get him a drink in.

He led the man to the fitting room and asked him to take off his clothes, he couldn't resist watching him, his body was quite something to behold, he could tell with a glance that his thighs were far too thick for the standard clothes. So rather than ask him to put a suit on he set at him with a tape measure.

his waist was small, but he struggled to reach around him to measure his chest, he asked him to tense his shoulders, the suit would need to allow him room to move, his muscles bulged, the fitter struggled to steady his breath. He bent to his knees and wrapped the tape around his thighs, his fingertips scraping against him. His eyes glanced up, he let them linger over his balls and he jumped when he noticed his bulging dick.

He looked up at the man's face, at work he never let his sexuality be known, he perved at his customers often but always keeping his feelings in, the man staring down at him, smiled though and he suddenly leaned forward and pushed his underwear down from his hips.

The dick encased within barely moved as the material dragged down away from it, it stood firmly in place and he could see the veins on it bulging. He didn't need any more encouragement, he lifted his weight to his knees and pressed his face towards it.

He wrapped his fingers around the balls, they swelled and jumped at his touch, he pursed his lips and dragged them down over the dick. He groaned as he sucked, he could feel the bulge against his throat, the body was swaying and leaning in against his face.

He wrapped his tongue around it, delighting as a trickle of semen escaped and lapped it up with his tongue, the man's hands were on his head, he pushed him closer as he moaned, he could hear the desperation in his voice and couldn't wait to hear him ejaculate.

He was pulled to his feet though and bolts of lightning struck as he pressed his lips to his, he felt hands on his body and rubbed his palms over his. His trousers were being stripped away and he felt himself being turned, he stared into the mirror before them and watched his dick being wrestled out of his clothes.

The man towered behind him, his lips were on his neck and his hands were on his dick, he let his body lean towards him, it was shivering in bliss. He watched as his dick throbbed, their faces were both glowing, he felt his body being pressed forward and eagerly lifted his arse to greet the massive dick.

He cried out as he entered, he had struggled to fit him in his mouth, his arse was almost being ripped apart, he pulled himself together, he realised he had been swooning, he stiffened his legs and let the penis pummel against him.

They both stared into the mirror, staring at each other's faces, he reached round and grabbed his dick closing his fingers over it and wrenching his wrist to match his pace. Their jaws clenched and they groaned, they had seconds left to reach their destination, when they arrived they both screamed, the intensity amazed them.

Breathing deeply, they rode the crest of the wave, letting their bodies sway gently together and once it crashed they fell to their knees, gasping for breath and shuddering. He pushed himself to his feet and carried on where he had left, taking the measurements of the man's calves and agreeing an appointment date for him to return.

Light relief

His frustration was increasing, he had sat at his desk for hours but seemed to be getting nowhere, the office emptied around him and still there was no chance of him leaving. He had been given a ridiculous deadline to complete his task, each answered question, asked more, he realised he would need to limit his scope and settled on making recommendations for a subsequent report.

His phone rang and he answered distractedly, it was his wife wanting to know when he would be home, he fobbed her off feeling guilty he would like nothing more to be home, but wouldn't be until after she was asleep. She understood, as always but he wished he could spend more time with her, they hadn't been married for long, she worked as hard as he did but not for as long.

He knew this task was important to the firm, if it went well it would firmly plant him on the path to partnership, his wife would have to understand. He began to put it all together a few more hours and it would be done, he tapped away at the keyboard and didn't hear the lift open or footsteps walking in to his office.

His wife stood before him, she had a cup of coffee in her hands, she placed it down on the desk before him and told him she thought he had sounded stressed out. He pushed away from his computer and thanked her, rubbing his eyes before gratefully sipping his coffee.

She asked if there was anything she could do to help him, he told her he thought it was all in hand now and there was nothing she could do to help.

She walked behind him and massaged his shoulders, he figured he could spare a few minutes, he told her he was frustrated because of the timescale. She told him she couldn't change time for him, but could help with his frustration.

She moved from behind and stood before him, she dropped to her knees and unfastened the buttons on his trousers. He stared wide mouthed at her, surely, she wasn't about to give him a blow job, she smiled, reached out and pulled his dick forward, before planting her mouth over it and sucking him in to her.

He laid back, no wonder he adored her, she pressed his dick against the back of her throat and long fingers pressed lightly around his balls. He cried out as the desire for her washed over him, she was so good, lashing her tongue across him, and ramming his dick against her face, once inside her lips scraped across the edges of him, dragging his skin down and jerking back over him.

He considered lifting her up so he could fuck her but it was impossible for him to stop her, he pressed his head against his chair and allowed his body to enjoy her, his pelvis was rocking, she was working diligently, she had no intention of teasing him, her aim was to make him come.

He groaned, he could hear his own heart beating, her hands spread to his arse and clenched as she pushed her fingertips in to him. Ever polite, he let her know he was about to come, he told her repeatedly placing her hand on his head, she looked up and stared into his eyes, she was as eager as he was for him to come against her throat.

It was too late for her to stop now, if she did it would be torture, he burst his groin upwards and pushed her head further on to him. He cried out, he was coming, waves of ecstasy ripped through him and he shot himself in to her.

She sucked harder, until he stopped moaning, then swallowed, gulping his sperm into her, she wrapped her tongue around him to clean him and tucked his dick back away into his trousers. She stood before him and took a sip of his coffee, before pressing her face to his and giving him a quick kiss.

He held her close to stop her pulling away and stood up beside her to walk her to the door, they kissed waiting for the lift and he thanked her, smirking as she left him. He went back to his desk and read over what he had written, and got on with his work, no longer frustrated with a smile upon his face.

Strip Poker

The friends were dropping like flies, a group of them had started, only three remained, the others were passed out in various positions around the furniture and floor. Connie could drink them all under the table, she had no idea why, she was smaller than most of them, her friends had abandoned the card game first, breaking off in pairs to chat about mindless girly stuff, or join their boyfriends in other rooms.

Greg and Martin were the only men remaining, neither would concede before the other, but both were about ready for bed, they felt as if they had drunk themselves sober. Greg suggested strip poker, convinced that Connie wouldn't agree and they could end the day, but when she nodded, he perked up, this may well be worth waiting for.

Almost an hour later the men were naked, she had laughed as she had watched each of them strip and declared herself the winner, they had insisted she stuck to the time limit, they had agreed to at the beginning that at the end of the game that the one with the most clothes at the hour mark would be the winner.

She tried to argue, but they convinced her that if she lost one more game there could be no winner as all would be naked at the end.

She reluctantly agreed, she had been lucky that she was wearing a body suit, rather than knickers and a bra, she hadn't had to reveal anything that they hadn't seen before in a swimsuit and wasn't sure she was prepared too. They stared greedily at her and though it made her feel uncomfortable it also thrilled her.

She was not used to the attention on her, she was pretty enough but not like her friends, her body was though, something she was proud of, she was on an athletics scholarship and worked out every day.

They stared at her wondering why they had barely noticed her before, she had made them laugh for hours and her body was hot, when she took a toilet break they each tried to convince the other to leave them alone with her, but neither agreed, the rest of the girls were asleep, this was their last chance of action.

She returned and as she lost the next game they almost felt sorry for her, not enough to stop her though and they clapped as they encouraged her to strip, their friends around them stirred and she lost her bottle, making the excuse that she didn't want anyone else to see her. Greg thought of the solution and they dragged her with them to the dining room.

They sat at the table and she stood before them, she knew there was no getting out of it and peeled off the body suit. They stared wide mouthed as she stood there and she realised it wasn't bad as she thought, at least she didn't have a flapping dick to hide as they had done.

She took a seat, butt naked like them and lit a cigarette, inhaling casually to prove she was unconcerned.

"I think we should play dare" Martin suddenly said.

The three of them laughed, she knew exactly what they were after, she could see that in their laps their dicks no longer flapped, stiff dicks instead where staring at her.

"Ok but only if I can go first" she answered.

They looked at each other, it was obvious what she was going to ask them, they considered whether it was worth it as would both get to ask her. They agreed with a nod and she asked what they had expected.

"Play with each other's dicks for one minute" she instructed.

They moved together knowing they would get her doing it next, they looked at her in their chairs, not acknowledging one another. She stared into their eyes then down at their hands, they were holding each other's dick, with little enthusiasm. She told them she would use as much effort as they immediately picked up their games, wrapping their hands around tightly and jerking from their wrists.

They tried to disguise it, but the pleasure was evident across their faces, she stared and let them run well over a minute, getting turned on as she watched them. They stopped and sat either side of her, it was her turn same dare.

She didn't hesitate, taking her hands to them, and working in unison. She felt them shudder in her hands, their eyes were closed as they enjoyed her, she felt powerful and horny.

The minute came and went, they waited with baited breath, she had no intention of stopping and they pushed their hands in towards her, her eyes closed as they touched her and they realised with a sigh that it was ok. Their hands pressed against her thighs and fingers walked to her vagina and clit. They rubbed and they pushed her, till she groaned out in ecstasy.

Her hands were still on them, she wrapped them around their balls and squeezed them, their fingers were working well together, taking turns, each moving aside for the other one. They glanced at each other and noticed her eyes closed, they were happy to come here, but wondered how far they could push her.

Greg made the first move and knelt before her, she opened her eyes and watched him as he smiled and pushed his tongue towards her. Martin moved his fingers away and looked at her, she told him to stand up, he stood beside her and she grabbed his dick and pressed her lips over it. She groaned as she sucked, the tongue felt amazing inside her, it reached all around the edges before pressing and piercing her.

Fingers were on her clit, they were rubbing perfectly softly, she clasped her mouth over the dick and sucked it relentlessly. Moans were raising from all of them, but the dick was about to burst, she put her hand on the man before her and instructed the men to swap places.

A fresh dick pushed towards her, she ran her tongue shaft to tip, the new tongue below worked across her clit and fingers pressed in to her. The three of them tortured slowly and time passed by quick. They were moaning and sweating, their bodies pressing closer.

She stopped them and moved, laying her body across the table, Greg's dick was throbbing it, he had almost found his release as she sucked, he pulled her legs up around him and pressed to the edge of the table and pushed his dick in to her. She reached for Martin and took his dick in her mouth, both men circled their hips towards her and she rammed her groin against the dick.

Greg shuddered as he came, gritting his teeth to stop himself screaming, he made way for Martin, who seized the opportunity without question, pulling out of her mouth and shoving in to her vagina. She had held herself off, determined to take care of both, she knew he wouldn't last long and let herself relax and come freely.

Martin stood beside them, watching as they groaned, he looked at the door, they were noisy, he hoped they wouldn't be disturbed. He shuddered and pummelled into her, biting his lips to contain his groans, her face flushed red and joy spread across it as she gasped and hit her climax, she grabbed Greg's hand and held it over her mouth, desperate for it to stifle her screaming.

He leaned in and kissed her, she stared into his eyes, her peak was never ending, Martin could tell and was endlessly ploughing in to her, he came with a loud moan and ground his hips slowly, at last the flames began to lower and he sensed her relaxing, Martin pulled out of her and Greg lifted her from the table.

They laughed searching for their closed and joined the others in the living room, they dropped together into the chair and finally let their eyes close.

London Bus

They sat at the back of the open top bus, it was not the best of days for it, the air was thick with misty wetness, they were only here for the day though and the tour was pre-booked, sitting on the ground floor would be pointless. At least they had the bus to themselves, which was a bonus as they could barely keep their hands off each other.

They had gotten married the week before and were on their honeymoon, they had dragged themselves out of the hotel room for their last day in London, tomorrow they would be moving on. As they kissed he put his hands on her leg, she let him push him up a little, enjoying the thrill but when he reached the top of her leg she stopped him, with her hand over his.

He left it there and distracted her by pointing out the landmarks in view, and whilst she stared he worked his fingers around the zip of her trousers and pushed his fingers against her naked skin. She looked down, nothing could be seen, her coat covered her and he did feel good so she decided to let him to it.

He had one arm casually draped around her shoulder, she leant against his shoulder, deterring him from kissing her to avoid the driver, who could see them in his mirror from guessing what they were up too.

His fingers casually twirled around her clitoris, it felt impossibly good to her, she struggled to keep her arousal from showing on her face.

He moved his hands down, letting his palm rub against her

clit and pushing his fingers in to her. She felt her mouth widen and lifted her hand to cover it, with her thumb on her chin and her fingers across her jaw, her breathing was becoming heavy and he smiled as he watched her.

She turned her face to him and he kissed her gently, the ignition had been lit, the fire in her eyes was addictive, his dick throbbed as he watched her, he couldn't wait to get her back to the hotel, he knew once she was this excited all inhibitions went out of the window, he continued to rub her and could feel her body shaking as he held her close.

She bit her lip to stop herself from moaning, he stopped her by pushing his tongue in to her, the skin of her face was hot and bright red, the light rain trickled through her hair, her eyes were closed. She sighed suddenly and fell away from his mouth to lay her head back, he moved his head in front of her to shield her from view and as he did she cried out in ecstasy.

He felt his own breath becoming heavy, if he allowed himself to lose it though, they could end up being arrested, he struggled to stop himself from losing control and closed his own eyes to enjoy her moans. He could feel her moisture spreading over his fingers, she was so close.

They had missed have the tourist attractions and he realised that it would soon be time to get back off the bus. He forced himself harder in to her, ramming his fingers in and roughly pushing himself against her clit. She was whispering to him, yes and had her hands over his, pushing him closer to her.

With a low groan it started, the rush to the finish and her body tensed as she came, stiffly she held herself against him and he couldn't resist glancing at her, holding her eyes to his so that he could enjoy the pleasure with her.

Once the peak passed her body softened and embarrassment washed over her, she smiled as he pulled his hand from her and refastened her clothing, he cuddled her, crushing her body to his and they kissed softly. She was worried about getting off the bus and passing the driver, he assured her that he wouldn't have seen anything, he had covered her face the whole time.

She ran her hand across his groin, smiling when she noticed his dick was rock solid, she let her hands trace the outline and suggested they go straight back to the hotel, he couldn't agree more.

The bus stopped and he took her by the hand and led her downstairs, the driver smiled as he let them off and waved, he had seen much worse.

The Massage Parlour

The friends bundled in laughing, it was Callum's birthday, they had pooled together to give him a joint present, they knew he would take some persuading, so had spent the last few hours getting him drunk and blindfolded him on the way here.

The girls sitting around looked far from impressed, the friends quickly and silently selected one for him and bundled the two of them off to the bedroom, settling his bill before piling outside to wait for him.

Callum had no idea what his friends were up to, but presumed he had arrived at a surprise party, his blindfold was pulled away and a girl stood before him and the two of them were alone together. She was clothed only in underwear, an extraordinarily tacky bra and a thong that left nothing to the imagination.

It dawned on him immediately that his friends had set him up, where he was and the fun they would have had selecting the girl for him. Callum was in his 20s, tall and skinny, the girl was at least 40 and must have weighed 300lbs. Her skin fell in chunks around her stomach and the top of legs and her breasts were huge, he considered walking straight out of the door, but figured a blow job wouldn't hurt.

She bent to her knees before him, and he slipped off his jeans, she put her hands behind her back and enclosed her mouth around his dick, it was soft and dangling, she sucked him hard, bending him in to her mouth and it wasn't long before he began to expand, filling her and she had to pull her head away from him and ram her mouth against him.

He closed her eyes as she worked, she was amazing, she dropped his dick from her mouth and it stood solid before her, she grasped his balls with her lips and tossed them around with her tongue until they swelled solid and she pressed her tongue around them, before returning her attention to his dick, licking it with her tongue and teasing its teeth against her lips.

He had planned to allow himself to ejaculate inside her, but as he looked down she began to push her breasts around him and he was amazed by the way his dick felt against her skin, she was holding her breasts together and ramming his dick between them, he moved his hips to assist her and groaned as the feelings of desire washed through him and grabbed her nipples and squeezed till they stiffened.

His desire got the better of him, he pulled her up to her feet and dragged her with him to the bed, he laid flat and let her sit over him. Her vagina pressed over his dick as she sat down, she unfastened her bra and her breasts tumbled down on to him, he held them in his hands, loving the way they the skin burst through his fingers, he held the palms of his hands against the bottom of them and shoved up to push her to a sitting position.

She grasped his dick with the muscles of her vagina, dragging him up and dropping down over him, her skin moved in waves, thrashing down on to him, her hair fell over him and her eyes stared. She was far from his usual type but there was something about her that turned him on that he couldn't put his finger on, he suspected it was her tits, he couldn't tear his eyes away from them.

He moaned as she rode, she was putting all her energy into it, enthusiastically thrashing her body and ploughing down on to him, her jaw set stiff, she was concentrating hard on pleasuring him, searching his face adjusting her pace to match the peaks in his pleasure.

She bounced quickly, his eyes widened and were fixed to her breasts, she took her hands to them, massaging her nipples and watching his desire grow. At this point she would generally fake it, to push her client over the edge, but she didn't feel the need too, his dick was solid beneath her, that and the pressure on her clit over his groin was enough to make her orgasm for real.

She exaggerated her feelings though, screaming as she came and letting her body shudder, without slowing her pace, yes, she screamed, fuck me, ah yes, he drove his hips up to thrash into her and held himself stiffly up until he felt himself coming in to her. He screamed as loud as she had, staring at her tits as the electricity hit him, she fell over him, ramming her tits towards his face and he ran his lips and tongue over them greedily, revelling in the peak.

Once it was over, she pushed herself off him and as she bent before him to cover pick up a gown to cover herself with, her arse was huge and dimply, what on earth had he been thinking. He allowed himself to be convinced that he had been too drunk to notice and stood and made his way out of the door, thanking her first without making eye contact.

He joined his friends outdoors and they laughed at him, he denied screwing her, telling them that he had just let her suck his dick. They dragged him in to a taxi and led him off to a club, where an actual surprise party was about to take place.

The Launderette

Belle was not having the best day of her life, she sat frustrated in the laundrette waiting patiently for the wash to finish so that she could move it to the driers and nip out quickly to collect some bits. She was going on holiday the next day, the washer had broken the night before, flooding her kitchen in the process.

She had hoped to drop the clothes off for a service wash, no such luck, the laundrette was unmanned at weekends, she wondered whether the clothes would be safe in the drier, no one had come in since she had been here but she was not in the best neighbourhood and if her clothes were stolen it would be a complete disaster.

It occurred to her too late that the washers – unlike the driers couldn't be opened mid wash, so she could have nipped out earlier and her clothes would have been safe. She rolled her eyes and realised that the way her luck was going lately she probably shouldn't risk it.

The washer finished and she passed them over to the dryer, an hour should do it, if they were damp she would hang them out at home. Having accepted that there was no alternative, she waited more patiently and was glad she hadn't left when a man came in moments later and filled the washing machine.

He chatted casually to her and she tried to deter him, answering in short polite sentences, but asking him nothing, he smiled at her and asked her what was wrong, she was surprised he could tell but he told her she was looking anxious.
When she told him, he offered to keep an eye on her clothes for her, she thanked him but said no, she had no idea who he

was anyway.

It took her a while to realise that he was flirting with her, she was flattered he was younger than her and very good looking, she enjoyed flirting back but had no intention of letting it go anywhere. With half an hour left on the dryer he leaned and kissed her, she did consider stopping him but didn't really have a reason too, she had only been single for a few months but it wasn't as if he was asking her to marry him.

His kiss was soft and sweet, he held her face, she relaxed against him, his hands began to spread down her back and she let them, his touch thrilled her, she reciprocated and took it further, pushing her hands up his t-shirt to touch the naked skin of his back. He sighed as she touched him and looked around, they were sat against a window, visible to everyone on the street.

He stood and walked towards the back of the laundrette, pulling her with him, he closed the front door on his way and they he pressed her against the middle row of machines and pressed his lips back to her.

She worked quickly, unfastening the zip of his jeans and pulled his dick out, she held it firmly, squeezing her fingers over him, he was shocked, his hope had been to get her phone number, he couldn't quite believe what she was doing.

His dick shuddered in her hands, his eyes glanced desperately around, if the door opened they would have seconds before being caught.

Hell, if she was willing to risk it he would, he pushed his hands up her skirt and lifted her, balancing her arse on one of the machines. He ran his hands up her legs and pushed his fingers in to her, she moaned, thrashing more desperately with her tongue into him, he rubbed his hands against her clit, she was wet already, hungry for him.

Her eyes were closed, their kisses grew increasingly passionate, their tongues and mouths spreading to each other's necks and chests, he nudged her top down, wrapping his tongue around her nipples. They were both groaning, when suddenly the machine before her came to life and began to vibrate as it moved to a spin cycle.

He smiled and grabbed her round the arse and pulled her towards the edge of the machine, he leaned his dick forward and rammed it in to her vagina. Their bodies shook with the machine, he thrust his hips slowly so that he rammed softly in and out of her, but he let the machine do most of the work.

Her body shook, he placed his fingers over her clit to let it vibrate over her, she shouted out, her clit was throbbing, the intensity shocked her, his finger moved over like a vibrator and his dick as well as stiffly stabbing her was sending vibrations through the lips of her vagina as well as deep within. Add to that the danger, the fact that they could be caught at any moment, pushed her right to the edge of ecstasy.

She clenched her jaw, forcing herself to wait for him, she stared into his eyes and realised he was as close as she was and as she stared he erupted, pumping violently into her and shouting out to express his relief.
She joined him, allowing her body to absorb his thrust and pushing her groin against him. Her body exploded and she shouted with him, as they rode the orgasm together, allowing the vibration of the machine to bring them home.

The washer clicked off and they smiled at each other at the

show their appreciation of the perfect timing, he tucked his dick away whilst kissing her and lifted her body back down from the machine.

Hook Up

He had never done this before and couldn't believe it would be as straight forward as his friends said, he had tried online dating but this was different – online sex hooks ups, he imagined it would be full of men but their seemed to be loads of women. He didn't see why there would be, as far as he could see women could end any date they chose to with sex, whereas men had to put in the time first.

He had just come out of a long-term relationship, he was in his 40s and not in the greatest of shape, he had no luck on nights out, he had been out of the dating scene for too long and it seemed as if everything had changed.

His blind dates had not gone too well either and it was probably his fault, he didn't want anything serious but the lack of sex was killing him, the dates seemed like interviews for a job he wasn't interested in.

He had selected her profile and sent a message, she responded and they had talked and a few days earlier he had had his first experience of phone sex with her, he knew where he stood the only thing he was concerned about was whether she looked anything like her profile.

She was supposedly his age, but looked very good, with a slim and athletic body and a pretty face, on the phone she sounded confident and steered their conversation to sex effortlessly. He hoped she was as easy in person, he had booked a hotel room at her request and was meeting her in the bar. Either of them could make the decision, yes or no, but he assumed that if she agreed to go to his room she would be up for it.

He arrived first and started drinking, she joined him, also early and looked even better than her profile, she was dressed casually in jeans and a vest top, he bought them both a drink and they sat together at a quiet table. They made a pathetic attempt at conversation, barely bothering to introduce themselves to each other, it was obvious what they were there for.

He told her he had more drinks in the room if she wanted to join him there and she readily agreed, rising to her feet and taking him by the hand to the lifts.

They had their first kiss on the way up to the floor and once they started kissing they couldn't stop, stumbling out of the lift and walking down the corridor together locked in a passionate embrace.

In the room, she crushed her body against him, and they drew away from each other in short bursts, allowing just enough time to rip each other's clothes off. Naked their bodies pressed close and they let their hands wonder, her arse was firm, he ran his hands across it, staring at her reflection in the full-length mirror before him.

They fell on to the bed together, tossing and turning taking turns to be on top, their mouths constantly locked together. Her clit ached for him, she rammed herself against his legs and groin, his dick was solid, she rubbed herself against it, not quite ready to push it inside her just yet.

It was impressive, thick and long, she pushed herself down to it, letting her hands run over it before licking it with her tongue. It pulsated as she worked and he groaned in appreciation.

Moments later he stopped her, twisting her beneath him and taking his own turn to lick, her legs shook as he kneeled between them, his tongue was magical, he licked and poked, she made no moves to stop him, spreading her legs wider and moaning to encourage him.

He added his fingers to the mix, walking them slowly up her thighs and pushing them into her, her back arched as she pushed her head against the bed and she was suddenly screaming, twisting her spine and turning her body beneath him. He continued to lick her, holding her down to lick her through her waves of ecstasy, she finally looked vulnerable and out of control.

Once she stopped groaning he moved his body over her and kissed her breasts as she lay, eyes closed beneath him. She lay motionless, he smiled and got them both a drink, she accepted hers and took a swig before setting it back on the table and saying it was his turn first.

She checked first, his dick remained hard, she crawled on top of him, facing his feet and directed his dick towards her.

She ground her hips slowly over him, her vagina had tightened and she had to force him in, once he was she clung to him, twisting her pelvis and reaching down to take his balls in her hands.

As his moans increased she knew she was torturing him, moving so slowly but she was giving her climax time to return, she pushed his balls against her clit, cupping and lifting them till they rubbed against her.

She glanced to her right and could see that he was watching her, their eyes met reflected through the mirror and she saw that he had quite a view, she watched as well, delighting in the expression on his face, he was close, his hands held her hips and he began to quicken her, lifting his hips and grabbing hers to ram her faster over him.

As she stared their moans increased, he screamed first, closing his eyes and hastening her, she rushed to join him, lifting and dropping over him until they came together, their bodies shuddering.

She let her back collapse, her face falling to his feet and raised her arse to let her dick fall from him, once it had she let her legs straighten and lay beside him until their breaths settled. Once they had, she twisted her body to let her head fall against his chest and he stroked her hair for a few moments, before sitting them both up and grabbing them both their drinks.

They sat together, he hadn't thought to ask his friends what would happen next, he felt like this was the point at which he would pay her, she was as easy as a hooker would have been. He wondered what was in it for her and she scolded him for being sexist, her reasons were the same as his.

She agreed to spend the night though and they hardly slept, making love throughout it, at breakfast he asked her if she would see him again, just for sex, he added hastily when he saw the look on her face, she smiled and agreed and they pushed themselves back under the covers.

The Crush

Laura was annoyed with herself, she had agreed to work overtime and had to cancel her plans for the evening, she hadn't been doing anything special but she couldn't say no to him. She stared as he worked and wasn't the only one under his spell, half the staff fancied him, he was good looking but it wasn't just that that drew people to him. He was aloof, arrogant, rich and sexy as hell.

Predictably he was dating a model, he didn't flirt with anybody, although the more confidant girls in the office continuously through themselves at him, he was oblivious, he was on another level, like a celebrity, his minions, irrelevant, scurried below him. Laura had more access to him than most, she was his assistant's assistant and one of few who spoke directly to him.

Three hours in he called her in to his office, he asked her to let the rest of the staff go and she did, she was nervous to be alone with him, he made her skin crawl but in an enjoyable way. She assumed he would dismiss her also, but he asked her to sit opposite him, she squirmed as he relayed his instructions for the next day.

He delighted in watching her face redden, she was obviously intimidated by him, most people were, he rarely fostered relationships with his staff, but this one intrigued him. She was too good for the position she was in, he knew that his assistant had been taking credit for her work and he could easily promote her to take her place but he didn't know if he could stand to be so close to her.

He spoke to her about her ambitions and smiled when she

revealed she didn't want to be his senior assistant, she wanted to be him, a partner in the firm. He was pleased and thought through the possibilities, the safest thing to do would be to send her to another office, miles away.

He was drawn to her, she seemed delicate and vulnerable, maybe he just wanted to take her under his wing, he knew it was more than that though, no matter how much he denied it he was attracted to her and could tell she was attracted to him.

He forced himself to end the conversation and let her go, he stepped from behind his desk and walked her to the door, they both went to open it at the same time and as their hands touched he felt a bolt of lightning flash through him. They both paused and stared at each other, she had obviously been hit by the same fork, her eyes were on fire, inches from his, he leaned slowly towards her and allowed their lips to press together.

Instantly, his heart soared, he put his arms around her and pulled her body close to his, she didn't resist, she lifted her arms and held him around the neck as she kissed him back passionately.

They fell back in to the office, their desire for each other pushed every other thought from their brains, without caution or doubt they tore clothes from each other's bodies.

Naked their skin ground together, there was no time for exploration, he just wanted to be inside her and she ached to get him in. He lifted her on to the desk, brushing its contests aside and forcing his body between her open legs.

She gasped as he entered her, she could hardly keep track of what was happening, one minute she was wondering if she was about to be promoted, the next she was laid naked across his desk waiting for him to penetrate her. He pushed himself in and she cried out, he filled her completely, briefly kissing her breasts before returning his mouth to hers.

They kissed as he ground, each tongue forcing their way in, succumbing to the greed. She wrapped her legs around him pressing her heels against his arse and he dragged her with his hands towards him, whilst his hips pummelled into her, shoving her away.

They clung together, groans escalating, her clitoris felt engorged, she had travelled quickly to the edge of her climax and lingered there, enjoying every second as she waited for him to overtake her and wrench her with him over it.

He couldn't even attempt to control himself, the urgency to have her was everything, he rode her straight to ecstasy and as his orgasm hit he thumped against her, stunned by the intensity of his release, he screamed out and stared as she screamed with him, her body shuddering. Their eyes and bodies, locked together, refused to release.

Their kisses continued, slowly softening and as their breath softened, awkwardness returned. He tore his lips from her and peeled his body away, she struggled to cover herself, retrieving her clothing and hurrying to get dressed.

Once she was she turned to him, he had dressed and was leaning on the edge of the desk, she was surprised to see he looked apologetic and embarrassed, as did she.

She shrugged her shoulders and began to walk out of the office, but he stopped her and hugged her body back close to him. He told her he was sorry, but couldn't resist, he had had a crush on her for months, but shouldn't have let himself act on it.

She stared open mouthed, he had to be kidding, it was her who had a crush, what could he see in her. He smiled when she told him, it was just as he had suspected, she had no idea that she was object of every man in the office's affection.

The Nanny

He knew it was a cliché, screwing the nanny but he had found her impossible to resist, she had offered herself up on a plate to him. His wife was oblivious, her life was dominated by her work, they hadn't slept together for months, since his affair had started in fact but he was convinced she didn't know.

The couple were in their 40s, the nanny was almost half their age, he had been surprised that his wife had employed her, she trusted him more than he deserved. He had no intention of divorcing her, he worked full time too but earnt nothing like her, he couldn't afford to live like this without her and as hot as the nanny was he had no intention of being with her.

She had made it clear on her first day at work that she was available, dressing in skimpy clothes and flirting with him, in front of his wife she acted completely differently and on the first night his wife had worked away, he had offered wine whilst they talked. They had gotten on so well, she hung on his every word, when he'd kissed her she had let him and they had made love on the living room floor.

His wife called, she was working late again, he pretended to be annoyed, at the end of the call, he ran off giddily to shower, it had been almost a week since they had had the chance to be alone.

She was settling the kids and he waited for her, pouring them both a drink, she entered and he closed the living room door and dragged her with him to the sofa.

She protested at first, telling him the kids were still awake, he told her they would be fine, they could listen out for them on the monitor, his wife would be back in a couple of hours so they had to be quick. He kissed her and soon, she had forgotten her concerns, their kisses were passionate and it didn't take long before they were pulling off each other's clothes.

He kissed her breasts, rubbing her nipples with his hands, she moaned as he rubbed them over her, driving them down between her legs, he pulled his mouth away from her so that he could watch the reaction on her face.

Her desperation for him made him feel powerful, he pushed her down to her knees and pierced his dick towards her lips, she kissed him gently at first, massaging his balls and then opened her mouth and pushed him deeply within. She sucked hard and he pushed his hips forward, leaning his hands on her shoulders, his legs shook, his dick throbbed, he moaned loving every second of it.

The lights on the monitor flickered and a child's voice shouted her nanny's name. He looked over annoyed and she pulled away from his dick, he held her though and rammed her back over him. The voice silenced and she stared at the monitor, waited a few seconds and then continued her work.

He noticed the lights flicker again before she did and he distracted her to stop her noticing, pulling her head up to his and laying her back against the sofa, he kneeled at the edge and opened her legs, he dragged her arse close and rammed his dick in to her.

He stared at her breasts as he fucked her, bouncing as he pounded himself against her body, her head pressed against the sofa, eyes closed, lips apart, she was groaning softly and he ground his teeth. He was about to ejaculate when the voice of his child once again rose, her eyes flashed open but he had no intention of stopping, he was far too close.

She stared hungrily at him, making no attempt to go, her eyes were begging him to fuck her, her voice telling him not to stop, yes, she screamed, he had had no idea she was so close, his pleasure wrenched higher and he allowed himself to pummel straight towards his release.

They screamed together as their orgasm hit, his body pressed over her and they ground their pelvis's close, hands on each other's arses, each pulling the other in. They kissed, greedily ramming their tongues together, until their peak finally settled and he pulled himself off her.

She dressed quickly and hurried off upstairs to sort out the kids, he threw his clothes in the laundry room and headed upstairs to take another shower, he was tempted to ask her to join him, but could hear her talking to the kids. His wife would be home in less than an hour anyway, he didn't want to push it.

The wife dialled the nanny as she looked at the screen, she had more than enough evidence now to get her divorce, she thanked her for her work, told her the job was complete and she could leave once the kids were asleep. She had been expensive but it had been worth it, the settlement she would have had to give him, was ten times more than her fee.

The MILF

He had always been jealous that his friend's parents were so much younger than his, he was 14 by the time it dawned on him that his mum was hot. He spent at much time at his house as he could, always offering to help in the kitchen so that he could perv over her. Nothing happened of course, he was a skinny teenager and she was a goddess.

Throughout college she was barely out of his fantasies and though he had had many girlfriends there, he had often thought of her. After graduation, he and his friends drifted apart but he was returning to town for his wedding and he couldn't wait to see her and wondered if she was still fit.

He knocked on his friend's door, she answered and he was blown away, she had barely changed but he certainly had and she struggled to recognise him, he reminded her and she stared in surprise, before pulling him in with a hug and a kiss. He felt like he was 14 again and blushed, she shouted her son down and the friends hugged.

He couldn't stop looking at her, his friend introduced him to his fiancé and the four of them sat in the garden, she had divorced several years earlier, her husband had been having an affair, he was surprised to learn that she was single. His friend soon shepherded his fiancé away, they had a rehearsal to attend.

He knew that his friend would expect him to leave but he made an excuse about waiting for a lift and told him he would see him later that day, once they were alone, he flirted quite openly with her, he had nothing to lose, he was leaving town again in two days.

She flirted back with him, amusement on her face. He suggested he should go, but she told him there was no rush, she pulled her chair closer to him and leaned in for a kiss.

Excitement washed through him, it was a fantasy come true, a few years late but still, he felt his dick stiffen immediately and he forced his mind to settle and not get carried away. He held her face as they kissed, inhaling her scent, her hands wrapped around him and she pulled him to his feet. He followed, gob struck, she led him by the hand up the stairs to her room, she closed the door behind her and stood there, stripping off her clothes.

He watched her silently, unfastening his shirt, her body amazed him, she was fitter than anyone he had seen naked before. Her breasts were small and pert, her stomach flat and toned, he stared, wide eyed as she peeled off her briefs, he shrugged his shirt off and she walked to him, placing her flat hands on his chest.

They kissed, urgently now and she unfastened his trousers and pushed them from him, naked he pulled her against him and they wrapped their arms around each other's waists. He ran his hands over her, rubbing her breasts, but settling on her arse and he lifted her with his strong arms and carried her with him to her bed.

He wanted to spend time on her, to kiss every inch of her body, he started at her toes, watching them curl as he sucked them. He ran his hands up her calf's and he let his tongue follow, she groaned when he reached her thighs and he ran his lips across her pelvis, he bypassed the goal, kissing her stomach instead, lingering on her breasts, he smiled as she began to moan.

He kissed her neck, snuggling against her and briefly let lip kiss lip, then he turned her body over and headed his lips back over her back. He kissed gently down her spine and pushed one of his legs over her, on his knees he massaged her back, reaching round intermittently to squeeze her breasts. Her arse was incredibly pert, his body moved down and he moved between her legs after spreading them.

She groaned as he ran his hands up the back of her thighs, he lingered his thumbs up the inside and let them push against her clit. He tried to ignore his throbbing dick, but delighted at the way it felt pressed against her skin. He lifted her at the hips, till she balanced on her knees and pushed his fingers through her legs and massaged her clit, her back arched and she groaned, her arse pressed towards him.

He ran his fingers into her vagina and she rocked against his touch, his breath was heavy, she was gasping, almost ready to come, he drove his body to his knees and positioned himself next to her. With his hands, he directed himself and she pushed herself over him, scrunching the muscles of her vagina and squeezing him in.

Electricity shot through him, this was the stuff of dreams, below him she began to scream, her body shuddering, he grabbed at her hips and ploughed himself in, within minutes he was joining her, the climax erupting like an explosion in his head. He fell over her as he withdrew and they collapsed on to the bed. They laughed, reminiscing, he told her he had wanted her for years, she told him she had always known.

He asked her what she was doing for the rest of the day and she answered – it was her turn, she made her way to his toes and began kissing his legs.

Physio

She had been visiting him for months, he was well on his way to recovery, her job now was to build his confidence, he had suffered a spinal injury and had had to relearn to walk, today they would head outdoors. He walked slowly beside her, he had been incredibly brave and never complained, the fact that he had a limp bothered him, she assured him it would soon go away.

He asked her how much time she had left to work with him, she reluctantly told him their time would soon be coming to an end, he looked pleased though which surprised her, she was beginning to think he had a crush. Her role was to begin rehabilitation, once her clients could walk unsupported, she passed them on to a colleague who would fine tune and take on the rest of their needs.

She would be sad to leave him, the two of them had become quite close, he was her age which was unusual, most of her clients were old. They had spent a huge amount of time together, it was not unusual to become attached, she had shared stories of her own life with him, to make it easier for him to open to her.

On her last day, they walked around the park together, it took a while but he got there in the end, she drove him back home in silence and she hugged him goodbye at his door.

The next day she received a call from him, he was asking her out on a date, she paused before answering, technically he was no longer her patient but she wondered whether seeing him would be ok.
He spoke before her, he told her he had waited for long

enough, he had asked her boss whether he could ask her out weeks ago and he had told him, it wasn't a problem if she wasn't seeing him as a patient anymore.

She smiled, no wonder he had been so keen for her to discharge him, she was flattered and couldn't think of a reason to say no.

He met her in the restaurant, his limp had already improved in the past week, she didn't mention it, she had no idea if this would work, but it wouldn't if she continued to think of him as a patient of hers. She already knew a lot about him, but over dinner she learned a lot more, he asked her all the right questions and was charming and sweet.

She was determined to treat him as she would any date, so when he took her home, she let him walk her to her door. He lingered on the doorstep and they shared their first kiss, it wasn't friendly or familiar, it was hungry and rugged, she leaned in to him, letting her enjoyment show and falling in to it, she felt a rush of blood to her face and their breaths hastened.

She forced herself to pull away, it was their first date after all and he laid a final kiss on her cheek before heading back to his car. She watched as he went, knowing it wouldn't be long before she saw him again.

A week later they met again and this time after it she invited him in, he looked around her living room, picking up her pictures and asking about each of them. She stood beside him, telling him about her family and friends and wasn't surprised when he held her hand and leaned in to kiss her, his kiss was so passionate, it almost took her breath away.

His arms reached around her and he pulled her body close, she could feel the bulge of his dick pressing against her chest, she had not planned to go much further but was powerless to stop him. He towered over her, but was bending to kiss her, she was returning his kisses on her tip toes.

He glanced to his side and pulled away from her, he led her to the chair and she realised he had been standing for too long, he sat and pulled her over him, pulling a leg either side of her. Their kisses continued, velvety and long, their heads twisted as they fought with their tongues. He moved to her neck and she threw back her head, his touch amazed her, her body was tingling with the anticipation of what would come next.

His hands cradled her breasts and he opened her shirt, his face pressed down to her nipples and he circled them with his tongue, his hands were on her legs and he pushed up her skirt, he pushed her panties aside and drove his fingers in to her. She gasped as he touched, her face was bright red, he pulled his head up and stared as she threw back her head.

He unfastened his trousers and pulled out his dick, he lifted her up at the arse and rammed her down on to it. She groaned as she wound her hips over him, showing no caution at all, her eyes were as hungry as his were, desperation rose in them both. Her mouth widened as she stared and she panted as she groaned, her hips were manically circling, he let her do all the work, his balls were engorged he was desperate to burst.

She screamed as she came and he studied her face, her jaws were clenched tightly and her eyes were squeezed closed, he joined her quickly, it was not optional, he felt as if he had been holding his breath, he released and ignited, moaning and gasping.

They rode the peak together, their bodies frozen, their heads pressed together and as it passed they kissed slower, before he laid back and let her rest on his chest.

Soccer Moms

The manager looked over at the side lines, it was impressive how many kids had turned up to join the team, there wouldn't be room for all of them, but the club did have a second team so he would take his pick of the best and they would take the rest.

The kids didn't really care, they were 6 and 7-year olds, they were more interested in being able to stay with their closest friends, the parents were anxious though and took it in turns to casually bump into him and introduce him to their talented kids.

At the first trial, he decided on the kids who were obviously the best, he dismissed them, to give himself time to look at the rest, he explained to the parents that he often switched the teams anyway sometimes one week to the next, some of the kids would drop out, others would drastically improve, the parents shouldn't take things too seriously and let the kids enjoy themselves.

It was obvious his thoughts had fallen on deaf ears, he was continuously being pestered and decided to call it a day, they could all return the next week. One mother, seemed more anxious than the others though and she followed him in to the changing room. He was barely listening to her but suddenly pricked up his ears, this woman was asking him on a date.

He looked at her for the first time, she was hot, but he wasn't interested, he was married, she was young enough to be his daughter, what did she want to go on a date with him for.
She smiled and explained how desperate she was for her son to join the first team, he shook his head not quite believing what he was hearing and joked that she didn't need to date

him, but a blow job would help.

She walked straight to him and dropped to her knees, he was speechless and stopped her with a hand on her head, he ushered her out of his office, stuttering and hardly able to catch his breath. When they had finished clearing the equipment, his assistants joined him, he told them what had happened whilst shaking his head.

When he left the assistants talked, they confessed that she had also approached them both, they hadn't accepted the date either, they were in relationships they didn't want to risk, they wished they had thought of the blow job though, if she had offered they wouldn't have said no.

The door of the room opened and she stepped in to join them, she had been listening and told them, if that's what it took she would do it, they laughed nervously, glancing at each other but doubting whether she was serious.

She dropped before the first of them and unfastened his trousers, they both stared open mouthed as she pulled the other man to stand beside him. She reached for their dicks and pulled them out of the gaps in their pants, she stroked them both with her hands and held her mouth towards the hardest.

She sucked as he groaned, leaning his hands on her head, he rammed against her throat looking down as she worked, his friends dick was being tossed swiftly in her hands.
She pulled away briefly and swapped the positions of the men, taking a second dick in her mouth and driving her hands down the first. She kissed the sides before pushing her head over it and squeezing it against her lips.

She alternated between them both, driving each of them to the edge, it would be easy for her to finish quickly but she took her time with them instead. She looked up before sucking each of them, their mouths hung open and their eyes were closed. She felt powerful and in control, she hadn't acted like such a slut before, but was becoming quite turned on herself.

She pushed to her feet and they looked surprisingly at her, she opened her dress revealing her nakedness beneath and leaned her body against the desk, the first man, with no hesitation pushed towards her, he took a grope of her breasts and rammed himself in to her, the second man moved beside them, watching intently.

She moaned as he fucked her, she was already wet, he grabbed her hips and rammed her against him but didn't last long, he screamed as he ejaculated and rammed his mouth against her chest. He moved away quickly and the second man entered her, his dick was thicker and harder and she cried out as he forced himself in to her.

She lifted her hips to press her clit against his groin and she circled them swiftly to feel the pressure on all sides, he leaned in to kiss her and she wrestled his tongue with hers, he froze for a second before pounding faster in to her. The orgasm hit her like a punch in the face, she shouted out in shock and pressed her back against the desk, he joined her, holding her arse in his hands and ramming her against the desk, he froze over her moaning softly before a smile spread across his face.

The following week her son made the first team, between them their boss wasn't hard to persuade, she was happy and showed them how much again and again.

Conception

The women laid in bed together and talked through their options, they had been together for years and had excitedly decided it was time for a baby. They had an appointment with an agency but came out disappointed, it was expensive, they couldn't afford it, they would need to find an alternative.

Friends had offered their services but they had decided against it, whoever ended up the father would be forever bound to them, they wanted animosity, so that the baby would be theirs completely, they agreed the only option was to have sex with a stranger. It wasn't hard to arrange it, they advertised themselves online as a bisexual couple looking for a man to join them.

They were swamped with offers of course, they were both attractive with good bodies, neither had had sex with a man before and neither of them were eager to try it, they agreed they would both need to sleep with him, it was the fairest option. It would double the chances of a pregnancy, they didn't want to have to do it again.

They laughed together looking through profiles, he had to be good looking naturally, the genes were important. They decided on the youngest of the bunch, he had little experience, so they figured he would be easiest to manipulate, they would put on a show and encourage him to join them.

He was thrilled when they chose him, they met at a hotel, he stuttered when he introduced himself and they led him straight off to bed. They undressed him and left him watching on a sofa next to the bed.

They imagined he wasn't with them and began to kiss each

other's bodies, they let their hands rub against each other, titillating each other's clitoris. Heads pressed to breasts and nipples were teased and tortured, it was enough for him, his dick was throbbing forward.

The first woman approached and straddled over him, she grimaced as she pressed his dick in to her, the other woman sat beside them to distract him, ramming her tongue into his mouth and turning him towards her face, he began to grunt within seconds and lifted with his feet to push in to her, his hands wrapped tightly around him and the three of them pressed together, each woman held her hand against the others clit and made each other moan till he came, he screamed out forcing himself up and into her.

The women moved to bed and dragged him along with them, the three of them took turns to kiss and rammed their bodies against one another, they let him lick their tits and push his fingers inside them. They moaned as he did, they didn't have to fake, it felt good. As his dick stiffened they kissed him right up to the last moment, the second woman lay flat and together they coaxed him onto her.

The women lay beside each other massaging each other's tits, they kissed as they touched, totally disregarding him. He was thrilled enough to be watching them and rammed himself in, within seconds he was screaming his climax impossible to miss.

He collapsed and lay beside them, spooned on the bed.

The Bank

Matts transfer had not been his idea, his head office had heard rumours about a rampant affair he was conducting with one of assistants, the fact that they had both denied it had saved his job but could not prevent his transfer to this place. Although this office was much quieter he couldn't help but feel relieved that he had moved away from her, towards the end she had been getting needy, he had a wife for that a lover was supposed to consist of hot sex with no strings.

The staff here did nothing to peak his interest, the women were his age, overweight and mumsy, that was until a position for an office intern was filled and he knew as soon as he saw her that he was in trouble. She was 21, the boss's daughter and one of the sexiest women he had ever seen, the fact that there were so many reasons she was off limits only increased his desire to have her.

She seemed as determined to have him as he was to have her, she flirted continuously, coming in to his office at every opportunity, wearing floaty dresses and perching herself deliberately on the edge of his desk as she chatted to him.

When she came in in a dress shorter than usual one day and reached up to the shelves in front of his desk, he joked that if the dress were any shorter he would be able to see her briefs, her answer that she wasn't wearing any left him gobsmacked and unable to respond, when she proved it with a flick of the skirt which revealed her bare arse he knew any further resistance was futile.

She laughed at the expression of shock on his face and skipped out of the office, her father had shifted her from one boring position to another, determined to get her into the business, this was the worse one yet and she couldn't wait to get herself sacked from it.

The women in the office cringed at the way he flirted, he was their age but refused to accept it, the fact that he thought she was seriously interested in him amused them, he had been nothing but rude since his arrival and they waited in eager anticipation for her to get on with it, so they could be rid of him.

The next time she walked in to his office he asked her to close the door behind her, she did as he asked her, leaning against it for a second before walking seductively towards him, he pushed his chair out as she neared and revealed that his trousers were open and he had taken out his dick. It throbbed impressively and he asked her to take a seat, staring into her eyes, before gesturing with them to his dick.

The intern obeyed eagerly, she lifted one of her legs, stepped over him and lowered her groin towards his, he sighed as the edges of her vagina hovered at the end of his dick and as she pushed herself on to him he groaned in pleasure, grabbing her by the hips and pressing his mouth in towards hers.

He circled her hips as he lifted himself up and rammed his dick in to her, once she had established her pace, he let her at it, lifting his hands to grasp for her breasts and pulling away the flimsy material that covered them. Her nipples were engorged and pink, he lowered his lips to them, sucking them into him and circling his tongue over them as they pierced towards him.

Her moans were getting louder, he pulled himself away from her breasts to shut her up, the office staff were feet away and the customers just beyond them, his job was the last thing on mind, but if he got caught, this would end and he was desperate already to ejaculate.

She kissed him greedily, biting his lips and thrashing her tongue in and out of him, his hands lowered to her arse and he lifted her, dragging her up before slamming her down again and watching her shudder as she began to lose control, he rubbed her hands against the inside of her thighs, letting his fingertips brush against her clit and delighting at the way she tilted her pelvis to exaggerate the friction against it.

Her mouth escaped his and she began to kiss and bite his neck and earlobes, she was driving him nuts, he closed his eyes and forced himself to concentrate, a countdown began in his head and he excitedly revelled in it. A sudden escalation in her moans rushed him and as she writhed erratically he grabbed her hips and ploughed with her to force their climax to hit.

With a sharp intake of breath, the explosion tore through him and he groaned loudly as it hit, everything else was irrelevant this feeling was everything, he bit his lip and tensed his body, she was desperately grinding against him, trying to extend the moment of ecstasy until finally she came.

He smashed his mouth against hers, and clamped her body towards him, he groped her as she pressed to him shivering, running his hands down her back so that he could press her against every part of his body and as the plateau finally ended, they pressed their foreheads together and slowly kissed, reflecting on the moment that had taken their breaths away.

It dawned on him what he had done and he hastened to push her away from him, she lifted her ass and let him drop and as she stepped away he pushed his dick back in to his trousers and pushed himself back under his desk with a smile on his face. Her cheeks were flushed and it was obvious she had just been fucked, so rather than let anyone see her like that he asked her to stay, she might as well make herself useful and get his filing done rather than give the game away.

Originally, her plan had been to let her father know straight away, but the orgasm he had provided had shocked her to the core, her job had suddenly become more interesting, maybe she wouldn't need to leave so quickly after all.

Sisters

Although his girlfriend was hot, when her sister returned from University for the summer break, Jon couldn't resist flirting with her, the girls were pretty much identical, but the youngest walked around in tiny shorts and vest tops all day without a care in the world whilst her sister rushed off stressed every morning conservatively dressed.

During the day, he should have been at work too, leaving her alone in the house but he had been switching a lot of shifts lately, just so that he could hang around the house too, his girlfriend had no idea, he always left with her before sneaking back. She had practically handed it to him on a plate, but he had not seen her with other men and had no idea if she was just naturally flirty, he didn't want to risk his relationship, he just wanted a fuck, to be 100% sure he was going to get away with it, he needed her to instigate.

This morning he had almost given in, she had walked into his room and lay sprawled across his bed as she chatted, he could see the edge of her arse cheeks as her shorts rode up and it would have been so easy to drop himself over her. As soon as she left he wished he had done it, he had had to take a shower and relieved himself with a quick toss, to relieve his tensions.

Tonight, the family were having a BBQ, he tried not to drink as much as the rest of them, it wouldn't take much for his barriers to drop completely, getting caught screwing around would mean he would be homeless as well as single, he had a good thing going and had no intention of losing it.
He watched her all night and her flirting continued, but his girlfriend had drunk too much and was feeling unusually horny, so he took her off to bed early and took his frustrations out on her.

Hours later whilst his girlfriend snored beside him, he headed to the kitchen to grab some water, on his way back to his room he noticed the sister's door was open and as he tiptoed by, he looked in and was shocked by the sight. She was laid on top of the bed, butt naked, with her head on her elbow, staring at him. He couldn't have resist if he had wanted too, he creeped into the room, closing the door behind him.

He pushed in to bed beside her and as soon as his head hit the pillow, her hands were on him, his shorts were off within seconds and her perfect body was balanced over his. He ran his hands over her back and down to her arse cheeks, his dick pressed solidly against her stomach, her lips rammed against his and he found himself desperately forcing his tongue in and out of her.

Two things dominated his thoughts, he had to be quiet and he had to be quick, she opened her legs and put her knees either side of his hips, he pushed his hands against her breasts to hold her before him, her body was perfection, pert little breasts, tiny waist. His stared at her as rubbed, lowering his hands across her stomach and tickling her clit as she sighed audibly and closed her eyes.

Her hands were on his dick, slowly she let her hands move from its tip to its shaft, he opened the lips of her vagina with his fingers and forced them in to her, slowly but deeply, her mouth opened and she moaned softly.

He lifted her hips and dragged her forward until she hovered over his dick, he brought her down slowly, feeling the muscles of her vagina drag over his dick inch by inch and once he was fully enclosed inside her he allowed her hips to circle and pulled her groaning mouth down to his.
Their kisses became more frantic, arms wrapped around

shoulders as mouths moved towards necks. As her moans became louder he tried his best to quieten her, but his lips were being bitten and tugged with teeth as he tried to cover hers and the passion was forcing moans out of him that were beginning to outdo hers.

The movement of her hips quickened, he ploughed his hips up to meet hers, holding his back stiff as she ground and as she took a sharp intake of breath and pulled away he realised she was about to climax.

As he held himself against her he stared intently at her face, her eyes were on fire, her mouth opened as she panted and her brows were stiff, when the moment hit she whimpered ecstatically, her rapid increase in pace spread her ecstasy to him and he grabbed for her arse, pulling her body back over him and ramming his dick in and out of her. Cries escaped him and he held her shoulder against his mouth to quieten himself as his dick exploded in to her.

They writhed together, stretching out the pleasure for as long as they could do before the guilt set in, she pushed her body away from his and he crept out of bed, grabbing his shorts and turning away from her without a word.

He half expected the whole family to be stood out there waiting for him, but knowing his girlfriend it would have been much more likely for her to run in and punch them both, than to patiently wait for them to finish.
The hallway was as silent and dark as it had been when he had left it, he closed the door behind him and tiptoed back to his own room.

His girlfriend lay where he left her, sprawled across the bed, snoring, he crept in beside her and closed his eyes with a smile on his face.

X-box

The fact that Tara worked with her husband was a blessing and a curse, they worked the same shifts and travelled in together, so there was no need for her to drive or struggle with parking, on the downside office flirtation was impossible, the hot guys in her office were off limits.

The same applied to him obviously, but the men in the office outnumbered the women five to one and she was arguably the hottest woman who worked there, she couldn't flirt back in front of her husband but they purposely flirted with her and took the piss of him when he showed any frustration.

Dan was his closest friend in the office and one of the few who paid her no attention, he was friendly but distant and often spared time with them at their home, playing on the x-box with her husband like a teenager, whilst they drank beers and ordered takeaways.

Tara tended to leave them to it, tonight she was painting her bedroom, he had complained to her about the smell before his friend had arrived but she had brushed him off, saying they could sleep in the spare room if it hadn't gone before bedtime. She could hear them next door laughing and shouting as they took turns playing football games.

She stepped back to check out her work, the voices next door had quietened but it was obviously her husband's turn, he cursed as he played shouting at the x-box and the imaginary competition, she suddenly felt hands behind her and jumped, dropping the paint brush on to the floor in her panic.
The arms stayed and dragged them back towards her, her head turned and she realised it was Dan, he dropped his mouth to her neck and pressed his body against her.

Tara knew that she should have pushed herself away, but before she had a second to consider it his hands were on her, they ran up her legs, over her shorts and pressed across her naked stomach as they forced their way up her t-shirt.

Hands held her breasts and she did nothing to stop them, her breath was coming in short bursts and it dawned on her that she was aroused and already desperate for him to bend her over and fuck her.

She reached around with her hands to feel his dick, she could already feel it pressed against her back, stiff and hard, but to her surprise it was free, she pushed her shorts aside and dropped the top of her body forward, pointing her arse towards him as she rested her elbows on the bed. Her husband voice was still piercing through the walls but how long could one game be.

He knew they only had minutes, he held his hands on her hips and pushed himself in to her, her legs shook as he pierced his dick in to her vagina and he bit his lip to stop himself groaning. He had been coming here for months and had been waiting for his opportunity to do this, resisting the urge to flirt so that his friend would have no reason to mistrust him but he had known he would have her since the moment he saw her and when he had seen her earlier in shorts, with paint in her hair he knew he couldn't wait any longer.

He held his breath to keep himself silent as he pumped, her ecstatic sighs encouraged him, he ground himself stiffly against her, reaching round with his fingers to massage her clit.

Her husband was still shouting at the game next door, there could only be a couple of minutes left to go, he blasted harder, unable to stop himself moaning as he felt his climax begin to hit.

Her face pressed closer to the bed as he ploughed in to her, she rammed her face against the sheets, clutching them in handfuls, she trembled as she orgasmed, the bed muffled her screams. His body froze as he let himself release, he twisted his pelvis intensely slow as his spine shuddered and he ejaculated in to her, he allowed him chest to collapse as he draped over her, kissing her back and rubbing her chest as he pulled his dick out of her.

She pushed quickly to her feet and moved her shorts back in to place without looking at him, he backed into the hallway and she heard the bathroom door close and the splashing of water in to the sink. She picked up the paintbrush from the floor and grabbed a cloth to wipe up the mess that she had made. As she scrubbed she froze as she realised it was silent next door, had the game finished and if so had he heard them, or even seen.

When he shouted out in celebration she breathed a sigh of relief, the bathroom door opened and closed and she heard Dan's voice congratulating him and the two of them chatting as if nothing had happened. Tara pushed herself up from the floor, and forced herself to look around to make sure that everything was in place.

She sniffed, paranoid, wondering if her husband would be able to smell him on her, or even worse they were sat in there next to each other, maybe he could smell her on him.

She listened for a few minutes, the two of them had started the next game and were laughing and shouting again, all was well it seemed. She cleared away the paint and locked herself in the bathroom, peeling off her clothes and scrubbing herself in the shower, once she was clean she allowed herself to breath and she couldn't help thinking how exciting the session had been.

In Custody

He had picked them up in town, a whole group of girls drunk and brawling, he wished he had left them to it, hours had passed and he had just finished the paperwork, they were singing and shouting, taking up space in the cells and causing nothing but grief. He had to get rid of some of them, the clubs were about to close and he needed to free up some space to make room for them before he finished work.

He asked the custody sergeant how many he wanted him to release, and was told to get rid of them all apart from the two who had fought, that meant five friends of one of them and one friend of the other, who hadn't been able to stop themselves getting involved. The one on her own was quiet, she had been since she had arrived and paced the cell, rather than sit on the bunk.

He dealt with the five first, giving each a formal warning and ordering them to disperse. He collected the last one and took her in to his office, she smiled as he read her the warning, leading him to give her a lecture about the seriousness of the situation she was in. Her eyebrows raised sarcastically and though she had stopped her lips from smiling her eyes were laughing at him.

He marched her behind him to the exit and passed her shoes to her, she slipped the heels on to her feet and fastening the thin strips of leather against her ankles, bending from her waist so that her skirt revealed the bottom of her arse cheeks. He couldn't tear his eyes away from her, her legs were long the skirt way too short. When she stood and turned she looked in to his eyes, smiling again as if to accuse him of staring.

Before he opened the door, another officer shouted him, the other girls were outside it wasn't safe for her to leave, he had two options, re-arrest the girls or lock this one back up. His shift was over, he wouldn't get paid for doing either, he told his colleagues he would drop this one home and they smiled at him knowingly.

He didn't bother answering but had no intention of touching her, he had a wife at home who had once been as hot as her, easy and hassle free. He signed himself off work and took her with him out of the side door, she climbed in to the front seat of his car and crossed her legs, revealing the top of her thighs to him.

He asked where she lived and she directed him to the end of her street, they drove there in silence, thankfully she lived not far from him, on the way though her hand moved to his lap and tough it was the last thing he wanted, the thrill washed through his body.

He didn't acknowledge her, but left her hand in place, he could see that she was staring at him, and that she knew his dick was straining to meet her. She opened her legs as he continued to drive, shuffled her body down the seat and lifted her skirt, she moved one hand up her thighs and rubbed it against her clit, he looked over and saw that her eyes were shining and she was biting her lip.

He struggled to keep his eyes on the road, his dick was now throbbing she unfastened his zip and pulled it straight out, he sighed as she rubbed, what the fuck was he doing. He pulled in to a layby at the side of the road, he had been planning to stop her but was powerless to do it. As soon as he stopped, she dragged her body over to his, covered his lips with hers and smashed her vagina over his dick.

His hands reached up to hold her, he held them to the side of her face, greedily they kissed, his dick clenched by the muscles in her vagina as she circled her hips. His hands dropped to her waist, he pushed them up her top, pushing aside her bra, he clenched his hands over her tits. She was writhing and moaning, her eyes tightly closed and he panted to calm himself, about to explode.

She cried out in pleasure and thrashed her hands against the roof of the car, she stretched out her arms and pushed herself down to him, solidly and hard, he lifted his hips to let her ride him, delighting in her plateau and as her mouth opened wide, he felt himself go. He thrust, desperately crying out, crushing her tightly against him with his arms, his orgasm rocked through his body, leaving him perpetrating and shocked.

Her hands fell from the ceiling and the two of them paused locked together, he kissed her lips leisurely before lifting her back to her seat and getting himself dressed. She sat silently beside him as he regained his composure and started the car, he cringed as he drove her the rest of the way, thinking about what would happen next.

He pulled on to her street and he asked her to tell him which house, she told him to stop where he was, she could walk the rest of the way, her parents were home and would kill her if they found out a cop was driving her home. He stopped where he was and she got out of the car, she smiled and kissed him on the cheek on her way out and told him he had her number and she hoped he would call.

He watched her walking down the street, before he continued she turned around and waved, he couldn't believe that he had done it but she was undeniably cute, he watched the skirt skim her arse as she disappeared up a driveway.

He forced himself to head home, he didn't know how he would face his wife, hopefully she would be sleeping and he would worry about it the next day.

The Thief

Dorothy looked around her room for her bag, this was the second thing that had gone missing in the space of a week, she lived in a shared dorm and kept forgetting to lock her door. She let herself fall to the bed and sighed in annoyance, a bag and a belt had gone missing, neither were worth anything who would have wanted to steal them.

She barely cared about the items but it annoyed her that someone had been in her room, she flicked through the options of culprits in her head, half her room mates were girls and she presumed it must be one of them. She visited the girls in turn, letting her eyes scan their rooms, they were all her friends though and all their stuff was much nicer than hers.

That left the boys, she couldn't go in to their rooms, she didn't know any of them well, most were shy and quiet, she rarely spent time in the shared spaces the girls usually gathered in each other's rooms, the lounge was set up for the boys with an x-box and pool. She studied the boys in turn, figuring the thief wouldn't make eye contact, they all looked the same though so she returned to her room.

As she pushed opened the door, she cursed, realising she had left it unlocked again, she looked around the room wondering if she would notice if there was anything missing. Wondering was driving her nuts, she decided to set a trap, she walked back out through the living room and let everyone hear she was going out, rather than leaved she slipped off her shoes and slipped back to her room.

Dorothy pushed herself under her bed and lay staring out, within minutes the door opened and a man's feet wondered in, the door closed behind them and they headed towards the bed, the bed pressed in over her, whoever it was, was sitting down. She hadn't thought about what she would do if she caught him, but her fury decided for her and she pushed out of the bed to confront him.

His name was Thomas, he had moved in a few weeks ago and had never spoken to her, he stared shocked at her as she looked at him furiously. As she continued shouting he stood up from the bed, told her he was sorry but she wasn't listening, as she pointed at him angrily he grabbed both her hands, apologised again and told her he liked her. She stared without speaking and he let go of her hands, he grabbed her by the waist and pulled her against him.

She was too surprised to stop him and let him press his mouth to hers, she was pissed off but flattered and as she acknowledged that his kisses were delicious, she decided it would be easier to forgive him. She returned his kisses eagerly, letting his hands unfasten her shirt. As he pushed it off he stared at her, his eyes widening as he unfastened her bra and clutched his hands nervously over her breasts.

Dorothy couldn't quite believe this was happening to her, she had never had an admirer before, whenever she went out men went for her friends rather than her. The desire in his eyes was new, it left her flush with excitement, she dropped her hands to his jeans and unfastened them, before pushing them down and reaching in to his pants.

His dick was solid, he pushed it eagerly towards her hands, she held it and rubbed it and his desire leapt out of bounds, he grabbed for her skirt and pulled it down to her knees, this was not his first time but was the first time a woman had stood naked before him. He had had girlfriends before but they had only ever done it in the dark and under the sheets, he had always been shy and the girls he usually went for were shyer than him.

Dorothy could see he was nervous and took the opportunity to take charge, she twisted his body and pushed him down to the bed, he stared, wide eyed as she crawled over him, scanning her body, when her mouth dropped to his dick, he gasped and pushed his hands to her hair to stop her. Once in her mouth though, he froze against the bed, her mouth, hot and wet was lifting and dropping over him, her hands crushed his balls and he cried out in pleasure. He couldn't bear it much longer his hips were grinding towards her, and he felt like he was floating to heaven.

She stopped abruptly and crawled further up him, aware that he was about to burst, his desire for her was liberating, she crawled further than she would usually dare. Her legs stopped by his neck and she forced her vagina towards his face, he grabbed her hips roughly and lifted his neck to ram his tongue against her clit. She tasted sweet, he couldn't stop licking, reaching in to her vagina and spreading her wetness with his tongue around his lips, he pushed his fingers in to her, ramming them as she began to scream yes.

His dick was yearning for her to sit on him, he dragged her body down and planted her vagina over it, she sat above him, winding her hips, her back was arched and he was pushing her up by her tits.
He sat his body up to her, clutching his hands behind her back and as she lifted and dropped over him, he kissed her lips passionately letting her taste herself on him.

The two of them were too close to try to linger, the climax was on its way and there no way of stopping it, he lifted himself deeper in to her whilst she crashed down on to him and as he grabbed her eyes to him he saw the explosion coming. They shuddered and screamed as their orgasm hit, hips grinding erratically, lips pressing lips. Their heads fell apart and as they let them roll back, each absorbed in their own pleasure, astounded and gobsmacked.

They laughed when it was over, she lifted herself from him and lay at his side on the bed, he wound his fingers in circles around her back and they waited for their breaths to settle. She asked why he hadn't asked her out, he had wanted too but every time he had come to her room she hadn't been in, she laughed when he told her he had hoped to get caught so that she would storm in to his room and he could finally get her alone.

The Underpass

The girl walking along the street read a text, a smile flashed to her face, she couldn't help it, it had started as harmless flirting but since they had each other's numbers it had been getting out of hand. He was texting to say how good she had looked today, he wanted to know where she was.

She had just left the office, he was her colleague and she barely spoke to him at work, they had travelled together from a business meeting the week before and she had been flattered that he was flirting with her. He had taken her number from work and started texting her, she texted back innocently at first but lately their messages were getting steamier.

She had not set out to cheat on her boyfriend, before this she would never have dreamed of doing so, she wondered if she was cheating already, if her boyfriend were in the same position sending messages to another woman she would be mortified. She kept telling herself it wouldn't go any further, but each time she received a text she laughed and smiled and shot a response back.

She told him she was on her way home, they never texted each other at night unless she was away from her boyfriend or he was away from his wife, he knew that she walked and only lived 15 minutes from home. He had offered her a lift numerous times, but she knew that if she did she would have to decide, was she having an affair or not, she had an excuse, she didn't want anyone seeing them together.

As she entered the underpass she didn't see him straight away, it was darker than usual, dreary and musty despite the sun above it, trucks thundered above her and she rushed along quickly anxious to get back in to the light.
She noticed the silhouette of a man first and her body tensed

as she wondered what he was up too, he must have noticed her pause because he shouted out to her.

She laughed in relief and asked what the hell he was doing there, he told her he couldn't resist he had hoped she would walk through here, she paused to speak to him, panicked, the moment was here, what the hell was she going to do.

When he kissed her, she kissed back, she knew she wouldn't be able to resist him, he was handsome and bad and everything she fantasised about. He pressed her against the wall as he put his hands on her, a voice in her head nagged her to stop him, but the butterflies in her stomach flew up and quashed it.

She was as bad as he was, dragging her hands down his back and kissing him like a crazy woman, her tongue thrashed against his and she pulled him closer to her, when his hands pushed up her skirt she did nothing to stop him, she just lowered his zipper and pulled his dick out from over it.

It never occurred to her that someone could walk in and find them, the only thing on her mind was her need to have him inside her. She lifted her leg up and he grabbed it over his elbow, he reached down for his dick and angled it towards her, before ramming his arse forward and driving it in to her. She moaned as he pushed in, her hands getting more desperate, she untucked his shirt and drove her hands against his naked back.

He knew that he had her, he had known from the first text, they rarely said no but this one had been hard to pin down to a date.
He had expected to have to persuade her for more than a kiss, but she was as desperate as he was, which had shocked and delighted him, her body was perfect, he had hoped to get her

into his car, it seemed there was no need though, she was dirtier than him.

He held his hands under her arse, kneading it with his fingers as he endlessly pounded himself in to her, she was crying out, but it didn't matter, the sound was being drowned out by the traffic. He let himself loose with her, screaming as his climax hit, her fingernails pressed against his back and she began to scream in ecstasy.

They shuddered pressing together, he let her leg lower, they kissed softly as he pulled out of her and she smoothed down her skirt. He had had what he came for but couldn't quite pull away, her hands were still up his shirt and he didn't want her to leave. She asked him where he was parked, he was going her way she told him he should let her go first, to leave together would look to dodgy.

They walked together towards the exit and couldn't stop kissing, finally as the light hit them he kissed her goodbye and watched her leave. He tucked his shirt back in, waited a few minutes and headed to his car, she would be home in a few minutes he had to text her once more.

She walked the rest of the way home slowly waiting for his next, when she received it she smiled again, knowing she had exactly where she wanted him.

Mission Impossible

He knew she was out of his league, she always had been, once he had realised he couldn't have her he had done the next best thing and befriended her. In High School, she had been one of the popular kids and barely acknowledged him, in college they became friends as his popularity grew and hers waned.

They had both moved back home, her to get married, him to work at his father's business and as the years passed and he married, the two couples became friends. They lived nearby and got on with their lives, both had kids and watched them grow quickly. His wife was as hot as she was and he loved her to bits, she always sensed his desire for his friend but knew he would never act on it.

When she died he was heartbroken, his friends helped him through it, he missed her more than anything and couldn't imagine going on without her, he did for his kids and more years passed by, his friends tried to get him back dating but he had no desire to see anyone else.

When her husband left her for a woman half his age, the friendship group splinted and most of them went with him, her old friend from high school was the only one of his friends who stood with her, when she fought with her husband about him, he told her he wasn't surprised because he had always been obsessed with her. She paid no attention, he really had no idea, when his lover got sick of him, he begged her to take him back but she wouldn't hear of it.

When the friends got together weeks later, drinking wine and catching up on each other's progress, she asked him about what her husband had said and was surprised when he answered honestly. She couldn't believe it when he told her about the first time he had seen her, what she had been wearing and what she had said, 20 years had gone by and she had had no idea.

She told him she could barely remember him from school but that in college she had had a quite a crush, she told him about the night she had realised, what they had been doing and what he had said. He laughed and she laughed with him, as they pondered what would have become of their lives, he told her they still had a lot of life to live and asked her if she wanted to go on a date.

She worried about the risk of ruining their friendship, she voiced her concerns and he asked her to think about it. He followed her into the kitchen to help her clear up, she watched him and decided they had wasted enough time. As he stood over the sink she wrapped her arms around him, he rocked as she cuddled him, as they had many times before, when her hand dragged to his groin he realised she wasn't being friendly anymore.

He moved her hands away from him and turned to face her, he put her hands to her face and leant down to kiss her, she kissed him back softly and wrapped her arms around him, both stared at the other lovingly and before their passion set in. Their kisses became more desperate, their hands pressed roughly against each other's backs, after 20 years of waiting, he was finally doing what he had dreamt of and it was better than he ever could have imagined.

They were so beyond dating, already madly in love, the only question to answer was whether they were friends or something more. Her touch set his nerves on fire, she reached beneath his t shirt and held her hands against his waist, his breathing was heavy, he had goose bumps, he was desperate to get her to bed.

His excitement was addictive, his desire for her felt insane, he traced his hands over her body, lingering over her hips, her arse and her breasts. She pulled his shirt away and pressed her lips to his naked chest, whilst pulling at his trousers till they dropped down his legs. He tried to steer her to the stairs but they were making slow progress, he bent to the bottom of her dress and ripped it over her head.

He grabbed his hands around her arse, sighing when he looked at her, he told her she was amazing, whilst reaching round to unfasten her bra, he lifted her by the buttocks and seated her on the kitchen counter, he pulled away and stared at her, again holding his face to both sides of her head, she pushed his underwear away and pulled him in close, opening her legs to pull his naked body against hers.

He pushed himself in to her, pulling her to the edge of the counter, her body was shaking, as desire flooded through her, they ground themselves together, moaning and panting. The heat was undeniable, they were so much more than friends he was desperate to please her but just as desperate to please himself.

She cried out as she climaxed, pushing her head against his neck, he pulled her chin up to face him and ignited when he saw the pleasure on her face, their kisses were soft again, satisfied and long.
He pulled himself out of her and it dawned on him that they were naked in her kitchen, he pulled himself out of her and carried her up the stairs, there was so much he had fantasised about doing to her she hadn't seen anything yet.

She laughed as he carried her, telling him to watch his back, the time that had gone by hadn't been wasted, they had had good times and wonderful kids, the time for them was now and they were going to make the most of it.

The Boardroom

The arguments were going nowhere, three days in and it was obvious that further progress would not be made on this trip, the only question was how to avoid wasting the next two days that had been allocated to try to thrash it out.

The only silver lining in this pointless exercise was the fact that his opponent had a hot assistant, the two of them were obviously sleeping together, hence the reason why he had not already thrown in the towel, it was worth wasting days in here for the nights of bliss at the company's expense.

Although she was screwing her boss, she was also making suggestive eye contact, she had positioned her chair just far enough behind him so that he couldn't see what she was up too. He wouldn't mind a bit of her himself, he allocated the next hour of thinking time to figure out a way to end this charade and have her.

Solution found, he declared a break for lunch and recruited his own assistant to do what he was paid too, assist, he gave him in his instructions and waited patiently in the boardroom. The hot assistant arrived 10 minutes later, she was surprised but pleased when she realised that her boss hadn't yet returned, she was sleeping with her boss to get herself up the career ladder, but the nights in his room had been more about fulfilling him than herself.

She didn't waste any time, she stood before him and reached forwards with her hand and placed it firmly over his dick, he made no move to stop her, his eyes shone as he stared and a smile tugged the edges of his lips.
She went further, unfastening his zip before stepping close

and placing her lips over his. He had known what she would do, but had not expected her to be quite so quick, his assistant would be returning with her boss in ten minutes, he had hoped that he would catch them in a passionate embrace but figured he might as well go for it, the more compromising the position, the greater likelihood that the two of them would up and leave and free up the rest of his week.

He kissed her back passionately, reaching his hands up and under her skirt to grasp her breasts and lowering his mouth to her neck. Her own hands were busy lowering his trousers and as she pushed him back into his chair, she dropped down to her knees and closed her mouth over his dick. She sucked deeply, dragging him in to her and whacking the tip of his penis against her cheek.

He lay his head back and enjoyed it, he wasn't sure how much further she would go, but knew he couldn't allow himself to come here, six minutes remained. She wrapped her tongue round his dick, driving him nuts, he was tempted to forgo his plans and just enjoy it, but stopped himself just in time and pulled her back to her feet. He shoved her skirt up to her waist, pushed her briefs aside and pulled her over on to him.

With four minutes to go her vagina closed over his dick, he placed his palms against her arse and bounced her up and off him, before dragging her down roughly. Their lips pressed together once more and she wrapped her arms around him. She rode him with clear intent, give herself an orgasm and get off him, she thrashed herself erratically, grinding her pelvis deeply over him.

His climax was near, he concentrated, the timing had to be perfect, her orgasm knocked all thoughts of waiting out of his mind though, she screamed out, whimpering and panting as she came. The explosions in her body spread like wildfire to his and he moaned, driving his hips upwards and clutching her tightly against him as he ploughed up and in to her. With a shudder he came, shooting himself in to her hungrily as she leant blissfully against him.

As they sat locked together allowing their breaths to settle the door opened and her boss walked in, she jumped from him, revealing their nakedness and whilst he sat calmly she blundered around, pulling her skirt down and pushing towards him, apologising and begging his forgiveness.

He turned and stomped away and she followed him, whilst adjusting her skirt and refastening her shirt.

The Hike

The scenery was as stunning as the weather, Carly perched herself at the edge of the rocks and unpacked her lunch. She had not managed to convince any of her friends to take this trip with her, this was not their type of holiday and they had chosen instead to spend their days at the beach and their nights drinking. It was not a typical holiday for her either but the last few months had been hectic and she had just wanted time to breathe and relax for a change.

She had signed up for this trip last minute, a weekend hiking through the countryside and camping, the rest of the group consisted mainly of elderly singles and couples, it didn't matter to her, in fact she preferred it, for the past 24 hours she had not had to engage in pointless conversations, she had kept to herself, left in peace with her thoughts as she walked.

The tour guide had attempted to engage her, concerned that she had spent most of her time alone, once she had told him that that was the point of her trip he had left her to it, telling her he would leave her be and to let him know if she needed anything.

The last remnants of the group were still catching up, she took a book from her rucksack and leant back against the rocks and spent a blissful hour reading in peace.

The tour guide had taken a seat by the couple sat in front of her, he was explaining the history of the area and telling them about his own connection to it, she stared at her book but couldn't help listening in, his enthusiasm was sweet, he was her age but got on well with the oldies, playing along as the ladies flirted, his cheeks blushing when they got carried away.

The men in her life were sharks compared to him, always busy, always plotting and not doing anything unless it benefited them career wise or financially. On her commute to work alone, she encountered at least 100 men his age, none of them gave her or anyone else the time of day. She hadn't realised before how much she missed normal relaxed conversation and kindness.

Lunch was over, the group packed away their dinners and continued their way, the tour guide dropped in to her pace beside her and told her that they would be walking till around six and then setting up camp, she smiled and thanked him and he let her continue in her blissful solitude.

By the end of the walk her legs were exhausted, she set up her tent slightly away from the others, and once she had finished, perched herself on a chair outside it and relaxed with a book again. The tour organisers had arranged a BBQ and there was no need for her to pitch in, once the food was cooked she put her book away and collected her portion.

She took a seat on one of the make shift benches and was soon joined by a group of fellow walkers, she joined their conversation casually, politely answering their questions and forcing herself to ask her own. Once her meal was finished she waited for a break in the conversation to make a polite exit, others bundled in though and she found herself stuck there.

Half an hour later when she was considering being rude and walking away mid conversation, the tour guide stepped in to save her, asking if she would give him a hand and she followed him eagerly, whatever he needed couldn't take a few minutes and she would be free to return to her tent in peace. She followed him away from the campsite and behind the tree line and he confessed that he didn't need her for anything, he had just sensed that she had wanted to get away.

She smiled and thanked him but offered to help anyway, he just had wood to collect, from the dry store a few minutes away, for the campfire that they would light this evening. They chatted as they walked and he asked her about herself, nothing too deep, just the polite stuff. She asked him what she had heard him talking about earlier, not searching for words to break the silence for a change but genuinely interested.

She carried a bundle of wood back with her and was disappointed when they arrived back at the tent and he deposited her at her tent, telling her he would make an excuse for her if she didn't want to join in later.

Her plan had been to disappear in to her tent before the evening began but she found herself joining in and a glass or two of wine later she was engaged in an interesting conversation with a retired couple who had once been just like her, spending all their time working and forgetting about making time for themselves.

It wasn't until they retired for the evening that she realised most of the campers had gone to bed and she had spent the whole night enjoying herself.

The tour guide was dampening the fire and he smiled when she approached him and told her he had been ready to jump in and excuse her but had thought that she had looked like she was enjoying herself. She admitted that she had been, it was still early and she couldn't go to bed until she had sobered up a bit.

He asked her if she wanted some company and she nodded, he sat close and she wondered what he would do if she leaned in to kiss him, she suspected that he would not be pleased, she had pushed him and everyone else away most of the weekend and had in fact acted as aloof and snobbish as the people she had needed the weekend to escape from.

She stared at the fire instead, until to her surprise he leaned in and kissed her, taking his arm and wrapping it around her shoulder and placing the other against her knee, she kissed him back, enthusiastically. Her desire for him rose quickly, the kiss was delicious and endless, he made no moves to go further and it was left to her to push to her feet and pull him with her to her tent.

He didn't resist, they kissed as they walked, pausing only to dip their heads in and they kneeled inside the tent, bodies pressed together until she reached down to grab the edges of his t shirt and pulled them over his head. Her hands ran over his body, he was toned and trim, he mirrored her actions, never going further than her but copying what she did, he took her t shirt off first and as she unbuttoned his jeans he leaned forward to do the same to hers.

Their bodies released momentarily as they each removed their own jeans and she settled on to the camp bed and pulled him down beside her, his underwear was still in the way and she pushed it aside, rubbed her hands against his penis and cupped his balls.

He pressed his hands down her briefs and held her arse in his hands pulling her close so that her pelvis pressed against him and he ran his stiffness gently against her clitoris.

She wound her hips to increase the friction, sighing audibly as the pleasure rocked through her body. As her moans rose he crushed his mouth harder against her, although she had distanced her tent from the others they were still only feet away. He pulled his body over her and as she opened her legs and angled her pelvis towards him he pushed his penis in to her, she smiled as he began to moan louder than her and whispered sarcastically that he had to make more effort to be quiet.

He didn't respond to her, his face was frozen in concentration, his eyes were staring hungrily at her and his stiff jaw made it impossible for their kisses to continue, she stared in to his eyes, sharing his pleasure and as his thrusts became more powerful she felt her climax near and grasped at his arse as she held him in.

He began to grunt and groan, his arse tensed and he froze, she lifted her hips frantically and circled her hips against him, he closed his eyes, he was coming in to her, clutching his hands at the sides of her hips as she rolled up and on to him. As his dick throbbed and his skin pounded against her clit she felt the ignition spark within her, she no longer cared about the neighbouring tents all she cared about was the final push of her body towards him and as she exploded she whimpered and pressed her face against his chest to stop herself screaming.

Their bodies shivered against each other until their movements slowed, they opened their eyes and smiled, neither could quite believe they had done it but it had been wonderful and they still couldn't bear to pull away, she held him close, totally content and fell quickly into a blissful sleep as he lay locked over her.

The Break

He had watched her all evening, he hadn't been able to take his eyes off her since she had stood at the bar and ordered her drinks. Beautiful women were the norm, rather than a rarity in this place, but she was nothing like the rest of them, her face was clear of make-up apart from her hot red lipstick and she was dressed casually, in a t shirt dress that skimmed at her feet.

Although her friends were dressed in next to nothing, short skirts and low tops, it was clear that she had a better body than any of theirs, the material fell casually over her hips and bust, accentuating her assets without clinging desperately to them.

She danced without inhibition, the smile that dominated her face never left her and she laughed raucously, throwing her head back and bending over clutching her stomach. Each time she came to the bar he served her immediately, the wrestling crowds around him grew exasperated but he ignored them, the smile she hit him with was worth the snide comments that would follow as soon as she turned and left him.

He wondered why her friends were not taking their turns getting drinks, she was surrounded by them but each time their drinks were finished they looked to her and she shuffled towards him.

He delayed his break, reluctant to leave in case she slipped away, and as the bar began to empty as their customers drifted off to the clubs, she made another visit to the bar and struck up a conversation with him.

He blushed as she spoke and cursed himself, he was acting

like a novice but picked up girls here every weekend, usually sluts though, the easiest girls he could find, none were like her. As he leaned in to take her order she surprised him by asking if he had a break due, he stared gormlessly back at her, trying to figure out what she was asking. He told her he was about to take his break now and was shocked when she asked if she could join him.

He smiled and nodded, turning to a colleague and telling him that he was taking it and headed to the exit of the bar, he had no idea why she had asked him and what she was expecting, he knew what he hoped she wanted, but surely, he couldn't be that lucky. She followed along the edge of the bar and once he had ducked under, she took his hand and followed him in to the staff room.

As soon as the door closed he turned to her and she reached down to the bottom of her dress and lifted it, her legs were endless but his shock came when she lifted it up to her shoulders and pulled it over her head, she was stood naked before him with the body of a goddess. He realised that his jaw had dropped and pulled his jaw up before rushing towards her and letting his hands get carried away.

He grasped at her arse and smashed his lips against her, quickly bolting the door and pulling her into the room, between feeling her arse and breasts he managed to unfasten and push himself out of his jeans. He would have loved to explore her body for hours but that wasn't an option, his break lasted ten minutes and if he was any longer than that his boss would start beating the door down.

His lips crushed against hers, he pushed her legs open and drove his fingers into her, smiling as she moaned and he realised by her wetness that she was as ready as he was. He dropped his arse down to a chair and dropped her down over him, clutching her arse and planting his dick firmly in to her. She groaned as he filled her, his dick was huge and she could feel its girth stretching against her vagina lips.

She ground her clit against him, pulling herself up and over him before launching herself down so that his dick ripped in and out of her repeatedly, the music blared through the walls, disguising the moans that were bursting from her lips.

His were no quieter, he rubbed his hands over hips, reaching up to cup her breasts before lowering his lips to suck the nipples that already deep pink and stiff. She threw her head back and cried out in pleasure as he closed his teeth over her, biting her nipples softly, introducing a hint of pain to increase the pleasure. Once she was shuddering in climax and erratically riding her plateau, he allowed his release.

He forced himself upwards, lifting her with him and crashing with her against the wall as he ploughed his dick in to her, her plateau escalated unexpectedly and she cried out again, frantic this time as she lifted her legs and wrapped them around his waist, clinging with her arms around his neck. The sensation in his groin exploded and he screamed as he fucked her, shuddering and thrusting with his last sparks of energy until he collapsed frozen against her and she dropped her feet back to the floor.

He panted to restore his breath and planted her with a quick kiss before pulling himself out of her, he grabbed her dress and lowered it back over her delicious body, patting it into place before forcing his jeans back on quickly.
He unlatched the door and sat quickly pulling her down beside him, just in time for his boss to walk into the room and remind him that his break was over.

Extreme Role Play

She lingered at the end of the alleyway, she was well of the danger that she was putting herself in, unfortunately it was that that had lured her in to this, she had tried pretending, to free herself of this compulsion but it was never the same, this was the only thing that did it for her, her version of self-harm.

Her childhood had been great, her family loved her to bits, she had a good career, great friends and a happy relationship, so why was she so damaged? She must surely be damaged to be doing this.

She tried to stay away from the main road, it wouldn't do to be recognised, not that the reflection that had stared back from the mirror of her apartment resembled her in any way, her make-up was thick, hair backcombed, she was wearing the tiniest skirt she owned, a push up bra covered by a vest top, bare legs and killer heels.

A car pulled up by the road side and she peered out at it, a man rolled down the window and beckoned her towards him, he looked normal enough, she wasn't too picky, if he wasn't too fat or smelly he would do for her. She sauntered towards the car and he asked her to get in, as far as she was concerned that was a good thing, he hadn't haggled about the price, he was in too much rush.

She walked to the passenger door and jumped in beside him, she told him her price, he nodded and drove away whilst she was strapping herself in. He pulled the car into the vacant space of an industrial estate and counted out the notes, she stuffed them in to her bag and joined him in the back seat.

As soon as he got in beside her he pushed his hands up her

skirt and smiled when he realised he didn't need to remove her knickers, he unfastened his trousers and put her hands on him.

She lifted his dick out, it was thick and stiff, she ran her hands up and down it a few times before leaning in to press her mouth over it. As she sucked, she rammed her hands down his trousers to feel his balls, they were already engorged, she handled them roughly squeezing as she sucked until he began to moan.

His hands were pulling her top up over her breasts and he unfastened her bra, freeing her tits and holding them roughly in his hands, he told her exactly how to suck him, faster, harder, slower, he spoke authoritatively until his voice began to shake and then he whispered desperately, telling her that was right, that was how he liked it, yes that's it.

His hands abandoned her tits and he shoved them back up her skirt, he rammed his palm against her clit and his fingers in to her vagina, she moaned in appreciation, he may have been used to hookers faking it, but her enjoyment was real, she waited patiently for him to say the words, she was desperate to clamp herself over his dick.

He didn't bother telling her, he shoved her head away and dragged her body over him, he positioned her on her knees first and rammed his mouth against her tits, licking with his tongue at full length, then sucking her nipples and running his fingers over her arse. As she lowered her body she could feel the tip of his penis pressed towards her and rubbed her vagina over it, delighting as it flicked at the edges and teased towards her clit.

His fingers pushed in her again, first two then three, his arm was forcing her upwards and she pushed herself down over his hand, determined to feel the full force of his onslaught. With a groan of pleasure, he ripped his hand from her and forced her vagina down over his dick. She tensed her thighs as she moved her hips in circles over him.

He smashed his face against hers, thrashing his tongue in and out of her, whilst he grasped her arse cheeks in his hands and pushed his fingertips in to her arse hole, she strained to push her clit against him, three points of pleasure were torturing her. His desperation ignited her, this was it, this feeling, she felt as if she were on fire, explosions were rupturing throughout her groin and she screamed out as he lifted his hips and thrust himself in to her.

She barely noticed that he was coming too, her head threw back as she pulled away from him and she let his dick satisfy the hunger that had been building for months, since the last time she had done this, her head tossed side to side as she cried out whimpering for him to fuck her as hard as he could do it. He dragged at her hips, frantically staring in to her eyes, her orgasm thrilled him, he knew hookers were good at faking but this was real, he could see the flames.

They collapsed together against the car seat once it was over, taking deep breaths and as it dawned on her that they were not lovers who had just had passionate sex she pulled herself off him and adjusted her clothing. The shame set in immediately, she didn't need the money, she posed as a hooker because it was her fantasy, the first time she had done it she had been drunk and horny.

The man who had picked her up had presumed she was a hooker and paid her afterwards without her asking, the orgasm she had had blown her mind, the only way for her to replicate it was to do this. He looked awkwardly at her and told her he would drop her back, they got back in to the front seat and he asked if she had a business card.

She tried to put him off by saying this wasn't something she did often, he told her he came in to town once a month and could give her a few days' notice, she was tempted, but would that mean she were having an affair, she couldn't resist, she gave him her number, before jumping out of the car.

The Steward

She had arrived in the car park before the restrictions had set in but he was having none of it, he had told her to move her car half an hour before and she had spent the time trying to convince him to let her stay. Since she had sneaked in here, every car park nearby had filled up, if she left now she would have to park miles away, she knew that she had been taking a risk, but couldn't accept that the risk had not been worth taking.

Her last option was to offer her body to him, she did so jokingly, but he smiled and nodded, she let out a sigh of relief, hell he was half her age and hot, she would have paid to have him screw her.

He shouted out to his colleague, planted a permit on her car and asked her to follow him, they walked into a security cabin and he closed the door, he took off his coat and signalled for her to do the same. Rather than remove his trousers he unfastened his zip and pulled his dick out of the gap, she looked at it disappointedly, she had imagined a passionate fuck but his dick was flaccid and she presumed he wanted it to be quick.

He looked down at his dick and at her, she presumed he was implying that he wanted her to work on it and walked towards him, holding it in her hands and rubbing before dropping to her knees. She sucked enthusiastically, and though it stiffened its size barely changed and she wondered if he would ask her to move her car if she couldn't get him to ejaculate.

She reached in to his trousers and rubbed his balls, tossed his dick in her hands and ran her tongue up and down, still nothing, she pushed her hand beyond his balls and stuck her finger up his arse, no response. Although she had been more than willing to screw him, there would be no point in attempting to straddle this, it would barely reach the sides and she certainly wouldn't be able to get any pleasure from it.

As her mouth tired she seriously considered getting in her car and leaving, blow jobs were only fun if they led to something, this seemed utterly pointless. She barely noticed when his hand dropped to her head, but he pressed against it suddenly and she felt him stiffen, his hand that is, his dick still dangled loosely when she pulled it out of her mouth to sneak a look at him.

His face was contorted in ecstasy and he was moaning, she tossed him stiffly for another few seconds and he shot his semen out at her, she shifted her head to avoid a direct hit and it fell impressively in an arch across the tables. She looked back down at it and shuffled it a few more times before tucking it back into his trousers.

She pulled to her feet and tried to avoid eye contact, presuming that he would be looking sheepish, he wasn't though a satisfied smirk covered his face and he thanked her with a kiss and told her to look out for him if she wanted to turn up early for a space again.

She grabbed her coat and walked out of the cabin and into the festival, wondering how it was that a man so unfortunate could look so arrogant and happy.

The Neighbours

The women in the flat above him were driving him nuts, when they had first moved in he had been delighted, both were decent looking and the absence of men helping, led him to believe they were single, he had tolerated their music whilst he had thought he had a chance with them, but once he had realised that they were not interested his mood soured and his generosity faded.

He had asked them nicely at first to turn the music off late at night and now resorted to pounding with a broom against the ceiling, they obviously couldn't hear it. He marched up to their room and pounded on the door, they either didn't hear or ignored him.

He marched back to his apartment and pulled open the window to climb out on to the fire exit, he could hear that they were in the bedroom, it sounded like they were having a dance off up there, he climbed the metal stairs and pressed his face against the window.

What he saw both shocked and froze him, he stared, unable to pull away from the site that confronted him. It was no wonder that they hadn't heard him knocking, the women lay naked on the bed with their fingers inside one another, eyes closed and writhing in ecstasy.

The window was netted and he doubted if they would be able to see him against the blackness if they opened their eyes, he doubted it but sill, they could call the police.

He told himself he would just watch for a minute and pushed his head in closer to get a better look.
The girls had better bodies than he had realised, the blond had

an amazing pair of tits, big and round with pert little nipples perched at the top of them, her stomach was flat and her legs were long, her head turned side to side as she moaned.

The brunette was smaller with tits that could only be described as a perfect handful, her long hair covered her face as her back arched. They turned to one another and he shrunk away for a second and held his breath, when they began kissing passionately he realised that they hadn't seen him and he pushed in close again, this time reaching in his hands in to his shorts to take hold of his dick and massage it softly.

Their lips took turns to press against one another's breasts, their spare hands rubbed over arses but their fingers remained entrenched in vagina's. The blond dropped her body down and she kneeled before him, he couldn't see what she was doing, he presumed she had her tongue in her friend's vagina but he was happy enough with his view to give it much thought.

The blond leant directly in front of him with her legs spread open, fingers pressed in and out of her and her arse rocked towards and away from him, his dick swelled in his hand and he began to toss it firmly with his wrist, she was feet from him and he imagined his dick pushing in and out of her. He allowed his groans to escape, the music was the only sound that anyone within ear range would be able to hear, hence his reason for the visit in the first place.

The blond shifted position, twisting her body so that she sat over her friend's face, he groaned as her tongue rose and pressed over her clit and positive whimpered, when she ran her hands over her tits and dragged one of them up to lick her own nipple.

Beneath her the brunette had opened her own legs and was

pushing her fingers over her clit and holding her vagina lips open before driving her finger's deep within.

He could barely wait, it was like live porn, he wished he was filming this, he forced his wrist to toss quicker, he didn't want them to change position, this one was perfect. As the blond began to climax he almost shot his load, she was riding her friend like a rodeo bull, her tits were bouncing as her body rocked and she screamed out in pleasure, shuddering.

As soon as she had finished she let her body fall forward and her tongue drag against the brunettes' clit, her hands held her thighs apart and he had the perfect view of her vagina as her fingers teased its edges. As her body began to push up he shot his load, his body fell against the railing behind him and he closed his eyes, gyrating his hips as he let the feeling wash over him.

He sighed and pushed himself straight, realising what a mess he had made, his cum splashed right across the window, he daren't risk wiping it away, the couple had collapsed together on the bed and he realised now would be a suitable time to escape.

By the time he got into his apartment the music had stopped and he wondered if they only played it to disguise the sounds of their screaming. The next night, he smiled when the music started, gave it half an hour and headed on out of the window.

The Bus Driver

He always looked forward to picking her up, she stood outside the hospital five nights a week and had lately been standing beside him, chatting as he drove her home, her journey only took 20 minutes and he drove as slowly as he could, determined one day to ask her out but somehow unable to build himself up to it.

Tonight, there was no exception he pulled up at her stop and let her go, but as she soon as she stepped away she turned back towards him, her face looked panicked and she told him that she had just realised she didn't have her house keys and must have left them at work.

He told her he would be driving to the hospital and back here again over the next couple of hours if she wanted to ride along, but he couldn't do it any faster, he had to stick to the schedule which included a break at the terminus at the end of the route a couple of miles away. He had expected her to tell him it would be easier for her to get a taxi, but she climbed back on board, thanking him with a smile on her face.

He felt relieved, perhaps she enjoyed spending her time with him as much as he did, but she soon explained that she was skint until her next pay day. He stopped at the terminus and turned the lights off, he had been driving for hours, this stop was a mandatory break and he had to get out of the cab for fifteen minutes.

She walked to the back of the bus with him and they sat on the back seats, her body was closer than it needed to be and he figured this was the perfect time to ask her if she would agree to go out with him.
He stuttered as he blurted it out and when she didn't respond straight away brought his eyes nervously to hers, she was

smiling at him and told him she had been wondering if he would ever ask her.

She leaned in towards him for a kiss and he held his hands around her, pulling her body close, her lips tasted sweet, her tongue pressed gently against his. He wished that this could be the start of something but the bus had to leave in ten minutes, the kiss would have to do, still he couldn't resist letting his hands drape over her body, he had stared at it for too long to be able to resist.

It seemed that she felt the same, her hands pressed in to his coat and across his back, before untucking his shirt and he shivered as she pressed her cold hands against him. He decided to push his luck, he moved his hands to the front of her uniform and began to slowly unfasten the buttons of her shirt, when she didn't object he moved more quickly, popping open the last few buttons and pushing his hands in and over her bare breasts.

He sighed as he held his hands over her, her hands had spread to his groin and she traced the shape of his stiff dick with her fingertips. He yearned for her to release it and when she did he moaned in delight, her hands ran over his dick slowly and he closed his eyes and enjoyed her touch.

He moved his hand to her skirt but she stopped him and held it there, he pulled away but stopped what he had been attempting and instead held his hands against her face and reassured her that it was ok.
She didn't lay off on him though and he groaned and let her know that she was getting a bit carried away. He pulled away and told her he had to drive the bus in a few minutes, there was no rush, they hadn't even had their first date yet.

She was determined to continue and he wasn't going to stop her, screw the bus it would have to run a bit late, he moved his hands back to her breast and rubbed them slowly, fingering her nipples, twisting them with his fingertips. Her kisses continued and he couldn't help but increase their intensity, his tongue thrashed desperately in to her and his passion was returned in bucket loads, as well as forcing her tongue deeper in to him, her pressure on his dick got firmer and she twisted her hands over its tip, tossing and turning her hands and squeezing his balls.

As the explosion threatened to hit he pushed his hand over hers to stop her, she struggled against his hand but he insisted, he was about to cover her with his mess. She conceded her hand to his and held it in her hands and without warning dropped to her knees before him and took his dick in her mouth, he held is hands against her head to steer her away, but she showed little resistance and he thought what the hell, it was far too late for him to do anything about it.

He leant against the bus seat and groaned loudly, he could feel himself pushing against her cheeks and her hands were crushing his balls, her suck was intense, rapid, deep and endless, he was about to ejaculate before, but now this, it was just too much, he burst himself forwards and into her, squeezing his eyes closed as he felt himself come into her throat.

She sucked him clean and he lay back, panting, once she had finished she pushed his dick away and sat back down beside him, he put his arms around her shoulder and kissed her once more, just as passionately as before and then apologised and told her they better get on their way.

She put her hands out of her pocket and pulled out a key, she had had it all along, she told him, she had figured he had needed a bit more time to ask her out. He laughed and pulled her towards him, giving her a quick kiss and telling her he would drop her back home. Whilst he drove he held her hand and at her house she kissed him goodbye and he promised her would call her the next day.

He watched her till she reached her drive before pulling away and on his journey with a smile plastered across his face.

The Loan Shark

Stacey had scrambled around asking everyone she knew if they could help her out, they couldn't and she had known before asking that they wouldn't be able too, in all honesty if anyone else on earth had been able to help she wouldn't have gone to the loan sharks in the first place.

She had been doing ok with repayments up to this point, but her wages, which barely covered her expenses, had been docked after a sick day and there wasn't enough money left to cover everything. The guy who collected her payments had offered her an alternative, weeks before and she had shaken her head in disgust, now she was seriously considering it, it was either that or no groceries for the week as well as falling behind in all her other bills.

When he arrived, she invited him in and told him the situation that she was in, she could pay half and would need to cover the rest in the next few weeks, he smiled and declined her offer, telling her that his offer still stood. When she asked what she would have to do exactly, he looked surprised, as if she hadn't been serious.

He told her he would cover the missing half for a blow job, or the whole amount for an hour session, though it disgusted her she couldn't help thinking, the offer was generous, it wasn't as if he was disgusting, he was old enough to be her dad but had always been kind to her up to this.

He was being kind now too, she knew that his offer was more than she was worth, she had hoped that the best that she could achieve was a delayed payment.

She agreed, nodding her head and he told her he would put the money in for her this week, but come around later to collect his payment, they set a time and she was relieved to see him leave.

Anthony had hoped that when he first met Stacey she wouldn't take out the loan, the interest rates were insane and it wasn't as if she were a loser or a druggy like the rest of his boss's client's. He had been pleased that she had made all her payments so far and she only had a few months left to pay, when he had made the offer he had been showing off in front of a colleague, he hadn't been serious, but she had featured in his dreams since the day he had met her.

He was used to roughing up clients who didn't pay, he wouldn't be able to do that with her, the problem was although he had managed to be the one to visit her for payments so far that might not always be the case and he knew that many of his colleagues would have no problem threatening or carrying out those threats.

He could afford the loan repayment no problem, but it burned him to know that the original loan amount had already been paid weeks ago, he decided to have a word with his boss to see what he could do. He had laughed when he asked him for a settlement figure, but was impressed when he said he had arranged her to fuck off her payments and wanted to clear the debt himself. His boss agreed on one condition, he would slash the remaining balance, but she could never know and he would therefore either keep taking payments or screwing her weekly till the end of the term.

He cleared the debt and smiled in agreement, it had been the first time he had made the offer, his boss seemed to be proud of him. When he turned up at her house he was nervous, she had showered and answered the door in a robe.

Stacey had dressed and redressed, she didn't want to dress up, it wasn't a date, it would be more appropriate to dress like a whore, she took a shower and decided not to dress at all. She was anxious, but also a little excited, he had been the first person who had shown interest in her for years.

When he came in she walked up the stairs and asked him to follow her, in her room she dropped the robe, she wanted to get the hour over with as quickly as possible. He walked straight towards her, put his hands on her waist and kissed her, she pressed willingly against him, returning his kisses without hesitation.

Her nakedness thrilled him, her hands helped him remove his own clothing and they fell, naked, on to the bed together. He lay beside her, studying her face as he investigated her body, she closed her eyes, giving nothing away, he lay her on her back and started kissing her neck, his hands dropped to her breasts and to her stomach. He moved over her and set off down her body, when he began to kiss her stomach he saw her mouth open slightly and as he moved to her groin she moaned softly.

He pushed her legs open and worked on her with his tongue and fingers, her vagina clutched his finger tightly, he was used to prostitutes, they felt nothing like this, he eased his finger slowly into her, astounded by the way her back arched and she groaned. He wrapped his tongue around her clit, her pleasure was electrifying, he could stay hear all day.

Her vagina began to loosen around him, he lifted himself up and dropped down over her, she clutched her legs around him and as he pierced himself in to her, her brows knotted and she drew her legs around his waist.
He held himself back for as long as possible, closing his eyes to stop himself looking at her face, his dick was throbbing, the

sensation alone was driving him swiftly towards his climax.

She moaned loudly and he could no longer resist, his eyes flashed open and met hers, her hunger for him was palpable, her stare desperate and ecstatic. Her jaw clenched and she came, he followed quickly, ploughing down desperately into her throbbing vagina before letting go and screaming out in pleasure.

He fell over her, and kissed her lips, he had no idea how much time had passed but presumed it was time for him to go. He dressed and she pushed herself in to the bedding, he pondered whether he should before he kissed her but was glad that he did, she kissed him back and she smiled.

Glory Hole

Although he had been out of the closet for years, Bill's celibacy had lasted almost as long, his gayness was intact and obvious but as he got older and without a long-lasting partnership, sex became an impossibility, a 60-year old man didn't belong on the new dating scene and he refused to pay for it.

He heard some men in a pub talking in disgust about the gay club that had opened in the area, intrigue led him to look for details on the internet, it had a sauna and a steam room amongst other things, a place for men to meet for sex. He figured it would be no good for him, who would be interested in picking him up, but when he read further and found out about the glory holes, he felt a twinge in his groin for the first time in years.

It took him weeks to build up the courage to consider it, the first few times he went he couldn't force himself to go inside, the fourth time he had a stiff whisky first and stepping over the threshold made it easier. He was surprised to see that there were other men his age there, the young men were few and far between and those he did see were not exactly prize subjects.

Staff explained the procedure of the glory holes, their entryways were at different sides of the club so that no one could see who entered, the rooms were thin and could be entered at any time, if the opposite room was occupied a green light lit. Customers entered the room whenever they wanted and could push their own dick through to the other side, or suck or play with whatever came through.

To enter the club he had to undress, he was given a robe and strolled around, he walked into the glory hole corridor and stood waiting, there was no green light, he wasn't sure whether to wait or go for another stroll around, but whilst he thought about it the light illuminated. He froze, unsure what to do next, a dick popped through the hole in front of him and he smiled and decided to reach out for it.

His fingers closed around it and the old feelings came flooding back, it stiffened swiftly and he twisted and tossed it before dropping to his knees and pressing it into his mouth. He sucked hard, remembering a time when this had been his speciality, the men he had in secret, at a time when it had to be secret. He pulled away and thrashed his tongue swiftly around it, before driving it into him again and forcing his head forward and back as held his lips tightly to increase the friction.

The next time he withdrew he touched it softly with his fingers, it shuddered against his touch and he could hear the man softly moaning, it would not be long now, he took his own dick in his hands, he may be old but his dick showed no sign of waning, it was thick and hard, anxiously waiting. He wondered whether he should finish himself as he sucked, he intended to stick his own dick through the wall as soon as he had the chance but there was no guarantee that there would be anyone there to receive it.

He decided to be patient, he sucked as hard as he could and as he felt the cum flooding in to his mouth, he sighed as the recipient cried out in pleasure, he took a gulp and quickly lapped up any remnants of cum with his tongue, before lifting his body up and sticking his own dick through the hole.

Seconds passed, the dick withdrew and he waited in anticipation, he pumped his arse forwards, his dick searching for attention and at last a mouth closed in over it and he groaned excitedly. Whoever it was had plenty of practice, the mouth was eager and strong, the thrash of a tongue teased him slowly before shifting out of the way and allowing the suction to pull him rapidly to climax. He leant desperately against the wall, crying out, begging yes, yes, hoping against hope that the sucking would not end.

Explosions racked through his body, the hairs on it stood on end and his arse tensed as he held himself inside the mouth that drew him in, it was hot, warm and wet, he filled it, throwing his head back as he orgasmed. It lasted for an eternity, hitting him in waves, he sighed as he relented, realising how much he had missed it. The mouth withdrew and he pulled away, he fastened the robe back around him and made a quick exit to the dressing room, where he sat in a private booth and waited for his breath to settle.

He dressed as quickly as he was able and rushed out of the front door, it had been wonderful but he had been tempted to sit there all day, sucking dick after dick. Once he had gotten half way home he calmed himself, no one had seen him there, he wasn't being followed. The paranoia he realised was what was stopping him from living his gay life, but he had taken a big step today, bigger than he had realised.

The Water Park

She ran up the stairs exhilarated and was swiftly stopped by the man at the top who shouted at her to walk, she forced herself to slow down, the water slides were fun but not the main cause of her excitement, he waited in the pool below. He had caught her eye an hour earlier and had been following her around like a puppy since, her friends had abandoned her and were lounging around drinking at the pool side, soaking up the sun.

They had had a brief conversation, within their groups of friends and he had followed her when she had allowed herself to be taken away in a float around the whirlpool, clinging to the side of her raft and letting his body press against hers, she hadn't stopped him which was a rarity and he had followed her since in the hope that he had a chance with her.

She was having fun toying with him, he had gotten a little carried away and she thought he needed a chance to cool down, as she ran up the slide in her skimpy bikini she knew he would be watching her. As she splashed down and swum towards him, he scooped her into his arms and carried her along with him. The pair were being watched though, touching of any kind was off limits and as he kissed her for the first time a whistle blew and the pair were asked to pull away.

She laughed delightedly and splashed herself away from him, she had copped a good feel as they kissed, his dick was solid, it would be impossible for him to get out of the water just yet without revealing it. She took the opportunity to escape, she did want him but teasing was the best bit and she expected him to at least buy her a drink before she went any further.

She swum to the edge and stepped out of the pool, pausing at the side and laughing at the expression of torture on his face. She skipped along to the dressing room, pausing and waving before slipping inside. She took her time in the shower, grabbing her shampoo and washing her hair, when she opened her eyes he was there, standing in the opposite shower watching her.

She smiled, she hadn't expected him to have the nerve to get out so quickly, the outline of his dick was obvious, she didn't go to him, she knew that if she did they would attract the guard's attention, instead she walked slowly away, indicating with her eyes that he should follow her. He took the hint and followed, she left the door to the dressing room ajar and he squeezed in behind her.

He grabbed her by the waist and pulled her towards him, she was standing on the shelf so that only one pair of feet could be seen in the gap below, and her face was level was his. He kissed her as his hands took in her body, she felt wet and oily and wonderful, his already stiff dick, throbbed. She pushed her hands in to his shorts to take hold of it and covered her mouth over his as he moaned.

His hands unfastened her bikini top and he stared at her breasts before enclosing his fingers around them, her nipples were stiff, he pushed his hands down to her waist and pushed down her wet bottoms, he pressed his palm against her clit and his fingers in to her and smiled as she pulled her head away, pushed her head back and moaned.

There was no way they were going to get away with it, they would be discovered within minutes if they carried on moaning at this rate, it was impossible to stop though, their desire for each other was insane.
He lifted her with his hands on her arse and turned to take a

seat on the shelving, he didn't need to consciously push himself in to her, his dick found its own way and as she ground down over him he almost came.

Her closeness to climax matched his, her hips thrashed around, their mouths were pressed together but neither of them made an attempt to kiss, they held stiffly together as they tried to shut each other up. The sensations rushing through their bodies took their breath away, they were oblivious to the sounds around them, if they had been listening they would have heard a knock and a warning that they were about to come in.

Circling her hips wildly she came, he drove himself up to her clutching her tightly and clenching his butt as he drove himself up, lifting himself from the shelf he exploded wildly, shooting up and into as he joined her and their bodies wrestled close in climax. They screamed out, abandoning any attempt to quieten as their emotions took over, their bodies shuddered but then froze as the door swung open and a security guard stared in towards them.

He grabbed for a towel and covered them both as she peeled her body away from him and clung at his side, the security guard was talking but she couldn't bring his voice in to focus, her face flashed red and she was struggling to catch her breath. Her locker key was taken and the boy, pulled from her side and taken away before the door closed behind him. She sat with her head in her hands until her bag was lowered into the locker and she dried herself roughly, before dragging her clothes over her body and pushing out into the changing room and away.

He was waiting outside for her and as he embraced her and apologised she began to relax against him, the pair of them were joined by a security guard and exited from the building. Both groups of their friends stood laughing, the boys grabbed him from her and patted him on the back whilst the girls kissed and hugged her and laughed. Both groups had been ejected as they had, just because they had purchased joint tickets, they apologised but didn't need too, it had made their day and they would never let them hear the end of it.

The groups headed to the beach together, the couple drifted by each other's sides and held hands as they walked, letting their lips meet occasionally already anxious to get their hands on each other again.

The Speaker

He looked down from the stage as he spoke at the eager faces watching him, the days of nervousness and scripts were behind him, he spoke with confidence, he knew everything he needed to know about the subject and was happy to ask questions after the session. The students raised their hands patiently and he moved through them swiftly answering questions in groups and ensuring everyone had the chance of saying what they wanted to say.

It was one of the lecturers rather than one of the students who asked the most intellectual question and he answered as fully and openly as he could, smiling appreciatively and noting that there was more than friendliness reflected in the man's eyes. After the lecture, he stuck around shaking hands and engaging in conversation, the lecturer thanked him once he had finished and gave him the opportunity to receive a further round of applause before stepping away.

The lecture shook his hand in the corridor and as their eyes met, clarification was made. The men walked together to the lecturer's office and as soon as the door closed behind them, their bodies pressed together and they began their passionate escapade. The lecturer pushed his hands into the speaker's jacket, and held his hand against his back as they kissed, he had admired and fancied him for years, but had never been aware before that he was gay.

Both men were in the closet, publicly at least but the look that had passed between them had given their secrets away, though only to each other. Hands clutched at trouser buttons and zips, the encounter would need to be quick, they were both due to join the university faculty for lunch in twenty minutes.

Once their trousers dropped to the floor, the lecturer pressed the speakers body against the door and he swiftly locked it, as soon as he had done so he dropped before him and drove his mouth over the stiff dick that throbbed before him.

The speaker froze against the door, his partners were usually taken into his confidence after he had established a relationship with them and he could be sure of their intentions, he never normally let himself get carried away but this man's stare had given him butterflies. He twisted his hair in his hands as he sucked him, slowly and deliberately edging him close to his climax, he sighed audibly, then moaned, Christ he was good at this.

He yanked at his hair to stop him just in time, a blow job was wonderful but he wanted to be inside him, he dragged his body up and kissed him passionately before turning his body round and walking with him to the desk whilst squeezing his hands around his dick. Once they reached the desk he pushed him forward and over it, separated his butt cheeks with his free hand and drove his dick stiffly into his arse hole.

As he pushed in he tossed the lecturers dick with his wrist, his arse was much tighter than he was used too, he had either not taken a dick for a while or was not used to doing it. He forced himself in inch by inch, gaining depth with each thrust and once he finally reached capacity he delighted at the way his balls hit his skin.

Both men were desperately trying to stop themselves moaning, sounds escaped their mouths in grunts and whimpers as they thrashed obsessively together.
The lecturers dick was thick, it throbbed and pulsated and the balls that he allowed himself to stroke were engorged and stiff, he knew that he could allow it to explode at any minute but he restrained himself slightly, determined to make himself

climax at the same time.

The arse clenched his dick tightly, once it began to soften slightly, he allowed himself to thrash freely in and out of it, he pressed his body forward to cover his mouth over his jacket to cover the moans that were beginning to escape and with a final intake of breath he allowed himself to stiffen and plummet his way to ecstasy.

The tightness of his fist stiffened, he tossed quickly, urgently dragging the lecture up to join him and when lightning struck it hit them both, piercing through their bodies as their backs arched and muffled screams escaped their lips.

It was minutes before he could pull himself away, he felt light headed and gasped in short breaths to settle his heart rate. Once he could, the speaker released his dick slowly and pushed it back into his trousers, once he had lifted his zip back into place, he dropped to the speaker's ankles and retrieved his trousers up for him, lifting them back round his waist and fastening him up.

The men faced each other and shared a light kiss, they each ran their hands down their bodies to straighten up their shirts and jackets and once all was presentable, the lecturer returned to the door of his office and unfastened the lock on the door.
The men's faces were red still and they settled in opposite chairs to allow themselves to cool down, they smiled at each other across the table and as the speaker requested that the encounter between them, the lecture reassured him that no one here even knew that he was gay and he had no intention of discussing it.

After Hours

The lovers waited patiently for the store to close, it was her job to clean it and his job to secure it but since they had discovered each other they had done anything but, she came in early and carried out her duties quickly before the store closed. It closed hours before the food courts in the mall did, so his job was to stay on site until the mall closed, the doors were locked so there was no chance of being caught and it was his job to monitor the footage from the day before.

It had taken him a few weeks to convince her and the first time she had allowed him to screw her she had been cautious and shy, since then though her confidence had slowly grown and they had made their way through the departments, screwing without restraint for hours each night until her shift finished and she ran outside in to the car park, where her husband picked her up.

Each night he assured her that he would finished her duties and he did, he had to stay for an hour later than her, he spent that hour clearing up the space where they had been, finishing any jobs that she had not had the chance to do and wiping the tapes, after replaying the events to get a second look at his performance of course.

Tonight, he had arranged a special treat, he had placed the lingerie that he wanted her to wear on one of the beds in the furniture department and dipped the lights low, he had brought along a bottle of wine and selected a couple of glasses from the kitchen department to pour it into. She lay waiting for him and he let himself take in her body appreciatively whilst he poured them both a drink.

He passed hers to her and downed his and as she pushed her head up by her elbow to take a sip he stripped off his clothes and knelt on the bed before her, spreading her legs open and pushing his hands up her legs. His head reached her groin quickly, he ran his palms across the silk of her French knickers, applying pressure softly, the red fabric looked wonderful on her tanned skin, her stomach was toned and flat and her breasts swelled over the bustier that he had asked her to dress in.

Of course, he wanted to rip her clothes off and ram his dick in to her, but they had two hours to spend and he intended to fill the whole of it, he let his hands stroll across her stomach and breasts whilst she relaxed and enjoyed her wine.

Touching her thrilled him as much as it did her, his wife had left her body go years before and though her curves didn't matter at all to him, it drove her under the covers and in the dark, squirming at his touch. He liked to make a woman to purr, and he liked to watch her do it.

He kissed her legs first, rubbing her inner thighs as he let his tongue follow on a route from her knees and up her inner thighs, once he reached the crease at the top of her legs, she put down her glass and lay her head back against the pillows to relax.

He licked her with the tip of his tongue, tracing the outline of her knickers, up over her hips and across her stomach, he pushed his tongue in and out of her belly button and reached down into the edge of her knickers towards her hips.

He allowed his hands to skim past her clit and she sighed as he did, in anticipation of what she knew would come next, first though he moved up to her neck and down towards her breasts.

The bustier fastened at the front and he brought his arms up to slowly release it, hook by hook it opened and as each inch of skin was revealed he kissed it softly. Once it was loose he opened it and dropped to her breasts, his hands teased first until her nipples stood on end and her head turned side to side, before letting his lips close over them and biting softly with his lips over his teeth.

He stayed until she released her first moan and that enticed him to go through the process again in reverse, but harder this time. He kissed her nipples roughly, before dragging his tongue over her breasts and neck, he let his mouth fall to her lips for the first time and kissed her roughly, loving the way that when he pulled up away from her, she lifted her head to follow him.

He pushed her back against the bed, she had a long way to go before she was ready yet, he had to wait until she was soggy wet and begging for him. He moved his mouth back down across her body, sucking and licking the skin of her waist and hips before returning to her inner thighs and stopping where he started.

He peeled her knickers down, slowly with fingertips, once his lips hit her bare skin, her moans became more erratic, he ran his tongue across her pelvis in zigzags, skirting close to her clit but not falling over it, she pushed herself around beneath him, desperate to direct him towards the spot that thrilled her.

He used his fingers to open her up to him, bending her legs at the knee and spreading her legs wide, his tongue pushed slowly in to her vagina, licking around the edges softly.

His tongue moved up towards her clit and once he reached it she cried out, grabbing her hand over his head to hold him there, he had no intention of leaving as she well knew. He increased the pressure of his tongue, thrashing it against her clit, before driving it in to her vagina and letting his palm cover her clit.

Her hands abandoned his head and clutched the sheets beside her, her body shuddered and she whimpered and she let him know that she was reader, eager and desperate for him to push his dick in to her.

All his efforts had driven him to this, he loved to linger slowly over foreplay but fuck quick. He removed his tongue from her vagina and she moaned as he did, but reached her arms up to greet him and wrapped her arms around his back as he fell over her.

His dick was larger than average, he had difficulty getting it in sometimes but that was not a problem here, she was dripping wet, open and ready, he drove straight in to her, thrashing his hips until he filled her completely.

She could feel the edge of his penis reaching his limit inside her, she had never been screwed by a man so big, but it was his girth that did her, it ripped smoothly against her vagina lips, stiffly and swiftly, she cried out, driving her hips up to meet him and feeling every twitch of his dick.
He kissed her neck, then lifted his head over her, to watch her come, he would continue until she did, no matter how long it took, she clenched her face unattractively, her eyes closed and then flashed open.
Awe and wonder, pain, hunger, need, desperation, bliss, heaven, joy, ecstasy, he recognised and felt every thought that flashed across her face. The noise she was making was irrelevant, the eyes gave it all away and each emotion wrenched his pleasure up with hers until she hit ecstasy.

He ploughed violently before freezing solidly over and grunting and groaning madly. He could never tire of this, he could spend hours licking and sucking all day if it led to this at the end of it, he felt as if he was burning alive, the flames licking over him greedily, sucking in all the energy and oxygen before releasing it in a massive blast and bursting all over him.

The level of intensity never failed to shock him, it left them both struggling to breathe and panting and he pushed beside her on the bed and held her close as they rested together for a few minutes.

The guilt for them both set in whilst they dressed and they would take it home with them as they faced their husbands and wives but by the next day it would diminish and the expectation and build up would begin again.

The Tapes

The idea that security filming was transferred to tape was long outdated but footage was still thought of as such, in fact footage was stored electronically and shot straight up into the clouds where it was stored indefinitely. The physical footage record was beamed back down to the stores for them to view and store according to their own requirements, which differed by place.

Although his security team had access to the tapes, the store owner, who had long been disabled and bed ridden, liked to pass his days watching live footage, he was able to flick between departments, checking what all the staff were up to and peeking at the secret cameras that he had installed in the dressing rooms and playing with himself as women changed.

He had watched the relationship between his security guard and cleaner develop, he couldn't hear what they were saying but it was obvious that he was flirting with her and that she would soon give in to him. Within a week when he noticed neither were doing the duties he was paying them for, he considered sacking them both, still he couldn't help hoping as the days continued that they get together and do it on screen for him to watch them.

That had been weeks ago, now their actions were the highlight of his days, he didn't care that she wasn't cleaning, he hired a separate cleaner to come in before they opened in the mornings, the presence of a security guard was a requirement of his insurers, he didn't need to guard anything. They were pushing it with the use of things in store, they had started with the furniture and moved quickly on to clothing and soft furnishing.

Most of what they used was put back on the shelves, the cost of the other stuff was worth it, it wasn't as if they were stealing, they never took anything from the shelves that they didn't use, so they certainly weren't thieves, just horny little fuckers he thought as he turned his monitors on and looked for them on the screens.

Tonight, they were in the display kitchens, the security guard was one of the most generous lovers he had ever seen. They had just finished eating, he presumed that they had ordered takeaway, once they had finished he had cleared the table and laid her across it.

As his tongue started his work on her body, he flicked back his sheets and took his dick in his hands, allowing his fingertips to close tightly around it.

He rubbed as he tortured her, zooming in to have her body on full display, her tits were the best he had ever seen, when his head was over her pelvis he concentrated on her face, he was excellent at this, her face was lit up, her mouth open and gasping.

The increase in pleasure on her face grew slowly before exploding, she looked like a desperate nutcase, thrashing her body as arcs of pleasure hit.

The guard climbed up and on to her, his arse pumped erratically over her, the boss stared at her face, he had seen the size of his dick, he was a lucky man, but she was a luckier woman. Her hands clutched round at him, her fingertips scraped against her back, he clutched his dick tighter, he would come at the same time they did and imagine it was he who was fucking her and forcing her face to contort in such a way.

His dick throbbed in his hands, he held his breath as he waited for the lightning to strike the three of them, once it did he cried out, revelling in his own ecstasy and his body shook, he caught his ejaculate in a tissue and shuddered and relaxed as he let the pleasure spread throughout his body.

His breathing was beginning to worry him, he probably should be feeling such excitement at his age but it was like porn for his eyes only and he just couldn't resist it.

He tossed the tissue into a bin and watched them scurrying around clearing their mess up, he would notice anything they missed and leave a message for the morning cleaner to cover it the next day. He waited for them both to leave, before closing his eyes and allowing himself to fall to sleep.

Printed in Great Britain
by Amazon